**Bruce stared at the ... for like a laser bea...**

She was tilting her head at him, focusing on him with those inquisitive blue eyes. To other people that might be a good sign, but not to him.

He wanted a distraction. That was all.

He held the glass out again. "I can't promise it's a good year, but I can promise a decent toast from it."

She smiled at him, a brilliant, relieved smile. "Then I'm glad I didn't leave and miss the opportunity."

He handed her the flute of champagne, his heart kicking up a notch. She accepted it with a small laugh, and for a moment their fingers brushed.

He lifted his glass to her. "To getting to know you better."

She took a sip as he did the same. The tart, bubbly taste jarred him as they watched each other over the rims of their glasses. The magnetism between them made his blood pump.

She was still looking at his mouth. Maybe she wanted him to stay for purely selfish reasons.

He could handle that.

"I'm Bruce," he said. "And you are...?"

Her brow furrowed. Her mouth opened, then closed.

Ah, hell. And they'd been doing so well.

Dear Reader,

I'm delighted to announce exciting news: beginning in January 2013, Harlequin Superromance books will be longer! That means more romance with more of the characters you love and expect from Harlequin Superromance.

We'll also be unveiling a brand-new look for our covers. These fresh, beautiful covers will showcase the six wonderful contemporary stories we publish each month. Turn to the back of this book for a sneak peek.

So don't miss out on your favorite series—Harlequin Superromance. Look for longer stories and exciting new covers starting December 18, 2012, wherever you buy books.

In the meantime, check out this month's reads:

**#1818 THE SPIRIT OF CHRISTMAS**
Liz Talley

**#1819 THE TIME OF HER LIFE**
Jeanie London

**#1820 THE LONG WAY HOME**
Cathryn Parry

**#1821 CROSSING NEVADA**
Jeannie Watt

**#1822 WISH UPON A CHRISTMAS STAR**
Darlene Gardner

**#1823 ESPRESSO IN THE MORNING**
Dorie Graham


Happy reading!

Wanda Ottewell,

Senior Editor, Harlequin Superromance

# The Long Way Home

## CATHRYN PARRY

HARLEQUIN®

entertain, enrich, inspire™

Recycling programs
for this product may
not exist in your area.

ISBN-13: 978-0-373-71820-7

THE LONG WAY HOME

Copyright © 2012 by Cathryn Parry

For questions and comments about the quality of this book, please contact us at CustomerService@Harlequin.com.

www.Harlequin.com

**Printed in U.S.A.**

## ABOUT THE AUTHOR

Cathryn Parry loved living and working in seacoast New Hampshire during the summers of her college years. She still lives close by with her husband, Lou, and her neighbor's cat, Otis. When she's not writing, she figure skates, plans as many vacations as possible and indulges in her genealogy hobby. She loves to hear from readers. Please see her website at www.CathrynParry.com.

## Books by Cathryn Parry

**HARLEQUIN SUPERROMANCE**

1756—SOMETHING TO PROVE

Other titles by this author available in ebook format.

This book is dedicated to my husband, Lou, who cheered me on every day, cooked me dinner and patiently listened as I talked through plot points.

I couldn't have done it without you!

## Acknowledgments

Thanks to Megan Long for all your patience and wisdom in editing this story.

Thanks also to Piya Campana and the rest of the team at Harlequin Books, who worked hard to make the book the best it can be.

Thanks to my brother Phil, from whom I've learned many things about being a lawyer in a small town.

Thanks also to my ear surgeons Dr. Fred (father and son), to my nana, Ruth, and to the "road warriors" in Annapolis for your inspiration and insight with some of the topics in this story. (Any errors are mine alone.)

Thanks also to my writing buddies at New England Chapter RWA for your never-ending support and encouragement. I know how lucky I am to be a part of you.

Thanks as well to Laurie Schnebly Campbell, who once again presented a great workshop where I was able to develop the characters in this book. (Love those enneagrams!)

And to my late uncle, Richard S. Parry, proud veteran of the U.S. Navy, whose adventures and stories always sparked my imagination.

I miss you.

# CHAPTER ONE

No one had ever promised Natalie Kimball that moving home to be a lawyer in a small town with people who still thought of her as a hopelessly shy nerd was going to be easy.

"I can do this," Natalie muttered for about the tenth time that morning, her hands clenched on the steering wheel of her secondhand Toyota as she drove out of town and north up the coast.

To her right, the waves crashed toward her in a spectacular show of whitecaps; the Atlantic tide was coming in. The narrow strip of beach beside it, usually so crowded with tourists in the summer, was deserted, and most of the seaside shops and arcades were still closed for the winter. She opened the window a crack and let the fresh, cold smell of ocean air wash over her.

For once, Natalie was exactly where she wanted to be. She loved this place; it was in her DNA. Even though her father, Asa Kimball, didn't want her at home working in his law firm, Natalie knew she could be happy here *and* do a great job, if he gave her the chance. More than anybody else he could possibly turn the firm over to, she understood the people of this town: their connections, their histories, their families and their secrets.

Especially the family secret of the woman she was

set to meet. *I wonder what became of Bruce Cole?* Natalie thought.

Bruce was her longtime high school crush, though Natalie hadn't seen him since the summer he left town. It was only wishful thinking to expect his sister would mention him today.

Shaking her head, Natalie watched for the familiar gazebo perched on an outcropping of rock. When she came to it, she parked in a vacant lot where the meters weren't set up for the season yet.

Grabbing the packet on the seat beside her, she slammed the car door against the wind. It was an unseasonably cold day in late April even by New England seacoast standards—blustery, with freezing rain that made her teeth clench. She shivered, wishing she'd brought a warmer coat.

But this was where Maureen Cole's receptionist at the real estate office had asked Natalie to meet her. And to shore up her position with her father as a lawyer able to "bring in business," Natalie needed to convince Maureen that she should work with them on future projects. To secure her place, Natalie would do whatever it took, even drive ten miles out of town to the Rosewood Nondenominational Chapel in order to bring Maureen her forgotten notebook.

Natalie glanced down the beach to the picturesque chapel on a bluff overlooking the ocean. Strange how this place affected her. Long before all Natalie's surgeries, this little church had figured prominently in her romantic fantasies. She hoped the quaint property wasn't for sale. But why else would Maureen be here? Natalie had hinted for information from Maureen's receptionist, but the young woman had only smiled mysteriously. "I'm sure Maureen will fill you in when you see her."

Sighing, Natalie picked her way over the sidewalk, still littered with sand and pebbles after a late winter storm. Outside the chapel, a winter-deadened lawn was ringed by a garden beginning to come alive. For now, yellow forsythia sparked open and lilac bushes budded with purple shoots. Later, the roses of June and the tall, spiked perennial flowers of July would join them.

When she entered through the side door, Natalie recognized Maureen Cole immediately. A year older than Natalie, she looked every bit the prom queen and student council president she'd been in high school.

Maureen was curvy, blonde and authoritative—in a good way Natalie admired but would never be at heart. Her booming voice carried across the church to a volume that even Natalie, hearing-impaired as she was, could clearly process.

"Over there! You stand over there and I'll walk around you." Maureen tugged on a measuring tape, directing her mother. Nearby was a baby carriage with netting thrown over it, though there couldn't be many flying insects inside the chilly church.

Rubbing her arms, Natalie stood back and watched the women chatter away, their voices lower now as they worked. To pick out the words, Natalie concentrated on Maureen's lips. Maureen wore bright coral lipstick. Her teeth were straight and perfect; she'd gotten dental work done in the years since Natalie had seen her.

"...red would look nice," Maureen was saying, "but white is more traditional, and that's what I prefer."

But then Maureen turned to the side, and Natalie

couldn't read her lips anymore. She caught only the muted words *wedding flowers*.

Was Maureen getting married? Natalie glanced from the measuring tape Maureen wielded to the pad of paper she wrote on. Maybe they were planning the placement of floral arrangements for the ceremony.

A pang went through Natalie. Ever since she was a child, she had gazed up at this chapel as her family drove past on a Sunday, looking at the brides and wedding parties, and wondering what it would feel like to marry a man she loved in this fairy-tale place.

But dreams like that didn't happen for people like her. She needed to be practical. Use her brain, use her legal training, use her knowledge of the town's past connections and histories and secrets, and maybe she could find a way to be of service to people. Even if she wasn't the world's best communicator, like her father said.

"May I help you?" Maureen was standing directly in front of her.

Natalie jumped, snapping out of her reverie. "I'm... sorry." She cleared her throat, then remembered the binder cradled against her arm. She held it forward, smiling sheepishly at Maureen. "This is for you."

"Right." Maureen nodded, sizing her up. "You're the lawyer Lyndsey sent over with my wedding organizer. Thank you." With a grudging look, Maureen took the notebook she had left behind at her office and turned away from Natalie, immediately flipping to a page and scribbling furiously.

No one had said this would be easy.

Natalie walked around Maureen, to where she could

see her face. "Ah…forgive me for prying. But are you getting married, Maureen?"

Maureen looked up, staring at her. "Do you need to buy a house or something?"

"No…not right now. I'm settled, thanks." From the corner of her eye, Natalie noticed Maureen's mom picking the baby up and sniffing at his diaper. The exaggerated grimace on her face told the story. Quickly, Mrs. Cole wheeled the carriage toward the restroom at the rear of the church, leaving Natalie and Maureen alone.

She might as well face the issue head-on.

Smiling, Natalie held out her hand. "Hi, I don't know if you remember me, but I was a year behind you in high school. I'm Natalie Kimball."

"Kimball?"

The real estate agent gave a sarcastic, unfriendly smile and pointedly neglected to shake her hand.

Natalie wiped her palms against her already damp raincoat. She knew what this treatment was about: her father's involvement with Maureen's brother Bruce, and what had happened that last summer he was in town. Part of Natalie was dying to ask about him. She would never do that, though. As far as she knew, Bruce Cole had never come home, not once, and was never likely to again. She remembered how much it had hurt Maureen when he left.

Maureen's gaze traveled up and down Natalie's body. She had the curl to her lips of a former "in girl" judging and dismissing an "out girl." Natalie felt deflated, well aware of every physical flaw she had.

"Nope," Maureen drawled. "Your name doesn't ring

a bell. I didn't go to school with any of Asa Kimball's kids."

She said "Asa Kimball" as if the words tasted bitter. And then she turned away.

Natalie nodded. She understood why Maureen was acting this way. Indirectly, her father had made Maureen's life hell. Lawyers in general had made Maureen's life hell.

Bruce's life, too.

But Natalie wasn't that kind of lawyer and never would be. She saw herself as a helper, not an adversary. Her father, and his father before him, and for all she knew, his father before that, had run the family firm in the traditional way, which had, in her opinion, often caused problems. Years of standing on the sidelines, watching and observing, had convinced her she could make a place for herself, that she had a unique talent to contribute.

Natalie may not have been one to speak to people much, but she noticed things about people, and that was important, too. Maybe it was time to take a chance on the new style she envisioned. She had always thought that if given the opportunity, she could make a difference.

Natalie cleared her throat and approached Maureen again. "I know it was a long time ago, but you and I were…friends, actually—at least I thought so—your senior year in high school."

Maureen's lips pressed together, as if she was reliving the hell of being a popular girl who was suddenly ostracized by her peers. Natalie had seen it happen firsthand.

Hopefully Maureen would understand that her intentions weren't harsh. "We had study hall together on Fridays, final period," Natalie said. "I always looked forward to it. I…drove you to the bus station once in the fall." *Remember?*

For a split second, she looked bludgeoned and she abruptly sat on the nearest pew. And Natalie felt guilty. She hadn't wanted to use that particular memory, but it was the incident Maureen was most likely to recall. Maureen had planned to run away to visit Bruce, who was in his first year as a midshipman at the U.S. Naval Academy in Annapolis, Maryland. Natalie had never forgotten that day for many reasons, the most important of which was that it was the second most daring thing she had ever done.

"You were nice to me," Maureen finally said, albeit grudgingly. "Not too many people were nice to me that year."

"At least they talked to you," Natalie said with a joking tone. "I was always so shy."

Maureen cocked her head and studied her. "You look pretty." Her voice was softer, as if she was starting to warm up. "You cut your hair. It flatters you."

By reflex, Natalie touched her head. "Thanks. I found a really great stylist when I lived in Boston."

"*You* lived in Boston?" Maureen actually seemed interested.

"I went to law school there. And then afterward, I had a clerkship."

Maureen squinted.

"It's…a job I had, at the Federal courthouse on the waterfront. I clerked for a judge there."

Maureen smirked. "And now you're back to work

with your father on small-time wills and real estate clos-ings." Her laughter was unkind, all trace of the former softness now gone.

Natalie smiled gently, refusing to take the bait. "It's always been my dream to go solo."

Maureen's eyebrows rose. "So the old man is retir-ing?"

"Not…yet anyway." Therein was the crux of her di-lemma. Natalie fiddled with the button on her coat. Her father wanted to sell the law firm and retire to Florida by the end of summer. She wanted him to pass control to her and take a cut of her future earnings, but he didn't believe she had the ability to *make* future earnings.

This mission with Maureen was part of Natalie's plan to establish a bottom line for the summer, to prove to him she could.

And if she couldn't, well…

There was no *couldn't*. The law firm had been in her family for five generations, and she wanted to be part of that link, too. If she didn't stay and fight for her connection to that legacy, then it would be lost forever.

She *would* make a go of it here. And Maureen could help her, at the same time that she helped Maureen.

Natalie smiled and looked Maureen in the eyes. "If I can't convince my dad to keep the law office in the family, then he'll sell to a big firm from Portsmouth or Concord. If that happens, then they'll make his place into a satellite location to theirs."

With lawyers who wouldn't know anybody in town. Not personally, anyway. Outside attorneys wouldn't be likely to float a loan for legal work for a small busi-ness starting out, or to spring a local's miscreant son from the drunk tank at the beach on a Saturday night. Her father's firm did, often without charge. As a local businesswoman, Maureen would understand the implications.

Maureen leaned against the pew and chewed her bottom lip, thinking. Then she rubbed her hands over her face, and Natalie couldn't hear what she said.

"…such a big problem…the wedding…" was all Natalie caught.

And then Maureen moved her hands away from her mouth, and stared at her, waiting for Natalie to reply.

The familiar panic crept over Natalie that she'd missed something essential, that she'd be found out. And she'd been careful to stand face-to-face with Maureen so she could lip-read what she couldn't hear.

*You communicate so poorly,* her parents had always told her.

No one wanted a hard-of-hearing lawyer. Natalie knew it made them uncomfortable. It made them think she was either a snob or incompetent when she missed something important.

Sometimes both.

"I'm…sorry," Natalie said carefully. "Could you please repeat what you just said?"

Maureen's scowl deepened. Natalie got a bad feeling, as if Maureen was holding her response against her.

"Do you still have any ill-feelings toward my brother Bruce?" Maureen demanded bluntly.

"What? No! I never blamed him." On the contrary, Natalie had always thought she understood him better than most people did. "I knew your brother once—I talked to him, and I…"

She felt her face flushing. She could never tell Maureen about that night. She had never discussed it with anyone, even when she should have.

She was fiddling with her buttons again, and Maureen was staring in curiosity.

Oh, why not admit she'd had a crush on him? It was so long ago, surely it couldn't hurt. Most likely Bruce was married anyway, making beautiful babies and saving the world somewhere as a navy pilot or intelligence officer, something heroic and swashbuckling and passionately emotional, like he was.

"I had a huge crush on him, truth be told." Natalie laughed, but knew it came out strangled. "Me and about a hundred other girls in town."

"A hundred other girls in town turned their backs on him after what happened," Maureen said flatly.

Yes. Yes, they had. "But I didn't," Natalie said softly. "I was loyal to you, remember?" Maybe because Natalie was the only person in town who knew the truth about how Bruce had felt and what he'd done after the accident that had killed his best friend. "I saw what this town did to you, and I stayed by your side. I talked to you after all your cheerleader and student council friends turned their backs."

"You must really want my business." Maureen's voice was hard and bitter.

*It's not her fault.* Maureen had been a sheltered kid who'd gone through a tough year that had changed her life. But the most important thing was that Maureen had overcome the trauma. She was a functioning member of the community. From her father, Natalie knew Maureen had built herself up from a single mom with few prospects into a successful real estate agent specializing in the million-dollar beach homes along the waterfront. It must not have been easy to compete at that level, and was certainly not a job for the fainthearted.

Natalie, especially, could respect that.

"It's not that I want your business," Natalie said. "Take your business wherever you please, as far as I'm concerned. What I came for is to let you know I'm back, and I'm not leaving. This is my town, too, and I love it. I…think I can do good here, if you'll let me help."

Maureen shifted in her seat and stared at her. Twirling the tape measure between her fingers, over and over, as if she was taking Natalie's measure.

Natalie stood straighter. *Go ahead. I'm not the same shy kid who left town after high school. I'm a whole new person now and I want you to know it.*

"All right." Maureen lowered the tape measure. "My brother is coming home at the end of next month for my wedding. It will help me if you stop by and say hello to him. I think he'd like to see a friendly face."

"I…he's coming home?" Natalie raised her gaze and blinked into Maureen's eyes.

This, she had never expected.

"If it goes well with him and you're able to help," Maureen said, "then I'll consider bringing some business to your firm."

For a moment Natalie couldn't speak. Had she heard this right? "I would like that very much."

She should be happy. She had almost won.

And yet…

Her hands began to shake.

The one night she had spent with Bruce was his last

one in town. He'd never spoken to anyone other than his family again. Nobody knew why. Not even Natalie. It was a complete mystery to her, because Bruce had told her his plans that night, and they certainly hadn't been to simply disappear.

He had meant to help before he left. Everybody had loved and relied on Bruce Cole, once upon a time. He'd been the natural leader of the kids their age, the center of all that had been fun and good. And then he had left town and suddenly, everybody hated him. It became cool to blame him, and his younger sister—who'd really had nothing to do with any of it—had suffered the brunt of the fallout.

What would he say when he saw Natalie? What would *she* say?

*"Bruce Cole made sure he kept his plum spot at the U.S. Naval Academy,"* she'd heard people grumble. That was the perception—that when it came down to it, Bruce Cole was a heartless bastard. A guy who used people for his own ends and then escaped the consequences of his actions.

But Natalie knew he hadn't been involved in the accident. And back then, when she should have spoken up, she'd kept silent instead. To save herself from getting into trouble.

How many people got the chance to fix their mistakes?

"I…would love to see your brother when he comes home," she breathed.

Her hands shook harder now. Maureen stared. Natalie was afraid Maureen could see how much she was affected by Bruce's memory, still in an awed state of mixed puppy-love and sympathy that was…silly, really. She was an *attorney,* for heaven's sake. The daughter of the man who'd been hired, once upon a time, to depose Bruce for a lawsuit in civil court.

Maureen bent and picked up the bridal veil her mother had brought, and placed it on her head. With the delicate white lace softening her face, covering the harsh lines her bitterness had given her, Natalie could see the beautiful, innocent girl Maureen had been, back when Bruce had been home to protect her.

Maureen spoke again, but the words were muffled and Natalie couldn't see her lips behind the veil.

"May I?" Natalie asked. She gently lifted the veil. "This is antique, isn't it? Does it belong to someone in your family?"

"It was my nana's." Maureen's lips quivered. "She died a year ago." Then she shook her head. But her tough mask had slipped, and for a moment, Maureen had looked like the vulnerable teen Natalie remembered.

"Will you be my bridesmaid?" Maureen blurted.

"I…" *What?*

Maureen's determination had come back, the fighting attitude that made her such a good salesperson. "Here's what I need you to do," she said crisply. "You said you wanted to help me, right? Well, this is the help I need."

She abruptly stood and stalked to the front of the church, and Natalie had no choice but to follow her. They stopped in front of the altar.

Maureen pointed. "Jim—my fiancé—will be standing there. You remember Jimmy Hannaford?"

"Yes." He was a former classmate of theirs, a skinny,

quiet kid who liked computers and reading science fiction. "James was in all my math classes."

"Yeah, well, he runs Wallis Point PC now. If you want your computer fixed, Jimmy is your guy. His office is two blocks over from your father's law firm."

Natalie nodded, but Maureen kept talking. "Jim will have four groomsmen—his best friend and my twin brothers. Bruce is the fourth groomsman, and he'll be standing here."

Natalie stared at the spot Maureen had indicated, and could easily see tall, good-looking Bruce Cole standing there dressed in a black tux and white tie. With his dark hair and his dark eyes, he would be heart-stopping.

She swallowed, missing half of what Maureen was saying.

"…then, on my side—" Maureen pointed to the left of the altar "—I have Jim's sister and my two sisters-in-law as attendants. Plus you." She suddenly turned to Natalie, and Natalie blinked at the undisguised pleading in her eyes. "If you'll do it. If you'll stand up for me."

Maureen clutched the veil in her fist, and Natalie felt her heart go out to this hard, hurt woman who didn't have a best friend or a sister of her own to stand up for her on her special day.

*Just like me,* Natalie thought. *Just like me.*

"I'm honored you asked me," she said.

"So will you do it?" Maureen stared hard at Natalie. "Bruce will be paired with you in the wedding party, first for the chapel ceremony, and then for the reception afterward. I won't have much time to spend with him, so I'd be depending on you to make him feel comfortable."

Natalie looked again to the spot where Bruce would

stand. Then to where she would stand, across from him. They would walk down the aisle together, and later, dance at the reception with the rest of the bridal party.

"Where…where is the reception?" Natalie asked, cringing inwardly because she was sure she knew the answer. Where else did locals host their parties?

Maureen's eyes narrowed. "The Grand Beachfront Hotel," she snapped. "Is that okay with you?"

Bruce wasn't going to like it *at all*.

"It's fine with me," Natalie said. But her knees were shaking and her tongue felt tied. Why had she regressed to a shy, awkward teenager? Maybe she wasn't up for this task.

"Bruce is single, by the way," Maureen said. "He's not bringing a date, so you don't have to worry about any awkwardness there."

*Lovely.* Natalie should say no. She should run away. This could be an absolute disaster.

Then again, if she was able to pull off what Maureen wanted, wouldn't it be best for everyone? She would help her father and Maureen and the Cole family and Bruce…heck, in a sense she could help the entire town by keeping the law firm local. If she had learned any of the skills she'd claimed to have during those years on her own, then she had to do this, for everyone's sake.

"Okay," Natalie said. "I'll do it."

# CHAPTER TWO

BRUCE COLE STOOD in the rental car office at Boston's Logan airport and shook his head in disbelief.

They'd assigned him a minivan? *Really?*

He glanced at the electronic board listing the last names of the arriving platinum-level customers. There he was, "Cole, B.," assigned to the vehicle parked in spot 367. Here he was at spot 367, and there sat a minivan, which was against the explicit instructions on his frequent-traveler profile.

Bruce sighed. The golden rule of traveling was that anything could go wrong, at any moment, for any reason. Terminal shutdowns, bad weather, airplane mechanical problems, a hotel closed by Legionnaire's Disease. He considered himself lucky he hadn't been a passenger in an emergency landing on a jumbo jet in the Hudson River. Yet.

But the corollary to the golden rule was that there were some things a frequent traveler could influence, even control. And road warriors, with their points and their elevated status, had more power than those people who only traveled once in a blue moon.

Civilians, the travel companies could afford to inconvenience. Customers like him, not so much.

He left his suitcase and his briefcase on the pavement and peered inside the van's window. Fate must be laughing at him, because there was a child seat strapped in the back.

Sorry, fate. That wasn't ever going to happen. Even though he was only driving back to Wallis Point for this one night—and against his best instincts— this van was the worst vehicle he could show up in. His parents and Mark and Mike wanted him to stick around and be part of the family. Maureen, the headstrong real estate agent, would be trying to sell him a town house right down the street from hers.

Not a chance in hell.

His life was exactly the way he wanted it. He was free. Independent. Unencumbered.

No close relationships.

The only reason he'd made room in his schedule to fly back to Wallis Point to be in his sister's wedding was that she had nagged him until he'd given in.

Not that going back made any difference to him. He didn't care what anybody thought of him.

He stayed out of their lives. He stayed out of everybody's life but his own.

Usually.

He grimaced, visually plotting the trip ahead, and his subsequent escape. After he got a decent car, he'd roll into town, witness the happy event for Maureen, raise his glass in a good-natured toast and then he'd roll right on out.

Be back in the air first thing tomorrow morning on the earliest flight out—that was his plan.

First, though, he needed a car that fit his image. Shuddering, he opened the van door, plucked the paperwork from the visor and then wheeled his luggage toward the customer service counter. A place that frequent travelers avoided like the plague.

The line stretched five deep, with even more people being unloaded from a courtesy bus at the curb. It was Friday evening on the Memorial Day weekend—the beginning of the summer season in New England—what did he expect?

By instinct, he scanned the parking lot and realized that, predictably, the rental service had run out of cars. The wait to snag one could last hours. Bruce was a road warrior by profession, he knew the ins and outs of navigating airports, hotels, car rental services and business conventions—it was his life. Normally he loved it.

Better than anyone, he knew that by flying on a Friday evening—any Friday evening, never mind the Friday before a long weekend—he'd broken a major rule of road warriors: never travel with the amateurs. They didn't understand the arcane system of U.S. travel—how to make it as smooth and problem-free as possible—and because they didn't get it, they made life difficult for the people depended on fast entrances and quick exits.

The thing was, road warriors stuck together. They knew all about traveling out first thing Monday morning and home last thing Thursday night. Fridays were for paperwork and telecommuting from home. Bruce did his laundry and errands on Saturday and relaxed on Sunday. Then on Monday he flew to whatever client site he was currently contracted to, fixed the computer systems and was a hero. Or a bum, if something went wrong. Either way, he was free. Nothing held him down. Nothing locked him in place.

*Don't make eye contact.*

He walked past the snaking line—caught glimpses of families and old people and young, wide-eyed couples—and ambled up to the counter. This wasn't his normal rental-car place—he knew the staff in the Fort Lauderdale office personally—so he opened his wallet to get his identification card, just in case. It was tucked behind his gold American Express card, which he removed gingerly. The fragile plastic had been swiped by so many machines that the card was cracked almost in half.

He caught the eye of a clerk on duty. *Desmond,* the clerk's nametag read. Bruce nodded at Desmond, and subtly flashed his platinum-colored customer ID.

Desmond nodded back, but continued listening to the customer who was venting at him, a guy about Bruce's age with a goatee and backpack—and absolutely no power to make anything happen in his favor. A guy who didn't stand a shot at getting a car.

"I'm sorry, sir," Desmond said patiently, "I know you have a reservation, but we are absolutely empty at the moment. There is nothing I can do."

Then Desmond hurried over to assist him. He took the paperwork Bruce offered. "Good afternoon, sir. How can I help you?"

"I need to switch this for a sedan," Bruce said. "Something smaller and low mileage."

The clerk glanced at the sleeve of Bruce's paperwork. "I'm sorry, Mr. Cole, but there are no cars available. We have at least an hour wait. Your best bet is to keep what you have." He tried to hand back the paperwork.

Bruce smiled slowly. Held Desmond's gaze. Kept his palms flat on the counter. With an easy look that said he understood, he felt for Desmond, he really did, but

he knew the rules—hell, he had his own rules, too—
and this was the way it was gonna go down. He'd do it
gracefully, without inciting a riot in the line—especially
from the guy in the goatee, practically blowing a gasket
beside him, but either way, they were going to do this.

"There are always cars," Bruce said, softly, his body
angled away from the waiting crowd.

The clerk swallowed, his Adam's apple moving up
and down.

And then he went to his computer. Bruce tucked his
customer ID card back inside his wallet.

Desmond glanced from the monitor to Bruce. Bruce
smiled at him. He knew that the computer system—
similar to the ones he designed himself—was telling
Desmond that Bruce had rented one of his firm's cars
every week, never fail, for the past eight years.

"Excuse me, Mr. Cole," Desmond said, reaching for
the phone. "I need to get an override from management.
Would you mind waiting a moment?"

"No problem," Bruce replied. He went to slide his
wallet into his back pocket, when his elbow bumped
against something soft.

Actually, against someone soft.

A kid, no more than six or seven years old, had come
up beside him. Well inside his personal space. Now
what? He raised one eyebrow at the kid, who didn't
take the hint.

Big trouble, he thought. Don't go there.

"My dad says you're cutting the line," the boy said.

Bruce had a niece about the same age. She was a real
firecracker, too. Maybe that was why he was considering ignoring his own rules about not interacting with

civilians. It seemed nothing was going to be normal about this trip.

"Does he?" Bruce replied. In curiosity, he lifted his gaze past the kid to the guy with the goatee who'd been expressing his irritation to the clerk.

"Daniel," the man said, his face red with either exasperation or embarrassment, "get over here right now."

But the kid didn't move. Bruce frowned, looking down at him. What was it about this kid? Thin and determined, he had a set to his mouth. The parents were just…tired and worn-out from their travels, and kind of clueless about what was happening around them, to tell the truth. The mother rocked and cooed at a toddler girl, cute kid, with wispy hair a blinding blond that was almost white. There were two older kids, eleven or twelve, but they were arguing over an iPod, or maybe an iPhone. The father was sidetracked now, distracted with reading them the riot act, and attempting to get them to line up and behave, although even Bruce saw what a futile gesture that was.

Bruce looked down at the kid again. This was none of his business. But he couldn't seem to help himself.

"I'm not cutting the line on you," Bruce explained. "This is a special line for people who travel a lot."

The kid stared at him. "How can we get in the special line? We need a car. We need to get to Grandma's house before the traffic starts."

Bruce had news for him; it was already well into rush hour. Waiting another hour for a car might be the best thing for them to do.

"I think you'll be stuck in traffic even if you leave now."

The kid's chin set. "It's better if my brothers fight in the car than fight here. My dad won't be as mad."

"That's uh…good thinking."

"I know."

Bruce blinked and looked at the boy again. Something about this kid was just…sucking him in. The thing was, Bruce could relate to parents who were absorbed in their own world and not paying attention to the wide world around them. To older siblings who were equally absorbed in their world of petty squabbles, of scuffling with each other instead of behaving. To the baby, so cute and helpless. And to this precocious middle kid, the only one who paid attention to the bigger picture. A leader in the making.

"What's that big ring?" The kid asked, pointing to Bruce's heavy gold Annapolis ring with the blue stone on his left ring finger. "Were you in the Super Bowl? Are you famous?"

"It's my Annapolis ring. I earned it at the U.S. Naval Academy." Bruce pushed away his unease. He didn't usually wear the ring, but this week he'd had meetings scheduled with the upper brass of the navy—captains and admirals. His life tended to flow more smoothly when the people in charge accepted him as part of their club. So he'd dug it out of his top drawer, and now he was stuck with it for the night.

"What's the U.S. Naval Academy?" the kid asked him.

"It's where the country trains leaders for the U.S. Navy," he said by rote.

"Is that like the Marines? I want to be a Marine."

Bruce had felt that way once, too. "Yeah, I get that. When I was your age, I had a buddy whose father was—"

*Whoa.* He suddenly felt light-headed. Where was *this* coming from?

He was over all that old stuff. Way over it.

The kid stared at him, but Bruce shook his head in response. He couldn't tell him that once, a long time ago, he'd had nearly the same conversation with his best friend's irascible father. Because Bruce had been the precocious kid in his neighborhood. The inquisitive leader who'd felt the burning need to take care of everybody close to him because they weren't doing such a good job of it themselves. Maureen was the baby sister his mom fussed over, dressed in pretty clothing and took to girly things like ballet class and shopping. His brothers, twins, older than him by eight years, were the ones always distracted by hunting and fishing and boating, and fighting with each other. Their father was cut from the same cloth as Mark and Mike, and though they were all three good guys at heart, they had never understood Bruce. He baffled them. He was different from everybody else they knew.

Slowly Bruce let out his breath. Desmond the clerk had returned. He was smiling now, suddenly willing to be Bruce's buddy. People loved being able help somebody else out, when their hands were no longer tied from doing a good deed for someone who would appreciate it of them.

*You could do a good deed, too.*

*No,* another part of him said. *Don't get involved.*

He closed his eyes. Alarm bells were going off all over the place, but he couldn't help it. He wanted to be that carefree kid again, for once.

This wedding was going to be a mess for him, he could just tell.

But he opened his eyes and glanced down at the kid. He was looking at Bruce eagerly, as if Bruce was a hero or something.

How could he say no to that?

"You want me to get you a car, little man?" Bruce asked softly.

The kid—Daniel, was it?—put his hands on his hips and nodded.

"Is a minivan okay? With a car seat for your sister?"

Daniel grinned. "That sounds real good. She isn't big enough to sit on her own yet."

"Got it." He looked at Desmond, who was clearly baffled. "You heard the customer. Give them the Chrysler van in space 367." He held out his old contract. "And while you're processing the paperwork, transfer as many of my points as you need to cover their full fee."

Desmond squinted at the computer screen. "You've used all your points, Mr. Cole. Transferred the bulk of them last week, to a...Maureen Cole. A Mark Cole. And a Mike Cole."

He'd forgotten about Maureen's honeymoon, along with his parents' and brothers' trip to Disney World with his nieces and nephews at the same time.

"Yeah, well..." Bruce reached for his wallet again, skipped past the almost-broken-in-half corporate card, and reached for his personal card, stuck way in the back. "Put the base rental charge on my credit card. Use the renter's credit card for their gas, insurance and security holds. I don't want to be liable if they lose the car or crack it up or something."

He was a good guy, not a stupid guy.

"Certainly, sir," Desmond said. And as he returned to the computer to process the minivan, Bruce accepted the paperwork for his sedan. *Luxury Collection,* the header read. And Bruce's heart beat a bit faster, because every road warrior had heard of the mythical stock of high-end luxury and sports cars that were reserved for the high-end customers, but also available at regular rates for platinum-level members whenever there was an out-of-stock situation. Such as this one.

Yeah, Bruce had hit the road warrior jackpot. What would he get? A Lexus? A BMW?

He felt so good he saluted the kid, who promptly saluted back. Then Bruce hightailed it out of there before the parents chewed him out for overstepping his boundaries. But really, he was only serving himself. Going about his business, the way he always did.

As he walked to the parking lot, he thought of sharing the news about the car he'd scored, but who would he call? It was the weekend. The guys he worked with, work buddies, were all at home, spread to the four corners of the country.

For a moment he felt all alone.

And then he saw the car. Gleaming white. Black-top convertible. A Mercedes.

Wait a minute—he was taking a *Mercedes convertible* back to Wallis Point? Was this some kind of sick joke?

Fate was really sticking it to him tonight. For a moment he wavered, thinking he might be sick, but no, he overcame the physical reaction. Trained his mind to control his body. Remembered the boiling anger he'd once felt. The unfairness of other people's attitudes toward Maureen. Recalled how stubborn she had to be not to leave Wallis Point as soon as she'd graduated high school, like he had.

And once he'd trained his mind to remember the sweet glow of righteous anger, his body followed suit and he was calm again.

It was as if a curtain of numbness had fallen over what a few moments ago had been…something else. Because the past didn't matter anymore. It hadn't for fifteen years. The car accident was a long time ago, with lots of water under the bridge since then. He was done thinking or caring about what anyone thought of him.

He tossed his suitcase into the trunk. Walked around the Mercedes, glanced at the miniscule backseat, too small for anything larger than a briefcase, certainly too small for kids, never mind adults. He had to admit, the car was perfect for his rules. He should concentrate on that.

He slid inside the driver's seat, feeling better now. Felt the cool leather slide beneath his thighs. Smelled the new-car smell of a sweet, sweet machine with only five hundred miles on the odometer.

Just him and a fast vehicle he could easily escape in. Too bad he was returning it tomorrow.

He started the engine and turned on the radio. Loud, so he couldn't think.

NATALIE STOOD BEHIND the three other bridesmaids, and knew that her presence at Maureen Cole's wedding was awkward and out of place. For a moment she wished she could disappear into the floor.

But feeling uncomfortable and doubting herself had never solved anything, so she stiffened her spine and renewed her grip on her bouquet. White roses interspersed with white lilacs, the bouquet was as fragrant as it was beautiful. Her dress, too, was elegant and flattering—Maureen had let them choose their own gowns as long as they were black, short-sleeved and tea length. The group photos would be stunning, with the men in black tuxes with white rose boutonnieres, the women in black gowns with their white bouquets, and the bride in a simply cut, white silk sheath with a long train and antique lace veil.

Natalie felt her spirits drooping lower. She had always hoped for a wedding like this, in the beautiful chapel on the beach in her home town, saying vows at dusk. The problem was, in Natalie's teenaged dream wedding, she had been imagining Bruce Cole in the groom's place. Which was insane.

And now Bruce Cole hadn't bothered to show.

Natalie swallowed her disappointment, staring down at her hands and purposely avoiding looking at the vacant space opposite her where he should have been standing.

She wasn't sure what was going on, but something was very wrong. More than once before the ceremony she'd seen Maureen huddled with her mother and her sisters-in-law, whispering.

One of the rose petals was coming loose from Natalie's bouquet, and she absently tucked it back in. No one else knew it, but Natalie had built up Bruce's arrival as a pie-in-the-sky fantasy in which he would see her, instantly be sent back to that long-ago night they had confided in one another, and only this time, with her newfound courage and the shyness she had overcome, Natalie could initiate…something…with him.

Wrong again. And the sooner she shook off her unrealistic expectations, the better she would feel.

For a while she had also fantasized that she and Maureen would become fast friends since their meeting last month in the chapel. That wasn't happening the way she'd hoped, either. Yes, Natalie had been politely invited to the wedding shower, to the rehearsal dinner and even to this morning's hairdressing session, but it was clear the Coles were a tight-knit clan that didn't trust Natalie at all.

Or maybe she wasn't hearing them well enough to know what was going on.

Natalie sighed. One thing she did know for a fact—intelligence gained from her father this morning, unfortunately—was that Maureen had closed on the old Gale place, a National Historic Register home originally built in 1810. Sold to wealthy out-of-towners, Bostonians moving north to take advantage of New Hampshire's lack of state income tax. Which was fine. Except for the fact Maureen had taken her business to her usual out-of-town lawyer, instead of to Asa Kimball.

Who, as a result, was not happy with Natalie.

True, the closing fees weren't a lot of money. But the fees added up. And Maureen's business, added up, would go a long way toward giving Natalie's father the confidence that he could leave the business safely in her hands, rather than selling out to a stranger.

Loud organ music burst forth from the choir loft. The bride's processional was beginning, and Maureen appeared at the end of the aisle, looking beautiful and composed as she held her father's arm. The guests, about seventy-five in number, rose to their feet with a collective sigh.

Natalie pasted a smile on her face. As much as her instincts told her to run away—to cut out early—she needed to stick it out.

BRUCE WAS IN NO MOOD to walk down memory lane. Sitting for two hours in Route 95 traffic tended to do that to a guy.

He parked the Mercedes at a lot a few blocks from the beach then cut through the laneway behind a nightclub. The music spilled into the open air, a song from twenty years ago when he'd been a kid. It reminded him of summer campouts and days spent with his buddies in the neighborhood. It made him feel old and nostalgic and depressed. Those had been good days, and they were gone. Good friends who he hadn't spoken to in years. Most of them he didn't even know where they'd ended up.

*Hell.* If he was going to survive this visit, then he needed to stop thinking like that. His lifestyle had served him well for fifteen years since he'd left town. So he yanked open the door to the hotel where all the trouble had started, and marched inside as if it didn't matter. He quickly checked his computer and his suitcase with the bellhop in the corner—a habit he'd adopted because valuables were generally safer when he tipped someone to watch them rather than leaving them alone in a car in a public parking area—and then shook out the tuxedo jacket he carried and shrugged it over his shoulders, where it weighed heavily.

The reality was, he was so late that for all practical purposes, he had missed his sister's wedding. His first responsibility was to find Maureen and smooth things over with her.

He passed behind a brass luggage cart and glanced through the lobby windows to the crowded boulevard outside. Darkness was falling. Tourists were wandering past, dressed in flip-flops and shorts. In all these years, not a thing about Wallis Point had changed. This beach town was small, provincial and predictable—and it made him feel trapped. He loosened his tie. He couldn't wait to get out of here.

As luck would have it, Maureen was standing alone, in the hallway before the ballroom. When he saw her, he felt himself smile. His sister broke into a grin and ran to meet him.

"Hey, Moe," he whispered, once he had her in a bear hug.

"You're late and I hate you," she whispered back, "but at least you came."

"I'm sorry, I got held up."

She pushed back and looked at him. "Don't think I don't know how hard it is for you to be here."

"I'm fine." He didn't want to talk about his self-imposed exile with her, especially today. "This is your wedding, don't let me ruin it for you."

He dug in his pocket. His sister liked pretty things, and he'd done his best to find her a copy of the earrings she'd been admiring in a jewelry store window last Thanksgiving, when the family had come down for their yearly party at his house in Florida. He pressed the box into her palm.

Her eyes widened as she opened it. "Bruce, these are sapphires."

"Yeah, something blue," he said.

She stood a long time, clutching the box and blinking at him. There were dark circles under her eyes, and her skin was pale.

His antennae went up. "Where's Jimmy? Is everything okay with you two?"

A big, sloppy smile crossed Maureen's face, which was great to see, because Maureen usually looked hard and focused. She'd built a solid career for herself and her daughter, and he was proud of her.

"Come on," she said, tugging on his arm, "I'll take you to see him."

"Wait." He pulled out an envelope from inside his jacket pocket. He'd stuffed some cash inside. He wouldn't do anything so tacky at any other wedding, but this was Maureen, and he knew the importance she placed on security. "This is for you. It's spending money for your honeymoon."

"Excellent," Maureen said, and tucked the money inside her bra.

He relaxed. That was the Maureen he knew.

"And now…" She poked him in the chest. "I want you to stop skulking around out here. Go into the ballroom and spend time with the family. Nina has gotten so big lately. She's been asking about her uncle and she's been looking forward to her trip to Disney World." Maureen put her hand to her mouth.

"What's wrong?"

But Maureen shook her head, blinking rapidly, as if she was upset about something. Before Bruce could question her further, Jimmy came over and put his arm around her shoulders. Jimmy was small and slight, shorter than Maureen. Where Maureen could be fierce and strong-willed, Jimmy was steady and calm. He ran his own independent home-computer consulting business, so in a sense, he and Bruce were in the same industry.

"We need to get inside for the cake cutting," Jimmy said to Maureen.

"Right," Bruce said. "You two go on. I'll join you in a bit."

"Where are you going?" Maureen asked.

"Ah…" Now that he was here, the best he felt he could do was to disappear into the woodwork and observe the festivities from afar. And there was only one other guy he knew who would be happy joining him there.

"I'm looking for Gramps," he said to Maureen.

Her mouth tightened. "He's not here."

But that didn't make any sense. Maureen and Bruce had lived with Gramps and Nana during Bruce's last two years of high school, when their parents had been in Florida on a long-term job assignment. Nana had passed on a year ago, but there was no way Gramps would miss Maureen's wedding. "*Why* isn't he here? Is he sick?"

Maureen sucked in her breath and stared at him. "He's fine," she snapped. "He just couldn't make it." She had a set to her chin that Bruce didn't like. He didn't like at all. "We'll talk about this later."

*Later* he was leaving. *Later* he had a flight to catch.

"Fine," he said.

He'd call Gramps and get the whole story when he had the time. Which right now, he did not.

Because he needed to get out of here. He needed to separate from these people and this life he wasn't a part of anymore. He needed to be free.

But this was Maureen's wedding day, so he gave her and Jimmy a lazy smile instead. "Sure. We'll talk later."

"Come into the reception with us," Maureen pleaded. "I have someone I want you to meet."

Nope, sorry. He wasn't being introduced to anyone. "Thanks, but I'll pass." He nodded to Jimmy. "You two go on. I'll meet you inside."

They nodded—Maureen reluctantly, Jimmy with more force, and they left for the ballroom, Maureen's train dragging along the carpet. Bruce watched them until they disappeared inside, then he headed in the opposite direction down a short, musty back hallway.

One of the advantages of working here in high school was that he knew the floor plan of the rambling old hotel. Rounding a corner, he ducked inside a doorway and climbed rickety stairs until he came to a balcony of sorts.

Years ago, during the hotel's big-band heyday, this had been the pit where the orchestras were set up to play. The bands were gone, but the dusty space still gave a great view of the dance floor.

He stood near the railing with a bird's-eye shot of the conga line that snaked around the room. The men wore dark suits and the women black dresses. He remembered the invitation Maureen had sent: black-and-white informal. Maybe that was the latest style. Maureen was always up on design. She had started out being interested in fashion, then interior design, and now she'd morphed into staging and selling beach houses. Hard-nosed and practical, that was always Maureen's thing.

He crossed his arms and glanced down. He knew roughly half the people—Maureen's half, and they were relatives. As for Jimmy's half, he didn't know many in that crowd. They were younger than him. Still, he couldn't be sure they didn't know who he was.

*Damn it.* He had done his job. He'd shown up, he'd greeted Moe and made her happy, now why couldn't he quietly escape through a side door, for her sake?

And then he saw the leggy blonde. Standing alone by the windows, she was the only person besides him who seemed out of place.

Sure, she was dressed like everybody else, in a black cocktail dress, but in every other way, she stood out from the crowd. She was…self-contained, for one. A real stunner, but in a fresh-faced, natural way, with little, if any makeup or jewelry. Her thick, honey-colored hair was long, loose, undone. It made her look sexy without even trying. But most of all, he liked that she wasn't driven to snake around the room in the communal conga line, or to belly up to the bar, joking with the families, or even to sit at the cleared dinner tables, drinking coffee and chatting with the more subdued relatives, because she was disconnected from them, too. That much was obvious.

And then she calmly pulled out her phone to check her messages.

He liked that. He liked that…a lot.

"Who are you?" he muttered aloud.

Jimmy spoke up behind him. "That's Natalie."

Bruce swiveled to face his new brother-in-law. "Is she a relative of yours?"

"No."

"A friend of Maureen's?"

"Yes."

His heart sank. Messing with a friend of his sister's was a terrible idea. Unless...

"Is she an old friend that Moe hasn't seen in a while, or a work friend she sees every week around town?" Because the former wasn't too bad, but the latter would be fatal.

Jimmy blinked and stared at him. Bruce waited.

"No," Jimmy said.

"No?"

"No."

Bruce waited some more, but Jimmy added nothing. Like so many of the hard-core engineers and techies Bruce knew, getting Jimmy to open up was like pulling teeth.

"*How* does Maureen know her?" Bruce asked patiently, figuring an open-ended question was his best bet. Enough of the yes/no conversation.

"They went to school together." Jimmy blinked at him. "I have to take you downstairs now. Maureen wants you in the ballroom with her."

"Right." Bruce swept his arm forward for Jimmy to precede him. "Don't worry, I'm right behind you."

As Jimmy traipsed down the creaking stairs, Bruce hung back for a last look at pretty Natalie. With her thumb on her phone's screen, she was scrolling through her messages, unruffled by the music and the dancers in the wedding reception swirling around her.

Like an oasis of calm.

He needed calm. He needed an oasis, too, since it was clear Moe wasn't going to allow him to escape until the very end of her reception.

Would it cause problems for Moe if he approached Natalie? If she and Maureen had gone to school together, then that meant Natalie had attended the state university where Maureen had majored in business. She couldn't be a high school friend because he'd known all her friends before he'd left home. Knowing Maureen, Natalie was a dorm-mate invited to the wedding as courtesy. She would be out of Maureen's life just as quickly as she'd been invited back in.

Like he would be, too.

No. It was too risky.

He was about to leave, when Natalie glanced up at him. He froze as she studied him from head to toe. Then she calmly met his gaze.

And smiled.

He felt hot inside. Maybe he was nuts, because suddenly, the course of action he was imagining seemed like the only possible one to take.

ONE MOMENT, NATALIE was checking her messages. Her father had sent her a text—all in caps, but still, it was progress in getting him to switch from his habit of phoning her all the time. She had felt the phone vibrating in her purse, and since she was just sitting there watching everybody dance, feeling disconnected and out of place, she'd read his message.

Tenant called. Check the mousetraps at 3 South Street before you come home.

She'd groaned inwardly. He wanted her to cover for him at the rental apartments above the building that housed the law firm. She'd tried to tell her father she was a lawyer, not his building supervisor, and that furthermore she had her own maintenance-needy cottage to worry about, but he was under the impression that she was at his beck and call, part of the package deal of her insisting on coming home to Wallis Point to work in the family firm.

*Just rebait the darn mousetrap for him.*

She'd suppressed the shudder. She hated mice.

*You have to do it. Besides, you're at a wedding. Think romantic thoughts.*

But Bruce Cole hadn't shown, and her pie-in-the-sky fantasies had lost their wings and fallen to earth.

Sighing, she'd tossed her phone into her purse and prepared to leave to find a hardware store open at this hour, in case the mice had escaped and she needed new traps. She'd almost made *her* escape, too, until she'd glanced up at the old balcony where the orchestras used to play.

And saw…him.

She'd blinked and gaped. She must be hallucinating.

But no, it *was* Bruce Cole. And he looked even better than she'd remembered. The sight of him still made her stop in her tracks.

Her heart had seemed to grow in her chest, squeezing her tight. He seemed taller than before. He was broader in the shoulders and he stood straighter. Then again, he'd been a navy lieutenant, although now he was dressed in a black tux with his tie undone. His dark brown, almost black hair was swept off his forehead in a tousled non-style that made her want to run her hands through it and gave him the old, passionate air she remembered. His jaw was edged with a five-o'clock shadow that looked sexy and dangerous.

She lifted her gaze to him. Those dark, intense eyes, so alive with fire, were boring straight into hers.

Her heartbeat sped up. The pull of his eyes seemed to tug on her, an invisible line straight to her…well, to parts of her anatomy that hadn't felt a man's touch in quite a while.

His eyes seemed to drink her in. Raked her from top to bottom. And she was standing still, letting him study her. This was what she'd been waiting for, after all.

No man interested her the way Bruce did.

As a kid, he had always known how to connect with people. He had that magical quality, a "people" gene that Natalie had been born without. And now all of his intensity was focused on her. She felt every muscle weaken, as if she were being swept away by his gaze.

A slow smile slid up his face.

*Make him feel comfortable,* Maureen had said. Well, here was a start, and she would do her best to keep it going.

But then she was distracted by her phone vibrating again, and when she glanced back, Bruce was no longer on the balcony. He was coming down to see her— she knew it in her bones, and, shy-person-at-heart she would always be, she couldn't help worrying.

What if she didn't hear him properly? What if she said something wrong, something he misinterpreted, and she was responsible for sending him away from Wallis Point again?

Glancing around her, she looked for an out. Somebody they both knew who could rescue her if she made a misstep.

But every other wedding guest was on the dance floor, singing aloud to Sister Sledge's "We Are Family," reminding Natalie she was probably the only person present who was *not* family.

*Okay.* She would have to handle the conversation on her own. Pay close attention, focus, and in doing so, hopefully help him see that not everybody in Wallis Point thought badly of him.

Once, he had trusted her enough to open up. Just by listening, she had helped him. A small thing she knew had brought him comfort because he'd told her so himself.

And that had been an extraordinary night to a girl of fifteen with little confidence in herself or sense of her worth. She needed to remember that she'd grown since then. She had achieved some extraordinary educational and career accomplishments, and she had found the courage to come home and carve out a place for herself. *Don't think of me as I was then. Let me show you who I am now.*

As Bruce walked toward her, smiling, she remembered Maureen's deal with her. But even if there hadn't been one dollar of business on the line, Natalie would be breathing just as hard, her hands sweating just as much, and her heart yearning for Bruce to trust her again, just as deeply.

He reached for two flutes of champagne from a passing waiter. He held one flute up, and the full glass obscured her view of his mouth. It was so loud and so confusing in the room that she had to lean in to catch what he was saying.

He lowered the glass and looked at her, his smile expectant, a gleam in his eye. "So what do you think?"

This close to him, his voice sounded so low and deep that it sent shivers up her spine. But at the same time, she panicked. Because all she could think was, *What did he just say?*

## CHAPTER THREE

BRUCE STARED DOWN at the woman he'd aimed for like a laser beam. She was tilting her head at him, focusing on him with those inquisitive blue eyes as if she were trying to figure him out. To other people that might be a good sign, but not to him. He didn't want to actually *talk* to anybody about anything more important than an offer of champagne or a stroll on the beach.

He wanted a distraction. That was all.

He held the glass out again. "I can't promise it's a good year, but I can promise a decent toast from it."

She smiled at him, a brilliant, relieved smile. "Then I'm glad I didn't leave and miss the opportunity."

Her voice was soft and pleasant-sounding. He had to lean forward to hear her, which was nice. She smelled great, something lush and sexy that came from soap or shampoo rather than perfume.

Once there, in her space, she didn't shrink from him, and he didn't back away.

He handed her the flute of champagne, his heart kicking up a notch. She accepted it with a small laugh, and for a moment their fingers brushed. Hers felt soft and slight, her nails short and free of polish.

*She's low-maintenance,* was his automatic thought. *Good.*

He lifted his glass to her. "To getting to know you better."

She gave him a smile that invited him in, like a blond Mona Lisa. He suddenly felt very predatory and very hungry. It had been…months since his last hookup, with an international flight attendant who led the same transitory lifestyle he did. They'd drifted apart, and he missed nothing about her but the sex. Maybe that was cold, but that's who he was. He just didn't feel things the way regular people did. Not anymore.

A shout went up from the dance floor. Maureen was dancing with her new husband and everyone was congratulating her.

"I hate these things," he said to Natalie.

She blinked for a moment, and then smiled harder. "I know. I'd rather be somewhere else, too. With you, of course."

"That's heartening."

She brought the flute to her lips and took a sip, so he did the same. The tart, bubbly taste jarred him. He wasn't a champagne guy, but he drank a swallow, both of them watching each other over the rims of their glasses. The magnetism between them made his blood pump.

"We should probably toast the bride," she said, licking the champagne off her lips.

He raised his glass. "To Maureen and Jimmy. May they have years of bliss ahead of them."

Her gaze moved from his mouth to his eyes, then back to his mouth. She kept doing that, and it made his groin tighten. It also told him to keep going, that she was interested. "How was that for a toast?"

"Scintillating." She lifted her glass and clinked it with his, her eyes sparkling. "And now it's my turn. To bliss. May you have a good visit in Wallis Point."

Yeah, right. If she only knew how short it would be. Then again, she was still looking at his mouth. Maybe she wanted him to stay for purely selfish reasons.

He could handle that.

He took a second drink of champagne and then put down the glass. "I'm Bruce," he said. "And you're a… friend of Maureen's?"

Her brow furrowed. Her mouth opened then closed. Then she pressed her lips together and glanced toward Maureen.

Ah, hell. And they'd been doing so well.

"I'm Natalie," she said finally. She was still staring at his mouth, so there was that. He needed to press on.

"Pleased to meet you, Natalie." He held out his hand to shake hers, but she didn't take it. For some reason, she looked disappointed.

"I'm up-to-date on all my shots," he said to lighten the mood, "and I haven't bitten anyone yet."

Finally she smiled and took his hand, and he felt himself exhale. At the soft press of her flesh against his, he felt a thousand sparks within him.

She didn't. Or maybe she did—he couldn't tell because even though she gave his hand a halfhearted shake, her sharp blue eyes were focused on his mouth. It was confusing as hell. Maybe she wanted him to shut up and take her to her hotel room for some quick sex.

That was fine with him.

But first, they needed to stop dancing around the one clarification they needed to get out in the open.

"Look," he said, steering her gently by the elbow away from some guests returning to their table with dessert plates. "I know you don't know me from Adam, and that's fine—it's how I prefer it, too. But since you're a friend of my sister's, I need you to tell me how you know her, so at least there are no misunderstandings between us."

Protecting his baby sister took priority over anything he would do in town during these few hours. Even over his own need to escape.

"What kind of misunderstandings?" she asked. At least it appeared she was considering his offer.

"I…" *When I leave, you might get mad.* It had been known to happen. She didn't look like the stalker type—he didn't get that vibe at all from her. His impression was that she was sweet and laid-back—exactly what he needed.

But a man with white hair was walking straight toward them. If Bruce wasn't mistaken, he looked like his old elementary school principal. "How about we take a walk on the beach and sort this out?" Bruce asked.

She frowned. "It's dark on the beach."

Wasn't that the point? He noticed, with alarm, that his niece Nina was skipping his way as well. "None of my family members or old teachers are there, either," he quipped.

Her head tilted as she listened to him. But it was too late. Nina ran up to them and came to a stop. Natalie put her hands lightly on his niece's head. "Hello, Nina."

Shoot. She knew his family better than he'd assumed.

"Hi, Natalie! Uncle Bruce, will you come dance with me?" Nina pleaded. She hopped up and down, clinging to his hand with both her tiny ones.

Aw, hell.

"Dance with your niece," Natalie said softly. It was

noisy, and he had to lean close to hear her. Then she turned and smiled at the white-haired gentleman. "I'll dance with Bill."

He felt deflated. He couldn't get a read on this woman, no matter how hard he tried. Altogether, nothing about her made sense. She'd come on to him, too, with her looks, her smiles. But then as soon as he'd asked how she knew Maureen, she'd turned…cautious.

But her expression was smooth, and she gave him no hint of trouble. Her face was…a mask. Happy-go-lucky. Agreeable.

Just not to him. Because as he stood there, staring, she walked off arm in arm with a guy two and a half times his age and a lot crankier. He didn't get it.

She had snubbed him. And good.

But he picked up his niece, tossed her over her shoulder the way she adored and headed for his own dark corner of the dance floor.

Because here, in this moment, he had figured it out.

Natalie *did* know him from Adam. She knew all about him from the court of public opinion. Anybody in town could have told her. Hell, Maureen could have told her.

In the three-hundred-and-fifty-year-plus history of their little seaside town, he was probably the only guy who had ever been blamed for killing his best friend, and then leaving town before the funeral to pursue his own agenda.

He willed himself to turn cold inside, still and unfeeling. No guilt, no pain. He'd had lots of practice, and of all the things he was good at, this is what he did best.

Feeling dead, he held his niece's hand as she twirled

around and around, her puffy dress expanding like a top. This was a favorite game for the "princess cowgirl," as she'd so seriously told him she wanted to be when she grew up, and though he loved her, he was afraid his heart had been pretty much burned out and shrunk to ash. There just wasn't much of anything…meaningful…he felt moved to give anybody. He wasn't sure he wanted to, even if he could. It just ended badly. The fact he'd shown up at Maureen's wedding at all…well, that was about all he was capable of giving.

"Okay, princess," he said, extricating himself when the song ended. "Let's go find your mom."

On the way to search for Maureen, he glanced to where *she* had been. Natalie. But she was gone.

*He had no idea who she was.*

Natalie walked on stiff legs across the crowded boulevard to the public beach. Overhead, a moon shone low and full. The waves lapped on the shore. A smattering of couples strolled along the wet sand at the waterline, lovers enjoying the first warm evening of this Memorial Day weekend, the symbolic opening of the season.

She'd had such high hopes with Bruce. She'd felt elated when he'd approached her, but then crushed that he didn't remember her.

Even if he didn't immediately recognize her— and she'd been willing to cut him some slack on that count—she had been the only "Natalie" in their small high school. There was no getting around the fact that he didn't remember her at all.

She sat on the sand and wrapped her arms around her knees. The breeze felt good against her face, though she still felt an ache inside. She had never considered that Bruce might not attach the same significance she did to their meeting that night—the night she'd stolen the key and unlocked the door to the room in the funeral home where the body of Brian Faulkner lay after the car accident that had killed him.

She had crouched beside Bruce in that horrible place, which smelled of chemicals and was filled with fear. The room was lit only by a tiny penlight, because she was too afraid to turn on an overhead bulb and risk them being seen. She had witnessed how Bruce had cried, listened to everything he'd told her when she'd answered the door. And after he'd begged her, she'd promised she wouldn't tell anyone. She'd thought she was special to him. Because of that, she'd never discussed with anyone how he had mourned, or how he'd sat with his friend's body, alone in the dark, all night, until the attendants came to work in the morning.

And through that night, she'd learned that what everyone else had assumed was guilt was actually something else. Yes, Brian had died in a Mercedes stolen from the valet stand where Bruce worked. But Bruce wasn't complicit; she was positive of that. After all, Brian had been alone in the car when he crashed.

For all she could see, it was obvious Bruce had not known about the stolen keys. He'd simply sat with his best friend, seeing his soul through the last of his ordeal, loyal to their friendship to the last. Everyone else in town saw guilt in his reactions, but Natalie recognized it as a heartfelt, bone-deep grief. One that came from losing his best friend.

She didn't know how to connect with people on that

level. She'd always tried—witness tonight's silly attempt at flirtation with him—but the truth was, she was inept at achieving that kind of friendship or intimacy. She had always wished she could have heard what Bruce had whispered to his friend at the end. Maybe she would have some inkling of the secret.

But she'd never know what he'd said to him, because Natalie couldn't hear very well.

That was her secret.

She stood and brushed the sand off her bottom. Now that she knew that she'd imagined the past connection with Bruce, she needed to move on. There was no point in considering him any longer; he would be leaving town soon, anyway.

Yes, it was true she was attracted to him physically. She could imagine what it would feel like to make love to Bruce Cole, to want that to happen, but it was a mistake to think about that now. She'd actually accomplished what she'd set out to do tonight, so she could forget Bruce Cole. She'd done everything Maureen had asked her to—she'd talked to him and made sure he danced with his niece when asked, just as Maureen had wanted. Natalie had fulfilled her end of the bargain. The rest was up to Maureen.

And, if there was one thing Natalie had learned today, it was that she needed to consider other ways to bring in business for her father's law firm. She had an open house planned for next week—one that she hoped would net her more contacts. A lot of planning was required, and she needed to step that up.

She found her shoes and headed back to the hotel. Her parents hadn't raised a rude daughter. She would gracefully say her goodbyes, and then extricate herself from a no-win situation. There was no one at this wedding she could help, and no one who could help her. Time to move on.

Still, she thought, as she pushed open the glass door to the hotel, it stung. It would probably always sting, but at least now she could chalk up the experience as one big lesson.

*Stay practical.*

BRUCE CIRCLED THE LOBBY three times, feeling unsettled. He'd danced with his niece for a few more songs, though it had taken all the effort he could muster to keep the numbness in place. Nina adored him and was begging him to stay. If he let her affect him, he would go crazy.

He needed to get out of here, now. Time to drive back to the airport hotel. He had a 6:00 a.m. flight out of Boston tomorrow.

But Maureen would never let him hear the end of it if he left without at least saying goodbye, so he had to stick around until he found her and his parents. He tried her cell phone but she wasn't picking up—understandable since it was still her wedding reception—and nobody knew where she was.

On his fourth circuit of the lobby, his sister emerged from the elevator. Maureen had changed out of her wedding dress and into more casual clothes. In each hand she held the chubby fists of twin boys.

Jimmy's kids from his first marriage. Maureen's new stepsons.

For a moment, something seemed to break through Bruce's self-imposed numbness. A faint tinge of...

regret? He didn't know the toddlers at all. He'd barely exchanged more than a hello with any of Maureen's new in-laws. Heck, he'd barely spoken to Maureen.

That was for the best, wasn't it?

He shook off the doubt. In the end, he made his way toward her, cognizant of the people in the vicinity, scanning their faces and wondering if he knew them.

But before he'd cleared the first set of lobby couches, Natalie appeared.

He faltered, then stopped. Why did this woman affect him so much? He couldn't help sensing something... important with her, but that didn't make any sense.

While he stood there, frozen by indecision, Natalie gave Maureen a quick hug. Then she knelt down to each boy and gave him a soft pat on the head.

Natalie was leaving the reception, too.

Without even knowing why, he switched directions to follow her. She was headed for the elevators that led to the parking garage. As he caught up to her, she stood before the closed doors, the down button lit up red.

He ambled up behind her. Leaned in close and said in a low voice, "I screwed up in there. What I meant to say is I think you're beautiful, and you look amazing in that dress. Of all the people in that room, you stood out to me. You still do."

The bell rang, the elevator door opened and Natalie walked inside. She didn't turn. She didn't look at him. She kept her face averted.

And then the doors closed, and he was left staring at his reflection in the stainless steel.

He began to laugh. If he'd been looking for a sign that he needed to get out of here, that was it. There was no place for him in this town. The old prejudices were still evident—why else would she have snubbed him? He was enough of a professional problem solver to know that some problems never got solved. They were just worked around.

He jiggled the car keys in his pocket and turned back to where Maureen had been. She was gone, but when he looked for her he found his brothers Mark and Mike instead, holding up one end of the bar, post wedding-reception.

Eight years older than him, his brothers had marched past forty with their trademark stoicism. Their only concession to a midlife crisis was that they'd each bought a boat they moored at the local marina. The two brothers ran Cole and Sons plumbing, and pretty much did everything together. They'd both married girls from their graduating high school class. They each had two kids apiece. Mark, two daughters, a toddler and an infant, while Mike had sons the same age. Their lives were mirror images of each other. Their dad was retired, but now and then when he was bored, he took a small job with them. Of course, there were always the customers who insisted on the "father, not the sons." That was because Mark and Mike charged top dollar, while Dad could be counted on to fall for a hard-luck story. And sometimes, he plain forgot to bill people.

Bruce stood and looked at his brothers, their backs turned to him. Their blond hair was getting thinner, and their waistlines thicker. But they seemed content with their lives. "Townies" at heart.

Still dressed in their wedding tuxes, they each grasped a beer bottle—Mike left-handed, Mark right-handed—and were watching the baseball game on the big-screen TV. At the bottom of the sixth inning, the local team was losing.

Bruce clapped Mark on the shoulder. "Marcus, I'm headed out."

Mark turned and blinked at him. "You just got here, B.B."

B.B. was short for "Bruce Boy." He'd forgotten that stupid nickname.

"Yup," he said. "And now I'm leaving."

Mark took a drink of beer and nodded. He had been in Florida on a plumbing job with their parents back when Bruce had gotten into all his trouble with the law. None of them had ever really discussed it. "Did you check with Moe?" Mark asked.

"What, she runs our lives now?" Bruce said.

"She tries." Mike took his hand and shook it. "How's the weather in Florida?"

"Dunno, Mikhael," Bruce said. "I haven't been home in a week."

"Where've you been?" Both twins stared at him. They were always slightly bewildered that Bruce traveled for a living instead of staying put in Fort Lauderdale and enjoying his boat and his motorcycle in the sunshine.

"I'm on a project in D.C. The navy hired me to analyze their procurement systems."

He earned blank stares from his brothers. But that was good—if they didn't know what he was talking about, they wouldn't ask questions, which meant he could bug out of town even sooner.

"Bruce! When did you get here?"

Internally he groaned. Mark's wife, Desiree, stood on her toes to kiss him on the cheek, and Mike's wife, Holly, followed suit. A real family reunion. At this rate, he'd never be able to leave.

But he smiled, gave each of them the requisite kiss, went through the motions of being a sociable brother-in-law. "You two are looking better and better. How are the kids?"

"My niece Kristen is watching them upstairs in the room," Desiree told him. "You should go see them." She scratched her head, and Bruce noticed she had a new tattoo on her wrist. Some kind of Chinese symbol. "Your mother is up there, too. I swear, she's in her glory. She loves it when we all get together."

"She'll be in heaven when we're all in Disney World together," Holly agreed.

It was Bruce's turn to stare. What was she talking about?

Oh, yeah. The whole clan was going together for the week of Maureen's honeymoon: his parents, his siblings and their kids, mainly so Maureen and Jimmy's three wouldn't be too upset by their parents' absence. Bruce had covered the airfare, hotel and the car rental with his points, so he'd contributed without having to go with them. "I'm sure you'll all have a good time."

"It was so great of you to agree to stay here while we're gone. We've got the house all set for you," Desiree added.

Wait, what? Warnings went off in his head. "No, I'm leaving," he stated as calmly as he could. "I'm taking the 6:00 a.m. flight out tomorrow."

"The fridge is stocked," Desiree continued rapid-fire.

Sometimes he wondered at their habit of talking over everybody. Maybe it was part of being in a big family. "And we changed the sheets on our bed, so you can use our room. There's a copy of the instructions tacked to the refrigerator. All you have to remember to do is to leave the screen door unlocked for the dog-sitter."

Mark and Desiree had two yapping dachshunds. "Sorry, you've got me mixed up with somebody else." He didn't do pets.

Holly shook her head. "I don't think so."

"You haven't talked to Moe yet, have you?" Desiree asked.

"Where is she?"

"She's up in the room with Mom and the kids."

His mother lived and died for her grandkids. She'd been sixty when Nina was born, and on that day, she had promptly retired from being the dispatcher and chief bookkeeper for the family plumbing business. Holly currently did the honors. Desiree was some kind of nurse.

"Or Jimmy," Holly added. "He's the one who organized it all."

What had Jimmy organized? "I'm not part of this plan, whatever it is," Bruce said coldly.

Holly and Desiree glanced at each other. He was getting all kinds of bad signals.

"I think," Holly said slowly, "that you had better talk to Maureen."

"Isn't she on her honeymoon as of now?" he demanded.

Mark ambled up beside him. The ball game had cut to commercial.

Bruce pointed to his brother. "Tell your wife I'm flying back to D.C. in the morning. Tell her that I work for a living. I've already used my two weeks' vacation, and I don't have time for a social call."

"We're having a family emergency," Mark calmly explained. "Everybody's got to pitch in."

"What are you talking about?" he demanded.

Everyone went quiet and he realized he'd been shouting. His brothers looked solemn. Their wives just looked sorry for him.

Bruce ground his teeth and got control of his emotions, waiting for them to explain. As a business consultant, he always waited for the people with the problems to speak first. But he suspected his family was all a little bit afraid of him now. He didn't blame them; he had reached the end of his rope. This trip home had left him edgy, and he didn't like it. This wasn't like him. On the job, he was known for being Mr. Cool. He skimmed the surface of life; he didn't get sucked into the muck. And if they weren't used to that by now, it was their problem.

"Look, I'll see you guys next Thanksgiving," Bruce said quietly. "In Florida, like always."

"You really need to talk to Maureen," Mike said.

"And why is that?"

Holly and Desiree snuck a glance at each other. A loaded glance, ripe with meaning. He just didn't know what it meant. Mark looked at his toes, and Mike was busy peeling the label off his beer bottle.

"If you can't tell me, then it can't be that important," Bruce said. "Now if you'll excuse me." He pulled out his phone and pressed the speed dial number for Maureen. Honeymoon or no honeymoon, he was solving this problem before he left.

Desiree put her hand on his arm. "It's Gramps. He's sick."

Everything within Bruce stilled. He should have known something would have been very wrong to keep Gramps from coming to Maureen's wedding.

"How sick?" he asked.

"They gave him a CAT scan this week," Holly said. "Gramps has beginning stages Alzheimer's."

Bruce felt as if he'd been sucker-punched. He needed to sit.

Leaning against a barstool, he tried to remember his last interaction with Gramps. Thanksgiving, six months ago at his place. Gramps hadn't been quite as strong as usual, but he'd been riding in Bruce's boat, for cripe's sake. And he'd seemed completely lucid.

"He's frail, Bruce. He's been going downhill rapidly. You won't recognize him."

Bruce turned back to his his phone. He'd have to check flight times for tomorrow afternoon. "I'll visit him early before I leave." He'd be flying out on standby, and that meant a middle seat in the rear of the plane beside the bathrooms, but for Gramps, he would do it.

He was glad that nothing had worked out with Natalie after all. He wanted to be alone tonight.

Now he needed a local hotel room, too. There was no way he was staying in Desiree's house with her dogs and her nosy neighbors.

Scrolling through his phone's contact list, he strode toward the bellhop stand, typing as he went. By the time he'd retrieved his suitcase, he'd changed his flight and canceled his reservation at the airport hotel in Boston. He went to the front desk to book a room, momentarily confused that there was no frequent-traveler check-in station, and that he had to wait in a long and snaking holiday-weekend line beside people who commandeered the luggage carts and loaded them with mounds of duffel bags, piles of grocery bags and cases of soda, water and beer.

When he finally got to the front of the line, he was incredulous to hear that there were no rooms available.

And he didn't have status here, because this wasn't a national chain.

*I'm in hell.*

"It's Sandcastle Weekend," the bubbly clerk explained.

"It's *what?*"

"You've never heard of it? Sand sculptors come from all over the world to compete for prizes. It's our second biggest weekend of the summer, after Fourth of July week, of course."

Great. His sleepy little hometown had turned international on him.

He was contemplating sleeping in his car when he bumped into Maureen. Without a word, just a shake of her head, she tucked a room key into his hand.

He opened his palm and looked at it. "*How* did you get this?"

"I reserved a room for you months ago, Bruce. It was booked for last night, too, in case you'd changed your mind about attending the rehearsal dinner."

He suddenly felt ashamed of himself. Moe rarely asked him for anything. She'd just wanted him to come to her wedding like a normal brother.

A tear had leaked out and was running down her

cheek. "Aw, honey." With nothing else to say, he put an arm around her shoulder.

"We need you to stay for the week, Bruce."

"You know I can't." He suddenly felt tired.

"If you don't, then I have to stay home from my honeymoon." "

"That's…blackmail."

She pushed her hair out of her eyes. "No, it's life, Bruce. We have to take care of each other. And frankly, you've been doing a piss-poor job."

"That is not fair," he said.

"Isn't it? How is it fair that we've all been taking turns visiting Gramps every day, making sure he sees a familiar face because he's terrified about what's happening to him, and yet, you're not a part of it? And you'll never be a part of it, because you never come home. If he's lucky, you might show up for his funeral after he's gone, but we can't even count on that."

She was referring to him missing Nana's funeral a year ago. Well, he'd been in China then. He'd had no choice. "Do not go there," he said coldly.

"Why not, Bruce? It's true. You've cut yourself off from everyone. No one knows you anymore. The only reason Nina recognizes you is that she sees your photo on the bureau when we visit Gramps every day. He can't remember me, he can't remember Nina, but he remembers you. The guy has one son, one daughter-in-law, four grandchildren, seven great-grandchildren and of all of us, you're the only one whose picture he displays. *You're* his favorite, and you can't even see fit to visit him for one week. To *support* us for one week."

"I support you plenty."

Maureen paused, and in her silence, Bruce knew exactly what she was thinking. "We're all tired of this, Bruce," she said quietly. "Get over it."

"I *am* over it." It was the nonfamily members who weren't. Natalie, for one. "I stayed away to make it easier for you and the rest of the family. I still do."

"You know, I used to think it was best you stayed away, too, Bruce. You're right...sometimes it's hard being here. But lately I've been changing my mind. Family is important." Her voice broke. "I waited until you got here to tell you, but if you really want to make it easier for me, then you'll step up and help me while I'm gone. Visit Gramps for the week. You're the only person left for him, and he needs you. Don't you understand?"

He did. And he couldn't even spin it anymore, not even to himself.

That was the worst part about it.

# CHAPTER FOUR

SOMEONE WAS JUMPING on him.

"Wake up, Uncle Bruce!" Nina screamed in his ear. "We're going to Disney World!"

Bruce opened one eye. Sunlight streamed in through wide-open curtains. His head ached. For a moment he struggled to remember where he was, a definite drawback to the traveling lifestyle.

Nina smacked him on the temple with a plastic magic wand. "Your hair looks funny. You have bedhead," she announced.

That was amusing, coming from a six-year-old who wore Mickey Mouse ears and a sparkly princess costume, complete with wig and plastic purse.

His raised a brow at her and propped himself up on one elbow, but his stomach seemed to turn over. Last night Mark and Mike had followed him up here—to this room Moe had reserved for him at the Grand Beachfront Hotel. They'd carried a case of beer with them. Bruce knew the only reason they had made the effort was that a woman in the bar—he thought she might have been one of Bunny Faulkner's former cleaning maids—had made a comment about him.

"Stole the keys from the valet stand here and got his best friend killed," she'd whispered to a cohort sitting on a stool beside her. He wasn't surprised to hear it, but he'd left because he didn't want his family to have to deal with that.

And they hadn't. Mark and Mike hadn't said a word about it, and neither had he.

He gave his niece one of his easygoing smiles. "Hiya, princess. Where's your mother?"

"I'm right here," Maureen snapped, both hands on her hips. Her face was pinched and she was looking around the hotel room like a superior officer getting ready to assess him demerits. "This place smells like a brewery."

Yep, the three Cole brothers had killed the case of beer between them. "You should be proud, Moe." He winked at her. "Your wedding brought about the first real Cole brother reunion in years. Makes me feel in the family mood, it does."

"Don't be a jerk, Bruce."

He rolled over and covered Nina's ears. "Think of the children."

Nina giggled and bashed him with her wand again.

"Ouch, that hurts," he said in his best cartoon-character voice. His niece shrieked with laughter.

"Bruce, I'm not kidding," Maureen said. "Get dressed. We don't have much time."

Apparently not. She was standing before him with suitcase packed, papers in hand. Well, it was for the best.

He gave her a mock salute, not willing to let himself get sucked into a bad mood, but her back was already turned and she was answering her cell phone. Her real estate voice was engaged. She stepped out into the hallway, momentarily bringing in the sounds of chaos before she closed the door behind her.

He turned and waggled his brows at Nina, who was

now clinging to his back. "Time for you to leave so I can shower and get out of here, princess cowgirl."

She whispered into his ear. "I wish you were coming to Disney World with us."

Again, that regret tugged at him, nagging him to *feel,* but he pushed it away. "Honey, I live near Disney World. Any time you want to come for a school vacation, ask your mom to give me a call and I'll pick you up at the airport."

She gave him a pout. "I want you to come back *here* and get me."

Nina had Maureen's long, dark lashes and the same big, luminous blue eyes he remembered on his sister as a kid. He suddenly couldn't do this anymore, sit and joke around with everyone as if nothing had happened, as if he was still that same guy, still a part of them.

He wasn't anymore, and never would be again. Last night had proved that.

But he couldn't say that to his niece. Instead he nodded. "Call me when you get to Cinderella's castle."

Then he opened the door and ushered Nina outside, and saw that, yes, the ruckus had been from his boisterous family, gathered in the hallway. Mark and Mike looked as if their heads felt fine and it didn't bother them that their kids were screaming and running up and down the corridor. Two of the older ones—cousins, maybe?—were playing keep-away with their sister's stuffed animal. "Lambie!" she screeched.

He smiled to himself. This crew was a danger to sleeping travelers everywhere. If he didn't know them, he'd be cringing.

"Here's the packet with everything you'll need for

Gramps." Maureen pushed her way back into his hotel room, shoving a manila envelope labeled in her big, bold handwriting into his hands. "The main thing to remember," she said in that drill sergeant voice, "is that he has an MRI scheduled for Wednesday at the hospital. The home has a van that can take him, but he needs constant supervision, so it's best that you go with him."

"To the hospital?" He looked at her as if she was nuts—because she was if she thought he'd be any kind of help there.

"Yes, Bruce, to the hospital." She stared him straight in the eye. "The Wallis Point Regional Hospital."

He felt his jaw grinding. *If he remembered correctly, Bunny Faulkner had worked there. The last person in the world who would want to see him.*

He hauled his suitcase upright and unzipped it to find his toothbrush. It was best he got all the details out in front, now. "Does anyone know me at this nursing home of Gramps?" he asked as calmly as he could.

Maureen sighed. "I thought you said you were over it."

He glanced sharply at her. "I don't want it taken out on Gramps if somebody petty remembers the gossip," he said quietly.

Her lips pressed tight together. She didn't like what he was saying.

"Your friend, Natalie," he remarked casually, as he rooted in the side pocket for his toothpaste, "gave me a strange reaction last night after I introduced myself."

"That's probably because you hit on her." Maureen snorted. "I saw you come on to her. Way to be subtle, Bruce."

He smiled and shook his head. He'd approached Natalie only because she'd been "hitting on him," too. There had been an attraction across that crowded ballroom. He couldn't possibly have mistaken that. "Do you expect me to be a monk?"

She rolled her eyes. "You're here to take care of Gramps."

Which he was going to do. Today. Today *only*. He'd thought about it last night and had realized what should have been obvious from the beginning: he had the cash, he could hire a great private nurse to give Gramps the extra-special attention that Bruce could not. And as soon as he got to this nursing home, he would make inquiries.

But Moe didn't need to know that. It would upset her unnecessarily, and there was no need for that as she got ready for her honeymoon. He wasn't that big a jerk.

Maureen's phone chirped again, and she glanced at it. "The van to the airport is here. Bruce, I have to wrap this up." She opened her purse and pulled out an envelope with a slip of paper attached by a paper clip. "Here it is. I went through hoops to honor your request not to stay in any of the family homes. I've been working the phones all morning to find you a rental that's still open."

He glanced at the bedside clock. "It's 8:00 a.m., Moe."

"And real estate never sleeps. Lucky for you I'm an insomniac, because this is beachfront. A private cottage." She pressed the envelope into his hands. "Close to Gramps's nursing home, so you can spend time with him without worrying about weekend traffic."

The address was for an exclusive area on the water and accessible only by private road. He whistled, suddenly intrigued. "How did you manage this one?"

"I pulled in a favor. I didn't particularly like doing it, which should show you how much I'm willing to go to bat for you." She glanced at her phone, which was beeping again. "Look, I'll call you from the road. I need to get everybody going." She leaned over and half hugged him around the shoulder. "Take care of Gramps," she whispered into his ear. "And thank you."

As a rule, Coles did not thank each other. That meant she was seriously rattled about Gramps's condition.

"He'll be fine, Moe," was all he said.

She nodded, her lips pressed together. "Please call me when you see him," she said. And then she began marshaling her caravan down the hallway.

The poor kid would never enjoy her honeymoon. He fumed with his impotence in this situation. This made it all the more critical to hire somebody great—somebody capable—to protect and take care of Gramps for her.

Once Bruce was showered and dressed, he cleared out, repacking the few items he'd taken from his suitcase. Just another anonymous hotel room in another anonymous town. He'd have to look at the situation that way.

NATALIE WAS SLEEPING soundly when the phone she always kept inside her pillowcase vibrated against her cheek and jolted her awake.

Her first thought was that she was late for the class she'd volunteered to teach. Berating herself, and without looking to see who was calling, she muttered a greeting into the phone.

"I wasn't expecting you to pick up," Maureen Cole said. "I was hoping to leave a message. We're on the way to the airport, and I didn't want to…" The rest of her words were blurred.

There was all kinds of background noise. A baby was crying—make that two babies—and it sounded as if a group of people were all talking at once.

Natalie turned down her phone's volume a bit.

"…and I wanted to thank you again for being in my wedding," Maureen was saying. "I appreciate that you went out of your way for me, and I won't forget it."

And just like that a glow filled Natalie. The disappointment of feeling out of place last night seemed to vanish. "I…thanks for saying that. I appreciate it, too."

Maureen kept talking over her. "…and also to let you know that I called your father and offered to bring him some new business because of you."

Natalie felt her jaw drop. "You're kidding," she squeaked. "That's great news."

*Beep.* Natalie had a call coming in. Her father's name flashed on the screen.

"Maureen, could you hold on for one moment?"

"No, I can't, we're almost at the airport. I wanted to prepare you for Bruce showing up at your house this morning."

Natalie sucked in her breath. Bruce was still in town?

*Beep.* She ignored her father's call. "Go on, Maureen. I'm listening."

"I needed a place for Bruce to stay," Maureen continued in her rapid-fire cadence. "I called your father and we came to an understanding about renting one of his properties for the week. He said there's an empty cottage where you're staying, and I told him that would be perfect. We just need you to tape an envelope with the key to the door. You don't even have to talk to my brother. I'm sorry he was such a dog to you last night."

Natalie sank slowly into her mattress. Was she hearing this right? Bruce was *staying in town? With her?*

"Natalie?"

A strangled sound came out of her throat. First of all, Maureen was mistaken. The cottage wasn't a cottage—it was a minuscule guest house, and it was on *her* property, not her father's.

This was Natalie's one inheritance from her grandfather. She'd wanted a stake in the family law firm, and instead, she'd gotten a falling-down dwelling that had so far eaten up more money than it would bring in for the next couple of years.

Still, it was the only significant asset that Natalie had ever owned, and she was grateful. She was currently in process of renovating it into two separate properties so that she could sell the guest house and earn some money to pay off her not-insignificant college loans.

*Beep.* Her father again.

He'd had no right to enter into this agreement without her okay. She could feel a slow burn starting, which was uncharacteristic of her.

"Hello? Natalie, are you there?" Maureen asked.

"I…need to talk with my father," Natalie answered.

"The deal is *done,*" Maureen said, with a hint of sharpness to her voice. Natalie blinked. She hadn't wanted to insult her. Ultimately, she needed Maureen on her side.

"Bruce will be over within the hour, okay?" Maureen said.

Natalie gulped in a breath. This could not be happening. "Just out of curiosity, why isn't Bruce staying at your house?"

"Maybe he wants a place on the beach. Is there a problem, Natalie? Because I really need to get going. I have three other calls I need to make before we hit the airport."

"No problems." Actually there were many problems. The apartment was a construction zone, for one, which was why she hadn't been able to rent it for the summer. But ten to one her father hadn't told Maureen that. Well, Bruce could see it and leave if he chose. All she had to do was her bit in helping Maureen. "Tell him… I'll meet him at noon."

Yes, she would assert herself. She needed Maureen's goodwill, but she also needed to stay on guard. As a lawyer, she had to be a diplomat who could balance everyone's needs. That's what good diplomats did.

"Sounds like a plan." Maureen sounded relieved. "And, Natalie, thank you again."

"Have a great honeymoon."

"I can't tell you how good it's going to feel to hand over Nina to my parents." Maureen suddenly sounded tired, which immediately made Natalie feel guilty. In the future, she should cut Maureen more slack.

But there was no helping Bruce. The guy that he used to be…that was lost.

As much as Brian Faulkner was lost.

The whole thing was too depressing to think of.

Bruce Cole had gone from being a guy who was soulful and intimate and a good friend to a guy who just didn't care.

Natalie headed for the shower. She had a busy day

ahead. She would not worry about Bruce, and she certainly would not succumb to his charms. At this stage in her life, she did not do flings or meaningless hookups—especially not with guys who couldn't remember who she was.

If Bruce had any other plans with her for this week, then he was mistaken.

BRUCE WHEELED THE MERCEDES past the Residents Only sign into the exclusive cul-de-sac at the north end of Wallis Point. The lots alone cost megabucks, and most were owned by wealthy out-of-towners, not the blue-collar guys he'd gone to school with.

He checked the address Moe had given him against the number on the mailbox. The cottage she'd rented for him was the only modest dwelling on the street, a one-story weathered home with a big porch, classical in its simple New England beauty.

He parked the Mercedes in the empty driveway and relaxed. The out-of-the-way place calmed him. It was perfect for what he needed today. No one would bother him here. This afternoon he could get some work done remotely and still be able to check on Gramps before he blew out of town for good. No one would even know he was here.

He grabbed his briefcase and overnight bag from the trunk and approached the front porch, surprising a big gray tomcat napping in the sun. A real mouser by the look of him. At Bruce's step, the cat opened his eyes and beat the hell out of there. Bruce knew how he felt; too bad he couldn't do the same just yet.

The door was locked. He glanced at his watch. If he

could get inside the house, he could check it out quickly before he visited Gramps. At some point, he could head out to the main road until he found a grocery store to buy something to eat. Maybe he'd even find a vendor's stall where he could pick up a bathing suit and a beach towel. It was hot outside, and the beach in back looked private. He would have a good afternoon alone, before he flew out of Boston this evening.

But he needed to get into the house first. He opened the envelope Maureen had given him, but other than paperwork for the nursing home, there was nothing there. And she hadn't said anything about a key.

Likely she'd forgotten in her rush to get to the airport. He jiggled the door, but the bolt was strong. The windows looked old; he could try to jam them, if worse came to worst. But for now, he was standing on a homey-looking doormat that said Welcome. He tried the obvious, stepped back and lifted it.

And found a single, shiny key.

This was too easy. He unlocked the door, stepped inside the small cottage and immediately knew that something felt wrong about this place.

The house was not an empty rental property. Somebody *lived* here.

He pulled out the slip of paper Maureen had given him and double-checked the address. Yeah, this was the place. The cottage was sunny, freshly painted and clean-smelling. Decorated nicely, actually, with posters of faraway places and shelves of books. But whoever lived here, well, they weren't the neatest people. The sitting room was cluttered with clothing and papers. In the kitchen, breakfast dishes were still on the dining table, a half-eaten bowl of oatmeal with spoon inside. Hello, Goldilocks.

He put down his suitcase. "Is anybody home?" he called out.

A shrill buzzing rang out. He jumped, then realized it was an old-fashioned telephone with the ringer turned up high, like the one his grandfather had owned when he was a kid. When the ringing stopped, Bruce picked up the receiver.

The dial tone also seemed extra loud. Bruce jerked and pulled it away from his ear. Wow, that brought back memories from living with Gramps during his senior year in high school. Bruce looked more closely at the plastic handle. Yep. It had that same super-loud volume-control dial on the side.

On a whim, Bruce picked up the TV remote from the coffee table. Clicked on the small, old-fashioned television. If he was right, the sound would blare like a dozen trumpets being blown.

But no, the volume was turned down. Instead he read the slow crawl of words across the bottom of the screen. Close-captioned for the hearing impaired.

Obviously an elderly person lived in this quaint, doll-size cottage. Only that didn't make sense, either, because beside the refrigerator was a pair of very high-heeled, very strappy, very sexy black sandals.

And on the couch, in a ray of sunlight, a plastic laundry basket contained a jumble of, ah…unmentionables. Sexy, lacy, girly unmentionables.

It didn't seem likely that senior citizens were wearing pink Victoria's Secret bras.

As he glanced up from the laundry, he saw a face in

the window beside the front door. Natalie—the woman from the wedding last night—the one who had snubbed him. She was leaning over, fumbling with her purse.

With one thumb he speed-dialed Moe's cell phone number.

She answered on the first ring. "Hi, Bruce. What's up?"

"This house I'm renting...it wouldn't happen to belong to your friend Natalie, would it?"

"Is that a problem?"

The door opened, and Natalie strolled inside, dressed in a loose skirt and yellow top, talking to herself in a voice dainty and soft, like she was. The big, gray-striped mouser she held in her arms seemed to hang on her every word.

"No, no problem," he said to Moe. "I'll talk with you later."

He stuck his phone in his pocket and felt himself grinning. Why not? Natalie didn't hate him. He'd been wrong about that. This was the problem he hadn't been able to see until now. Her reaction to him last night hadn't been about him at all—he simply hadn't realized that she'd been keeping her own secret safe.

Whistling, he leaned back against her kitchen counter and waited for her to see him. Because she certainly wasn't going to hear him.

Natalie was deaf.

# CHAPTER FIVE

NATALIE POCKETED HER KEY so she wouldn't lose it again, fumbling with Otis's weight as her neighbor's big tomcat hung over her left elbow. The neighborhood hunter had wooed her until she'd finally let him into the house and fed him during the lunch hour when his owners were at work. That one weakness of hers, sharing the milk from her cereal bowl with him because she'd wanted so badly to connect with somebody—some living thing— had been enjoyable at the time, but in the long run, she knew it was a mistake.

Otis was not her cat. If she let herself get attached to him, she would only get her heart broken. But the feline couldn't care less about that; he was doing everything he could to ingratiate himself into her life and her good graces, to make her fall for him.

Well, she was going to stop that, as soon as her supply of cat food was gone. She dropped Otis and let him attack the bowl of kibble she kept beside the door for him. She would not share a can of tuna with him—her lunch—no matter how he attempted to charm her.

"Hello," a loud, cool-toned voice called from inside her house.

She screamed and jumped. Otis bolted over her bare feet and up the staircase to her bedroom, where he'd never been before. She whirled blindly, her instincts shouting for her to grab for a weapon, something to strike out with, but in the next split second she saw him—

Bruce Cole.

He looked as calm and unruffled as he had last night. He was wearing a navy blue T-shirt that brought out a hint of midnight-blue in his dark brown eyes, and a pair of khaki shorts. This was the first she'd seen of Bruce's body, his bare skin, and for a moment she couldn't think of anything else.

This man had a way of reminding her about sex whenever she was around him. His hair was damp as though he'd rolled out of bed and into the shower. His presence in her kitchen seemed…intimate in a way she'd never imagined. He leaned one hip against her counter as if he belonged there. His arms were crossed and he was smiling mysteriously.

"You aren't supposed to be in here," she said.

"Sorry." His lips curved, and when she dared to look into his eyes, she saw that they were twinkling.

"Maureen gave me the address, but she forgot to give me a key," Bruce said, pushing away from the counter and walking toward her. "I found one under the mat. Once I was inside, I figured I'd made a mistake." He stopped, inches from her. "Is it a mistake, Natalie?"

No matter how she'd wanted to resist him, she couldn't. With one look, one tilt of his charming mouth, that crinkle to his eyes, Bruce made her feel as if she were in a magic bubble with him and they were the only two people in the world.

This was how she'd fallen for him as a girl. She'd thought that part of him was gone, that he had lost it.

Maybe it was still there, hidden deep.

"It's…not a mistake," she said.

He nodded. "I'm sorry we got off on the wrong foot last night. I tried to apologize to you."

She hadn't expected this. Her nails dug into her palms. She couldn't stop looking in his deep brown eyes, not even to cut her gaze to follow what his mouth was saying.

"I saw you at the elevator," he said. "I wanted to clear up the misunderstanding we were having when I asked you to leave with me."

She was caught on his every word, forgetting why she was supposed to resist him. "There's no need for you to apologize."

"Why didn't you tell me you're hearing impaired?" he asked.

What? How could he possibly know that about her?

Then she saw the TV remote in his hand. Last night she'd been watching a movie before bed; the actors had been mumbling behind too-loud background music, poorly edited. With old movies, they'd at least enunciated so audiences could hear. She'd had to turn on the captions just to figure out the dialogue.

"My hearing is fine." She snatched the remote from him.

But her hand had touched his. She looked up and his eyes were warm with regard for her. As long as she lived, she'd probably never get over her silly crush on this man.

"What do you propose we do about it?" he asked.

"I propose that we drop the subject entirely," she snapped.

His smile grew larger. "I didn't say anything, Natalie. I moved my lips but I didn't make a sound. I wanted to see if you could lip-read."

She gasped. She'd never been more mortified in her life.

"My gramps didn't have that skill," he said, his voice clear and loud now, "and that's why he couldn't hide his loss, but you can. It's true, isn't it?"

"You're wrong," she said.

"Why are you so defensive about it?"

Natalie blinked. Bruce was standing in her space with that focus, as if she was a problem to solve and he enjoyed figuring her out. That was even more painful to her, because even though he knew her secret, he didn't know who she was—not really.

But even more than her silly leftover disappointment that he didn't recognize her, there was a new, worse danger: What if he exposed her? What if people in town found out that she couldn't hear well? She had a terrible insecurity that nobody would trust her as a lawyer if they knew.

She swiveled away from him, stalking into her living room to put her remote away. If she could calm down and think…

She looked out the window at the beach and watched the waves roll to the shore. She had two choices: she could diplomatically handle Bruce's probing questions, or she could protect herself by going on the attack.

The threat was real. Rubbing her bare arms, she nibbled at her lip. Last night had shown that she and Bruce would not connect, that the fantasy she'd had of the two of them together would never happen.

*Push him away.*

She normally didn't behave like this. She felt heated from the inside and was sure her cheeks were bright red.

She marched back into the kitchen and confronted Bruce, who was waiting where she'd left him. "This is *my* house," she said. "You are not staying *here*...you are staying in the guest house next door."

"Why are you mad?" He stepped closer. He was on the offensive as well. "Are you afraid I'll tell people what I know about you?"

"No!" she blurted.

He snapped his fingers. "*That's* why you didn't want to walk on the beach last night," he said loudly, so she could hear him clearly. "Because you couldn't see well enough to lip-read."

"Stop that!"

"You look at my mouth when you talk." He grinned. "I like it."

"I am not interested in your mouth!" Edgy and close to tears, she pulled open the screen door and headed down the cement pathway that led to the small guest house next to the cottage, hoping he would follow without comment. The sun was hot, beating on her bare head as she passed the spot where Otis liked to stretch out like he was king of the property—she'd left him in her bedroom alone, but there was nothing she could do about that now. The cat she could handle; Bruce was her bigger problem.

She dug in her pocket for the key she'd gone into town this morning to copy for him. The wisest thing to do now was to show Bruce the space she'd agreed to let him stay in, and then if he chose to settle in, to evict herself for the week. She could always stay at her parents' house if she needed to.

She glanced back and saw Bruce strolling behind her with a lazy, athletic gait, his laptop bag slung over his shoulder.

"I lived with my gramps, you know," he called out so she could hear him without lip-reading. "He had a loud TV and a phone turned up all the way. I know the signs."

She covered her ears, and he stepped in front of her. "It's too late—I know your secret, Natalie." He winked at her. "Cat can't go back in the bag."

"Why are you doing this to me?"

He leaned closer and dropped his voice. "I promise I won't tell anyone." He waited until she looked back at his mouth again, and said, "Not even Maureen."

"Don't you *dare* tell her!" Oh, God, she was close to tears.

"You're good at lip-reading," he said, catching her arm as she turned. "I wouldn't have guessed if I hadn't spoken to you at the elevator last night. But I was behind you and you didn't know I was there."

She sat on the bench in front of the guest house and sniffled. It was no use. Lowering her head to her hands, she gave up.

Aw, HELL. Bruce had enjoyed pushing Natalie, just to shake her out of that buttoned-up stance she'd taken with him, but the last thing he'd wanted was to make her cry.

He sighed and sat down on the bench beside her, dropping the laptop bag to his feet. Should he attempt to console her? He was out of practice with these things. But the truth was, he was still sitting beside her instead of gunning it out of her driveway, just because he was so attracted to her. Everything she felt showed all over her face, which gave her a fragile air and made him want to protect her. Her curtain of hair fell over her face. Thick and light brown with sunny highlights.

*She wears it long like that to cover her ears.* Maybe she *did* wear a hearing aid? He wanted to pick up her hair, uncover her poor, faulty ears. Bring the hair to his nose and smell it. Touch it with his fingers.

Where was this coming from? This wasn't him. He didn't feel anything for anybody, especially not a stranger.

He pushed away from her and stood. Moved back from that garden bench where she was blinking fast to keep the tears from coming.

He bent and retrieved his laptop. He was two steps up the pathway when she spoke.

"I got earaches all the time when I was little," she said.

He turned, and saw her pressing her wrist to the corner of her eyes. He paused.

"My parents took me to doctors," she continued. "They gave me antibiotics. I missed a lot of school, but I still kept getting earaches. It was chronic, the medical people told us."

Unable to stop listening to her soft voice, he sat down beside her again.

"They said my Eustachian tubes were too small to properly drain any fluid that got inside. After a while, I needed surgery. Tubes in the ears." She glanced up at him, her tone steady. "Have you ever heard of that before?"

He found himself nodding, responding to her. He couldn't help it; he was drawn to her calmness. She was like a sunny meadow after a hurricane.

"I've been fortunate with my health," he said.

She nodded back. "I'm lucky that it happened when I was young."

Something in him moved. "Did the tubes help you?"

"No." She shook her head. "They kept falling out. We switched doctors a few times, but it was always the same result. More antibiotics and tubes in the ears." She smiled wistfully. "I got to be an expert at hospitals."

"How old were you during all this?"

She shrugged. "Young. When I was about ten or twelve, I…" She paused. "Well, the long and the short of it is that I stopped telling people when I got an ear infection." She fiddled with the key she held in her lap. "Nobody noticed. For about six months, I taught myself to lip-read in school. They used to give us hearing tests every semester, but I fooled those nurses, too. I would watch when the other kids were raising their hands, and every so often, I raised my hand, too. Nobody realized."

She was so quiet, so shy and unassuming, he could totally see it. "Didn't you have siblings? Anyone older who would've noticed?"

"No, there was just me. But that has nothing to do with it." She smiled tightly. "When I was being fitted for my yearly earplugs for summer camp, the technician looked in my ears, and saw the infections. She referred my parents to someone—a surgeon we hadn't been to before and…" Her voice turned soft. "He was the best person who ever could have come into my life. He treated me as an adult, explained everything he was doing and fixed my ears completely. He saved my life, possibly. I almost became a doctor, too, because of him. But…"

"What did you become?" he asked gently.

She took in a breath. "The important thing is, I don't want anybody to know or to talk about my ears." She turned and gazed long and hard at him. "Just as you don't want people to talk to you about Brian's accident."

He stared at her. Nobody had dared to say Brian's name to him in years.

But she kept talking as if nothing was wrong or out of the ordinary, in that gentle, matter-of-fact voice of hers. "So that's why I'm going to ask you to keep my hearing problems a secret, Bruce. To protect me from having to address it with people."

"Wait a minute." Bruce stood, blocking her exit. Yeah, he was way too close to her. In her face, almost, but he couldn't help it. "*What* did you just say to me about Brian?"

"COME INSIDE," Natalie said quietly, "I'll show you the space."

Yes, she was ignoring Bruce's question, and on purpose. She had hoped to make a point with him—that while he might have discovered her painful secret, she knew he had one, too. And it seemed to be working. He was quietly thoughtful, no longer probing her.

"First," she said, standing and brushing off her skirt, stepping sideways so he wasn't quite so close. "I have to warn you, the room where you're staying is unfinished. I mean, completely unfinished. The walls inside are studs. It's wired for electricity and basic plumbing, but that's about it. There's not even a working shower hooked up yet."

He stared at her. She smiled sweetly at him, turned and led him to the entrance, hidden off the pathway near the beach. He followed, but didn't speak—she checked once or twice by turning her head, and each time he looked at her with haunted eyes.

She felt ashamed of herself for having been rude to him earlier. That wasn't her normal behavior at all. But everything about Bruce Cole's presence had thrown her off her stride.

In the end, she'd decided that the best way to disarm him was to tell him the truth. Not because she'd wanted him to know—nobody had *ever* heard this story—but because it was easiest. Life worked better when she was nonthreatening and diplomatic. That's who she was. It was her personality and her strength, and it was comfortable for her, so why should she change into something she wasn't?

Unlike Bruce, she didn't have a direct personality; she wasn't confrontational, and the few times in her life that she'd been angered into going on the attack, she had only made things worse for herself. Witness the earlier exchange with him.

She made it up to him by smiling at him as she threw her weight against the sticky, creaky door and gently budged it open. "This place may be a work in progress," she explained, "but it has awesome potential. Wait until you see the view."

He tilted his head, assessing her. She held out her hand for him to enter.

A moment passed, then another. Curiosity seemed

to get the better of him. Squinting, he looked up at the recently redone roofline.

"I see why I missed this place from the road," he remarked, waiting to speak until she was looking at him. He enunciated his words loudly and clearly. Not in an overt, cartoonish manner, but in a way that showed respect for her.

She appreciated that. Maybe she'd been wrong to judge him so harshly.

Standing aside, she held open the door. He accepted her invitation and crossed the threshold. Then she followed him inside the guest house, waiting for his reaction.

When it was finished, this would be a beautiful space. The small dwelling she'd inherited from her grandfather faced the ocean on one side of a spit of land, giving them a slice of beach that appeared private.

He whistled. "Do you have workmen busy here?"

"Mostly me."

He stared at her.

She paced the room, which was overheated because there was a land breeze blowing through the screens rather than a sea breeze. She gathered her hair and lifted it from her neck, fanning herself. The guest house was tiny—it felt even smaller with Bruce inside—and she tried to imagine it through his eyes.

Set up like a studio apartment, the footage was long and narrow. The windows let in nice light, and that was good, but the harsh truth was that the interior was a construction zone.

"While you're staying here, I'll suspend the renovation project," she said. "We'll find you an air mattress, and I have some extra pillows in the cottage, along with sheets and towels and dish sponges and such."

He gazed at the corner with the small kitchenette. The cabinets were ripped out, and the refrigerator was unplugged. She didn't show it to him, but the bathroom was only half finished, too. The space was a glorified crash pad, and even then, it was devoid of furniture. No couch. No table. No bed.

He took it all in without any emotion crossing his face. He was completely stoic.

Finally he turned to her, and in a clear voice that rang to her soul, he said, "Looks like a person couldn't get into much trouble here."

Through her nervousness, she smiled. "Yes, if you do choose to stay, you'll be roughing it. I'm sorry I don't have better to offer you."

"I appreciate your offer. I know the hotels are full. I'm told there's a sandcastle competition in town. What's that all about?"

"We'll find out together. I've never been to one before."

He glanced sideways at her. She got the feeling he was assessing her more than the apartment. Well, that was fine—she was assessing him, too. "Have you been away from town for a while?" he asked.

"I moved back only a few weeks ago."

His brow creased as if he didn't know what to make of her. She supposed she had dropped a bombshell on him when she'd made the comment about Brian. But he wasn't asking how she knew him, and she wasn't going to spell it out for him, not unless he brought it up.

He strolled the length of the room then stopped before the lone electrical outlet in what would be the living area. He knelt, inspecting it, though he made sure to turn to her before he spoke. "Does this work?"

"It should." Maureen had told her that Bruce was a technology consultant, so maybe he needed to plug in his equipment. "If it doesn't, I'll call the electrician. He'll come right away."

"On the holiday weekend?" Bruce stood. "What is he, a boyfriend?"

That was a laugh. "No," she said simply.

"I'm relieved, I think."

He was? Why? Even though she'd lost her composure with him and was sticking him in this…renovation nightmare?

He peered at her. "Do I know this electrician?" he asked cautiously.

"Are you asking if he went to high school with us?"

"With *us?*"

She drew in her breath. "Yes, Bruce, I went to high school with you."

He smiled tightly at her. She could read the tension all over his face.

She told herself to keep going…that she could smooth over any potential trouble. Isn't that what she kept telling her father—that she had the ability to be a successful lawyer and advocate while at the same time, make people feel good about the situations they found themselves in?

"I…admired you when I was young," she said. It was sort of a lie, because she'd been hot for him more than anything. She was still hot for him now, if she were being truthful. The snug way his shirt pulled over his shoulder muscles as he knelt at her feet kept drawing her attention. She fidgeted, trying not to cross her legs. "You were two years ahead of me in school. I was hoping you would remember me last night at the wedding, and when you didn't…"

She feigned a shrug, because the confession hurt her more than she wanted him to know. She had *wanted* him to ask her to dance knowing that she was Natalie Kimball, the girl he'd confided in on the worst night of his life. She still craved his confidence, it seemed. *And* his embrace.

She gazed at the ancient flooring that she was preparing to replace soon. Instead of reading his lips she wanted so badly to kiss. "I guess I was upset with you," she finished lamely.

"It isn't personal to you, Natalie," he said, looking more at the wall behind her than at her. Maybe he felt the same way she did. There was…something…a zing between them every time their eyes connected. "I don't think about anything from back then." He knelt to zip open his computer bag and untangle his laptop cord. "I've got a busy life that keeps me occupied, and that's what I focus on."

"I think that's admirable," she said, glad he was concentrating on testing her electrical outlet rather than looking at her. Maybe what she needed to say would be easier if they weren't staring so much at each other. Her instincts were telling her that discussing it with him was the best thing to do, for both of them. Either way, they needed to have this conversation. It would be difficult, but ultimately it would smooth his way and make him feel more comfortable during his week in Wallis Point.

"So you know, for transparency's sake…" She took in a deep breath and crossed her fingers, praying he didn't bolt on her again. "I was the girl who let you into the funeral home the night of Brian's accident."

Bruce's hands stilled. His face became so pale his skin looked translucent, almost ghostly. His eyes lost all of their light. "I don't remember a damn thing about that night," he said woodenly.

"Nothing?" Natalie asked. "I know it wasn't your fault, and I—"

"Nothing." He stood. "And frankly, that's a chapter that won't do anybody any good to reopen. So don't."

His eyes were blazing at her now, and she let out her breath as she stood as well. The last thing she'd wanted to do was upset him. She wanted everything to be fixed, peaceful and happy.

"I thought if I reminded you," she said quickly, "then you might remember who I was. When you met me last night, you acted like you'd never seen me before in your life."

"Because I haven't," he said flatly.

"Yes. Well, now that I know," she babbled, following him to the door, "I'm glad it's cleared up. We don't have to speak of it again if you don't want to."

"I don't." He turned when he got to the threshold. "And I don't want you discussing it with anybody else, either."

"Of course not." She nodded solemnly. "This is the first time I've spoken about it, ever, and it's been what, fifteen years since it happened."

His gaze darkened. This line of explanation was

going nowhere—he looked more guarded the longer she spoke of it.

"I'll tell you what," she said. "How about if we make a deal to help each other for the week? You keep my secret, and I'll keep yours. You go about your business and say positive things about me to Maureen, and I'll assist you wherever I can. The town has changed since you lived here, Bruce, and if you need to find something, well, I could be your guide."

Yes, she was running on, but if she wanted to calm the beast, she needed to keep soothing him.

"Truthfully," she continued, "I'm more concerned about you keeping my secret. Believe me, in my line of work, any kind of weakness is seen as a handicap, and people could try to take advantage of me."

That made him pause. "What is your line of work?"

She had to tread carefully. Likely, he felt worse toward her father than Maureen did. "I'm trying to become a small-town lawyer."

"Trying?"

She smiled. "I *am* becoming a small-town lawyer."

"And nobody knows about your hearing impairment?"

"No one, as far as I know."

"What about your friends and family? Parents?" he pressed. "Haven't you told anyone?"

"No." Her voice wobbled. Of course her parents knew, but they never discussed her ears with her, not directly. And friends, well…

His voice turned softer. "Do you confide in *anyone,* Natalie?"

She looked away. She was a private person and didn't

like to tell people her troubles. She didn't have any troubles, really, as long as everybody else was happy. When other people were happy, life went more smoothly.

He must have noticed her distress, because his expression was compassionate. "What do your doctors say about it?"

She relaxed. He seemed more on her side now. Maybe he was calming down, considering her point of view.

"They say the damage to the hearing is in the middle ear," she said, "and also to the mastoid bone nearby. Typically when professionals first look at my ears, they want to operate. Surgeons like to cut. But when I explain to them what my original doctor told me—that after the infection ate away the living tissue, that the nerve to the face is nearly exposed—then they take another look and change their recommendation, because no doctor wants to risk paralyzing my face. That would be awful."

"It would." His tone was gentle. "You have a nice face."

"Thank you." She smiled at him. "I'd like to keep it that way."

"What about hearing aids? Don't they work for you?"

"Every few years, I try the latest model." She shrugged. "But so far, they're not made for my issues. I get echoing and feedback." And grosser side effects, like sweating inside her ear, that but wasn't necessary to tell Bruce. "I've found that it's best to work with my natural strengths instead. Lip-reading, as you said. Positioning myself so I can see people's faces when they talk. That sort of thing."

WAS HE FORGETTING his code?

Bruce stood back and took a breath. He had never

met anyone like this woman. She was brave. And kind—there was a lot more to her than what he'd originally seen on the surface. And the longer he interacted with her, the more he wanted to stay and get to know her better, even though it was in his best interest to get out while he still could.

With her, it might be too easy to slip into letting himself care again, and that would be risky. Natalie was the worst possible person for him—she was the only witness present the night he'd said goodbye to Brian. She knew too much about it already for his comfort level and if she thought she was getting closer to him, or getting him to confide in her, then she was wrong.

He just didn't do that. He couldn't form connections like that anymore. He didn't have it in him, and he didn't *want* to have it in him. He *liked* his life the way it was, rootless and unencumbered.

Turning, he packed the computer cords back into his briefcase. Testing the room's electricity had been a distraction to tinker with while she talked. He couldn't help it; with every sentence she uttered, the more he'd been drawn to wanting to learn more about her—about her struggles with her hearing, about her plans to renovate her cottage.

What was happening to him? Part of him wanted to pull Natalie to him without comment or preamble, just meld with her, the length of her body to his. Feel her heat, drown in that soft perfume. Devour her in a kiss that would satisfy the ache all this past history had put in him today.

She was dangerous. Staying here with her was a time bomb waiting to go off.

He stood, abruptly glancing at his watch. "I need to go now."

"Yes." She pressed her lips together and tilted her head. "So…can I count on you to keep my secret?"

He laughed; he couldn't help himself. "You're not like any lawyer I've ever met before, you know that?"

She dimpled. "I'll take that as a compliment."

He'd meant it that way. *Go, go, go,* his mind was telling him, *do not fall for her.*

But his body stood rooted, drinking in sweet, leggy Natalie. A smart, tough-in-her-own-way blonde, his new favorite type.

"Should we seal our deal?" she asked. Without waiting for him to answer, she stepped forward. He figured she would shake his hand, but no, she placed two fingers to her lips, kissed them, and then pressed her fingers to his lips.

He nearly jumped out of his skin. No one had *ever* done that to him before. The warmth of her fingers felt unexpectedly erotic.

He touched his mouth, not able to tear his gaze from her.

"To my silence," she said in all seriousness. "And to yours, as well."

He opened his mouth, but no words came. Just then, her phone buzzed with an incoming call and she took it, thank God.

"Yes, I'm coming," she said to the caller. "I'm sorry I'm late."

She glanced at the time, then back at Bruce. When she hung up, she smiled at him. "I have an appointment now, but I'll be back at five o'clock. Here's a house key for you, and a business card with my phone number. Do with them as you will. I hope you'll be here when I return, but that's for you to decide."

Feeling as though he'd been turned upside down, he clutched the key and the card in his fist, watching her walk away, her blond hair swinging in the wind. She sashayed down the lane, leaving him outside her unfinished guest house with all its possibilities; the key and the contact number an offering, but not a commitment.

*She's Switzerland,* he thought. A safe, diplomatic country that looked out for its own interests and didn't take sides. She'd turned the tables on him, and in a style he'd never encountered before. *She'd* handled *him.* Not at all what he'd expected.

Still, he could live with the results. For the first time since he'd stepped foot in Wallis Point, he felt relief.

## CHAPTER SIX

AFTER A FEW MILES of riding with the top down in the rental car he was fast regarding as his, zipping along the beach road with a coffee in the cup holder and breakfast in a bag on the seat beside him, Bruce was feeling back to normal again.

He had one more major errand before he hit the road, and this task played to his strengths: assess the situation with his grandfather, figure out what needed to be done, and then arrange for somebody qualified and topnotch to do it.

Basically what Bruce did for a living every day.

If Gramps needed extra attention from a healthcare professional, then Bruce would find someone affiliated with the nursing home and pay that person a few more dollars to give Gramps some additional consideration.

In Bruce's experience, people were always looking for money. A well-placed tip could get him a nicer hotel room upgrade, faster service, bags taken care of, preferred seating.

No, it wasn't precisely what Maureen had asked him to do, but he wasn't the right person to give Gramps the personal care that Moe said was needed. She was forgetting who Bruce was. Gramps himself would laugh at the ridiculousness of Moe's request. If Bruce had ever had a role model, then Gramps was it. His strong grandfather defined the words "aloof and independent."

Bruce's GPS alerted him that he'd reached his destination, and he pulled his car up to the nursing home.

The first thing that struck him when he exited the Mercedes was that this squat institutional-type building was not a "rest home." Not in the sense that it was a beautiful old private home as Bruce had envisioned. This looked more like a hospital, which did not bode well. It also looked like the type of facility people were sent to, not of their free will, when they didn't have any place else in the world to go.

*Probably where I'll end up,* he figured with a shiver down his spine.

He grabbed the breakfast that he and Gramps would share, and slammed the car door, not liking the feeling he was getting.

His phone rang, and he checked the call display. Maureen.

"What's up, sis?" he said into the receiver as he walked across the baking-hot parking lot. He pulled open one of the double-glass doors and found himself in an entryway, cold with blasted air-conditioning. Beyond that was another set of glass doors and a huge lobby with couches and fake potted plants. "You need me to take care of something else?"

"Bruce, I'm just checking that you're okay," Maureen shouted into the phone. Airport loudspeakers sounded over her in the background; somewhere, rows one to ten were boarding a flight to Fort Myers. He was jealous of everyone on that plane.

Sighing, he turned back and faced the window. There

was his white rental car, ready to whisk him away. "Everything's under control," he said into the phone once the boarding announcement was finished. "I handle problems for a living, remember? I'm not one of your kids you need to check up with every hour."

Moe laughed. "Sorry, it's habit." He could hear his sister more clearly now, even with Nina chattering somewhere nearby. "Jimmy and I talk on the phone all day long, about anything and everything."

Jimmy of the yes/no answers? It must be love, because Bruce just wasn't seeing it.

Although, it did make him think of Natalie. She'd said she'd had an appointment this afternoon, and she'd been dressed in business-type clothing. What was she doing working on the Saturday of Memorial Day weekend?

Maureen gave him a loud sigh, and he was jolted back to reality. "In future, Bruce, when somebody takes the time to communicate with you, it means that they love you."

"Yup," he said. "Got it." And he did appreciate his sister, but if she wanted him to hang out on the phone with her and spout about feelings, she would be disappointed. "Look, Moe, I gotta run—"

"So how did it go with Natalie?" she interrupted. "Are you settled in with her?"

"Ah…" Funny they were both thinking of Natalie. *She's amazing. Incredible.* Inexplicably he felt a twinge in his chest. He would probably always regret not seeing her after he left this place again. But, he didn't see any way around it. She simply knew too much, about him and Brian and the past.

The *funeral home.* God, of all the people he could have bumped into…

"I'm hearing an ominous pause," Maureen said.

"There's nothing ominous. Natalie's great. She's fine."

He set Gramps's breakfast down and leaned his forehead against the cool of the glass window. He really should hang up; the ham-and-egg sandwich was getting cold, and he had a job to do. Somehow, though, Bruce couldn't help asking his sister one last question. "How close of a friend are you to her, anyway?"

It was Maureen's turn to pause. "She seemed to really like you. That's partly why I asked her to be in the wedding party."

Natalie *liked* him? That was…well, it made him feel good. Who wouldn't want to be liked by a beautiful, kind, accomplished woman?

"And," Maureen continued, "truthfully, because Meredith—my counselor—had given me an action plan of making friends outside the family, and I sort of had a moment of weakness."

He felt his jaw drop. Two things were wrong with this statement. First, that his sister had problems that warranted her seeing a counselor, and second, that someone had told her she needed to make friends.

Back when he'd lived with his sister in Gramps's house, she'd had boatloads of friends who had dropped by the house day and night.

"What's the counselor for?" he found himself asking. Now why had he opened that can of worms?

"Jimmy and I are creating a new, blended family in case you hadn't noticed," Maureen said.

Bruce felt relieved. He'd thought she was going to give him an answer that somehow traced its way back to Brian's accident.

*Brian's accident.* Great, the conversation with Natalie was putting thoughts into his mind that he'd successfully kept out for years. "Okay, well, I don't want to sit in a coffee klatch with you. Gramps is waiting," Bruce said. "Enjoy your honeymoon. If you call again this week, be forewarned, I'm not picking up. You're supposed to be having a good time, not worrying about stuff back here."

"Bruce?"

"Say goodbye, Moe."

She sighed. "I'm glad you're back."

"I'm glad, too." Not about being in Wallis Point, but about talking to Maureen again. "Now say goodbye."

"You'll sit with him for two hours in the afternoon, right? Just try to connect with Gramps. Promise me, and then I'll be okay to go."

The pleading in her voice really got to him. Obviously she felt bad that Gramps was stuck in this place instead of at home. Well, he felt bad, too. And he would do everything to fix it so that Gramps was better taken care of than when he'd arrived.

"I'm headed up to see him now," he said. "I'm already in the lobby."

She let out a breath. "Thank you. I really appreciate you being there."

That was the second time she'd thanked him. She must really be scared for Gramps. "I have it under control. Don't worry about it for the rest of the week, okay?"

"Goodbye, B.B.," she whispered.

He couldn't help smiling as he hung up. Amazing how being home had hurtled him back to the relationships of childhood. He was living both the past and the present, intertwined. Contrary to what he'd thought, there had been good parts about those days. He'd liked his family then, and now that he was getting to know them better again, he found he still did.

Then again, at this point in his life, Moe was probably *his* closest friend, and that was a scary thought.

His smile dying, he grabbed the takeout bag and hustled inside. Beyond the entrance was a desk, but no one was behind it. He saw a sign-in sheet. Years of being forced to follow instructions blindly ("Yes, sir. No, sir.") had left him with a healthy skepticism of authority, so he ignored it, heading down a beige linoleum corridor past two unattended men napping in their wheelchairs. One of the men's heads was thrown back, his mouth open. A deep snore cut the quiet.

Another ominous sign. Gramps had always been active; he didn't belong with these old men, each with a foot in the grave.

Bruce remembered the slip of paper Maureen had given him. Room 203. There was an elevator straight ahead, so he took it up one level. He wouldn't stay as long as Maureen had asked—that was overkill, and Gramps would agree once he saw him.

He and Gramps didn't need to "connect." They'd always understood each other. If Gramps was up for it, they could turn on the radio and listen to the ball game while they ate their meal and talked sports. The baseball standings, the hockey playoffs, Indy cars. Gramps could choose the subject.

The elevator door opened, and Bruce moved with purpose past the nurses' station where three women in uniform were chatting amongst themselves. He breezed down the hall as if he belonged there, because he did belong there; he was there to visit his grandfather.

He strode past rooms with open doors, trying not to look at the patients. He came to room 203, the last in the corridor, and stepped inside.

Gramps was standing, facing away from him. He noticed right away that Gramps was leaning on a walker.

Bruce froze.

His grandfather looked nothing like the man he'd remembered, even from six months ago. In his late eighties, he'd been a bit frailer than usual, but now…

He seemed to have shrunk into himself.

Bruce's heart dropped as his grandfather turned. He wore gray elastic-band sweatpants and a Gone Fishing T-shirt. His feet were encased in Velcro slippers. A shock of white hair stood up straight.

The worst thing of all was that Gramps's eyes were completely uncomprehending.

"Who are you?" Gramps asked.

Bruce felt light-headed.

"I'm Bruce," he managed to say. "I'm your grandson."

"Who?"

"Bruce," he said, straight into Gramps's face so Gramps could hear him. Gramps didn't read lips the way Natalie did; people needed to speak loudly for him to understand. "Your grandson."

"No, you're not."

Bruce's heart sank. How could this be the man who, less than a year ago, had been zipping around the sea outside Fort Lauderdale with Bruce in his boat? What was he supposed to do to fix this? How was it even possible?

Bruce glanced around the small room, painted beige, with a dirty view of the parking lot. Inside were a cot, a chair and a tiny chest of drawers that held an undersized, outdated television. This was Gramps's world now.

But beside the television was his framed photo—Bruce's photo—taken of him at age twenty-one, in full dress uniform during Commissioning Week at the Naval Academy. Bruce didn't need to study it to be reminded of that time, even though he'd never kept a copy for himself. His parents had been so proud, but he'd just…been going through the motions those four years. Which had been ironic, given all the work and sacrifice it had taken him to get there, and to stay there. Now, he grabbed the photo, link to the past that it was. He held it up to Gramps's face and pointed. "I'm him. Don't you see?"

"No, you're not him. No." His voice shaking angrily, Gramps tottered over with the aid of his walker and took the framed photo from Bruce. He held it against the front of his Gone Fishing T-shirt then sat, clutching it as he rocked back and forth on his cot.

There was a tightness in his chest that Bruce didn't think he'd ever felt before.

*I have to show him that he knows me and that we're important to each other.*

It was an urgency he couldn't shake. He couldn't leave without helping Gramps remember that he was his grandson. He could not walk out that door, knowing that he might never see Gramps again and that their time together had ended like this.

But *how* could he help Gramps remember?

Bruce glanced again at Gramps's T-shirt. Gone Fishing. Gramps had been the person who'd taught Bruce to cast a line, to bait a hook. His grandfather lived to fish. Even in high school with all Bruce had participated in—baseball, homework, his part-time job parking cars at the hotel, his leadership activities—he'd still spent most spring and summer Saturday mornings at sunrise, sitting on a camp chair with a line in the water beside his grandfather. He and Gramps had drunk coffee from an old thermos and stared at the water. No talking allowed, or very little, anyway—just enough to alert one another to the necessities. Because talking scared the fish. Only when they were ready to leave had they packed up their gear and discussed the haul they'd made, or hadn't made. And then came the best part—the drive to the donut store to pick out a box, and then the drive home, where they woke everybody else.

*I need to take him fishing.*

If they went fishing, then Gramps would remember him, guaranteed. With Bruce, Gramps, a cooler and a thermos, the memories would come back. Maybe during the drive over, they could find a baseball game on the radio to listen to. Icing on the cake.

It was the only way.

"Come on, we're going outside," he told Gramps.

"Okay," Gramps said, surprisingly. Perking up, he steered his walker out the door like an expert in Olympic shuffling. Bruce felt a perverse pride as he walked slowly beside his grandfather, bee-lining it on two legs and four wheels to the elevator.

The nurses' station was empty this time; a few doors back, they'd passed one of the attendants. Bruce didn't know where the other two were. He and Gramps were about to make a clean getaway.

And then a screeching, loud alarm went off, blaring up and down the hallway. Red lights flashed on all four sides.

Bruce paused, his finger still not touching the elevator down button. And then he jabbed it. *Hurry up.* He willed the doors to open. But Gramps scooted backward, away from him. Another resident came over to investigate, a woman in a walker, with gray, wispy hair sticking out every which way. She stood beside Bruce, peering at him without saying a word.

He was starting to get seriously creeped out.

"Effie!" a nurse in pink scrubs exclaimed, hurrying over to the woman. "You know you're not supposed to go downstairs without somebody to help you," she chided. Then she smiled at Bruce. "I'm sorry, but the elevator won't work again until Effie backs away with her ankle bracelet and I press in the code to restart the elevator." Busily she unlocked a keypad and began to type out a series of numbers.

Bruce looked over at Gramps, who was grinning at him like he'd gotten away with something.

"What set off the alarm that locked the elevator?" Bruce asked the nurse.

"Some of the residents wear ankle bracelets that activate the alarm system when they get too close to an exit," she said, relocking the alarm box.

Bruce glanced to Gramps. He bet that beneath those new gray sweatpants that Moe had probably bought him, Bruce would find an ankle bracelet.

"Why?" Bruce asked the nurse. "Shouldn't those residents be allowed to go downstairs or walk the grounds if they want to?"

Her brows rose slightly. "Not if they're under security watch because their families have requested it for safety purposes. If they want to go downstairs, then a nurse will certainly accompany them."

"Okay," Bruce said. "Well, I'm his family, and I want to take him outside. I'll have him back for you in a couple of hours. How's that?"

The nurse smiled at him. "You're related to William?"

"Yes," he said. The nurse looked to be in her mid to late forties. There was no way she'd gone to school with him. "I'm Bruce, Maureen's brother. I'm William's grandson."

"He is not my grandson," Gramps said in a matter-of-fact tone. The weight on Bruce's heart seemed to press down even more heavily.

The nurse leaned toward Bruce in a confiding manner, which made the situation feel even worse. "I do recognize you from the photo in his room," she whispered.

He felt even sicker. "I need to take my grandfather out for the day. Please disable his bracelet."

The nurse looked at a clipboard at her station and then returned to him. "I'm sorry," she said, still smiling, "but your name is not on William's paperwork."

"I have updated paperwork," he said as he suddenly remembered. Maureen's packet was down on the front seat of his car. "I'll get it and bring it back to you."

"I'm sorry," the nurse explained in a patient tone, "but it's a holiday and I'm not the regular supervisor. We're short-staffed at the moment. You'll need to bring the forms back when the regular manager returns."

"When will that be?"

"Tuesday." She smiled sympathetically. "It's a long weekend, remember?"

He was speechless. He couldn't arrange to take his own grandfather out of this old-age home for a two-hour fishing session, one mile away?

The nurse had returned to her desk, so he strode after her. Why not? He could go to any commercial institution in the world and get logical-minded employees to listen to reason and common sense, and he would do so here. When he had her attention, he placed his hands on her desk, and gave her that calm but confident "You're going to help me and give me what I want" look that never, ever failed him.

He looked for her nametag, but it was covered by her sweater. Undaunted, he reached into his wallet and pulled out his Florida driver's license. Handing it to her, he said, "I am who I say I am. I need to take my grandfather out this afternoon, please."

"I'm very sorry." She was still smiling, damn it, not seeming sorry for him at all. "I understand your frustration, but I'm afraid there is no possible wiggle-room for me. I'd get in terrible trouble if I were to allow you to take William off the premises. I'm sure you understand."

And then she escorted his grandfather back to his room.

That was when Bruce finally understood what was

different about this place: he had no status, so to speak. No mileage, no points.

He was just a civilian.

Reeling, Bruce punched the button for the elevator, and then took the slowest ride in the world down one floor to street level. Once outside in the dry, sunny heat, he pulled out his phone.

Suddenly this was a matter of the utmost urgency to him. He was *not* leaving Wallis Point until he got Gramps outside, with a fishing rod in his hands. He didn't care what some bureaucratic nurse said.

But who would he call? Gramps's son, Bruce's dad? He and Bruce's mom were both sitting in the airport beside Maureen, waiting to board a flight to Orlando. Besides, they had deferred all decisions regarding Gramps's care to Maureen, the new, de facto family leader. Bruce had given up all rights to that position when he'd exiled himself from Wallis Point so many years ago.

He sat on the curb and put his head in his hands. He was not calling Maureen and interrupting her honeymoon. Somehow, he would solve this problem.

He trudged back upstairs feeling hollow to his soul.

"Where is Maureen?" Gramps asked, his mouth full, when Bruce saw him. He was sitting on his bed eating the breakfast sandwich Bruce had brought him, but left, forgotten on the chair. "And Marsha? Where is Marsha?"

Marsha was Bruce's mother.

"They're both on their way to Florida," Bruce said woodenly. "I'm here instead."

"Who?"

Bruce didn't know what to say anymore—he just

didn't. This wasn't a problem he could easily solve with logic. It was messy and full of feelings.

He wasn't going to let himself care. Everything that was happening had come about because of choices that he'd made. He'd committed to those decisions, and he would make the best of the consequences.

The next two hours were the slowest of Bruce's life. He sat on the only chair in the room while Gramps sat on a cot covered with a blue blanket that looked as if it was washed in cat hairs. Gramps had never owned cats. Gramps hated cats. Gramps liked dogs. The television was tuned to the local news station, and the headlines played over and over and over again on a fifteen-minute loop. Tragedies recited in mindless monotone. There was real human grief and suffering, but no one seemed to acknowledge that. No one seemed to care.

Gramps didn't speak, and Bruce didn't try to talk to him. They were a two-person theater of silence. Completely disconnected. And that was Bruce's fault.

Bruce hadn't been in torment like this—real torment—in a long time. And he was reminded of exactly why he'd built his wall of numbness around himself. Shutting down his feelings was the best thing for dealing with loss. Sometimes it was the only thing.

Because the grandfather of his youth was gone. Bruce didn't know who this man was. And this man, "William," didn't know who he was, either.

At the end of the two hours, a teenage attendant who looked like she was nine months pregnant came into the room without knocking. "William, are you ready for your bath?"

"I don't want the scrub brush," Gramps boomed.

Bruce stood. "Do you want me to stay?" he asked Gramps.

"Who are you?" Gramps asked.

"I'm your grandson."

"*He's* my grandson." Gramps pointed to the photo of Bruce at his Naval Academy graduation. He picked it up and shoved it at Bruce, who took it, like a hot potato.

He was forced to look at himself. The younger version of himself. The dress whites were fresh, but there was a dullness in his eyes. They'd been dull for his four years at the Academy.

Brian was supposed to have been with him.

Gramps pulled the photo back.

"That's me," Bruce said.

"It's not."

No, he supposed it wasn't. Too much time had passed since then.

Once he was outside, breathing fresh air again, Bruce took his phone out of his jacket pocket. Then he pulled Natalie's business card from his wallet and stared at it for a long time.

Should he call her?

He wanted to, desperately. Maybe she was dangerous for him because of who she was, but she *had* promised him silence when it came to Brian. She'd seemed so diplomatic. Maybe he could test that vow.

Yeah, he must be crazy for sure. But he felt just… overwhelmed with the desire to talk to someone who understood where he was coming from. He felt so disconnected. He was *always* disconnected, though, and that usually made him happy. One long escape from dealing with anything unpleasant.

Right now, though, he didn't feel like he'd escaped. Instead he was…adrift. Abandoned. Lost. Worse off than he'd ever been.

He needed to make changes.

## CHAPTER SEVEN

NATALIE STOOD ON TIPTOE in the Wallis Point Town Library and strained to reach the faded, half-hidden street directory from 1890.

Yes, she'd left Bruce Cole, the guy she'd been crushing on since adolescence, in order to rush across town through Saturday traffic, just to teach a genealogy class.

To an audience of one. Who wasn't even paying her.

Natalie had lost her way for certain.

Still, she brought the dusty book with the falling-apart binding to the table where Margery Whiting, her former elementary-school principal's eighty-year-old wife, waited expectantly, her gray perm failing to hide two oversize hearing aids.

Natalie felt a jolt every time she looked at them.

"Did you find any Hannafords, dear?" It turned out that Margery was related to Jimmy Hannaford, Maureen's new husband.

"Not yet. Why don't you take a look?" Natalie opened the directory for Margery, but the older woman smiled and shook her head.

"Oh, no. I have cataracts, dear. I can't see print that tiny."

"Then how about if I read it to you?" Natalie asked.

"Speak up, dear, you're mumbling."

A teenage boy following his girlfriend to the computer terminals rolled his eyes in their direction. That pretty much summed up how Natalie felt, too. No way was she ever letting on to people that she heard about as well as an eighty-year-old.

Bruce already knew. He'd heard her entire, embarrassing story. It was a relief he hadn't been turned off by her, physically at least—she'd seen how he'd reacted when she'd touched his lips with her fingers—but then after she'd left him and settled into her car, she'd felt... upset by what she'd told him.

Even now, an hour after the incident, she still felt out of sorts. Natalie excused herself from Margery Whiting. Taking the book across the library, nearly empty for the holiday weekend, she headed for the photocopier and charged up the machine.

Unlike Mrs. Whiting, Natalie may have had impaired hearing, but there was nothing wrong with her vision. She saw the situation clearly with Bruce.

She had shared her secrets with him and how she felt about them. It had not been easy. But...what had he told her of himself in return?

Nothing.

She lifted the cover to the heavy machine and settled the battered directory inside.

She had no illusions about the future. The odds were minimal that Bruce would decide to stay in her guest house. He would blow out of town, and she would never see him again. She had already faced that fact when she'd handed him her business card and her key. But if she could relive today, if she could do it over again, would she really want to expose herself the way she had?

It was painful. The agreement with him had been necessary, but in retrospect, it didn't have to be so one-sided. Next time, she would remember that. If there was a next time. And speaking of one-sided agreements, it was time she took a stand with her father, too.

The bright flash from the photocopier brought her back to reality, and Natalie collected the page of "Hannafords" from the paper bin and the directory from the scanning bed. On a whim, she flipped the pages to the Ks. She already knew the Kimballs had been around then; one summer she'd traced them and found that they'd settled the area in the earliest Colonial times.

Without thinking about what she was doing, she'd opened to the business end of the directory. "Kimball Family Law Firm." There was an ad for her family's offices, located at 3 South Street even back then, in the same downtown village section of Wallis Point as today.

Maybe that was her sign. She copied the advertisement, too. It would make a great addition to her souvenir collection of historical memorabilia. She was the last in the line of Kimballs to practice law in Wallis Point, stretching back five generations. *She* was their link to carry on. The only person left once her dad retired.

And she'd never directly confronted him about that. Was she a lawyer or wasn't she? People hired attorneys to fight for them, and here she was, avoiding advocating on her own behalf.

Bruce wasn't shy about making his desires known. He'd asked her outright about her hearing. He'd expressed his opinions about what he'd wanted, and he'd stopped her from discussing topics he didn't care to address.

Was she in charge of her own future, or was she not?

If her life was to change, then she was the only one who could change it.

Twenty minutes later, she unlocked the front door to their law office at 3 South Street.

She'd texted her father, asking him to meet her there, and surprisingly, Asa had complied, though dressed in his red golf shirt and tan pants. His neck was pink from sunburn and his nose was peeling, and it was still only the end of May. By August, he would look like a lobster.

"What's so urgent?" he asked her. "I was on my way to bring ballots to the Sandcastle event."

She'd forgotten he was on the committee. "Hi, Dad, thanks for meeting me. Come on back to my office."

She carried her copy of their 1890 advertisement to the minuscule back room that she used as her private space. She unlocked her bottom desk drawer and pulled out the collection she'd been amassing for the past several years.

Her father followed, dropping a stack of folders onto her desk. She ignored it. He'd made a habit asking her to put his files in order. For the weeks since her return, she'd been running errands and performing tasks that were better suited to a minimum-wage assistant, not a fellow attorney, and doing so without a fuss. Miss Diplomatic, proving her usefulness to him, listening and learning and waiting for the right time to speak up. Well, now was that time.

She took a seat and folded her hands on her desk. "I need to talk about my open house next week."

"What are you so dressed up for today?" he asked.

He was always diverting her like this. She glanced down at the summer skirt and sandals she wore. "Saturday morning is my regular genealogy class, remember?"

"Your dead-relatives obsession." Asa sighed. "And what are we getting for business from that?"

She smiled brightly, ready for the challenge. "I wrote a will for the assistant librarian this week."

"Yes, I saw the invoice. You undercharged her."

"That's because she wanted a relatively simple document. She's not married and has no children."

"And how many hours did you spend there today?" her father pressed. "How many people actually showed up for this class of yours?"

Why was she even letting him bait her? "It's Sandcastle Weekend, of course the numbers were down." She hadn't canceled the class only because Margery had asked the librarian to call her and Natalie had agreed, even though she'd known there was a carnival going on over on the boardwalk. Face painting and free samples of chowder—how could she compete with that?

Her father groaned. "Natty, you're putting in too much effort for too little gain."

"Which is why I want to talk to you about my open house next week." She flipped through the stack of historic postcards of Wallis Point, pulling out those that she thought would look great framed on the lobby wall. She hoped that would spur local interest when people came in. "I've sent out invitations and made up flyers, but now I'm trying to think of other interesting ways to draw people out and get them into the office to meet me. Wills, probates, estates and minor criminal cases. I've decided that's what I want to specialize in, the same as Granddad Asa did, but I need a renewed push to remind people I'm here. This winter I took a course on going solo and—"

"It's a hard life," he interrupted, "and one I'm doing you a favor in avoiding." Asa splayed his hands on her desk. "I've been delaying talking to you about this, hoping you'd get the hint, but no more."

Natalie was getting a sinking feeling in her stomach.

"I've been making inquiries," her father continued, "and I've found a lead. It's not too late for you to apply for a clerkship up in Concord."

Concord was an hour's drive away. Working there was not her dream or her intent. "I want to work *here*. I'm a Kimball."

"Yes, and you're a Kimball who's better suited to clerking. Come on, Natty, it's more rigorously academic, like you are. It involves research, drafting and writing—your strengths. You won't have to deal with the general public."

"I *like* the general public," she said stubbornly.

"Do I have to spell it out for you? You communicate so poorly. You put people off."

She could feel the blood leaving her face. *You're hearing-impaired,* is what he was really saying.

"Look," he said, "if keeping the practice in the family is so important to you I'll talk to your cousin Kyle."

Her second cousin Kyle lived in Massachusetts, and he hadn't grown up Wallis Point. "No," she said, "I can do it. I *want* to do it."

He shook his head at her. "You're setting yourself up for failure."

"Please show that you have confidence in me, even if you have to fake it."

"You're right." Her father nodded. "You asked me when you first came here to train you. Instead I've been protecting you. I've been shying away from giving you the difficult assignments, but clearly I can't do that anymore." He picked up the stack of folders he'd dropped, and left her office. When he returned, he carried an accordion file stuffed with papers. He dropped it on her desk, letting it land with a thump. "Next week, deliver these completed scholarship applications. The high school graduation is next month, and a choice needs to be made. I want you to sit with Bunny Faulkner and help her make that choice."

Bunny Faulkner was Brian Faulkner's mother. Good grief. Natalie shook her head. She'd been back in town a few weeks and everywhere she turned, she was reminded of that night. From being Maureen's bridesmaid to having Bruce possibly stay in her guesthouse and now to her having to work with Bunny, it was impossible for her to avoid thinking about Bruce and the connection she thought they'd made. Natalie could feel her mouth going dry. What would Bruce do if he knew?

"Are we really still working with Bunny?" she asked.

"We've done substantial trust work with her. She's a major client and has been for years. You should know that if you want to work here."

Natalie ran her hand along the bundle. Great. "Are these applications specifically for the Brian Faulkner Memorial Scholarship?" *Please tell me they're not.*

"The one and the same. You won it your senior year. Remember?"

She did. As the valedictorian of her class, she had walked in her white cap and gown up to the award stage where Frederick and Bunny Faulkner had presented her with a certificate. The two of them had saddened and scared her with their grief. She didn't relish this assignment.

"Why the glum face?" her father asked. "It's Saturday night. Don't you have any plans?"

She felt herself drooping lower. "I thought I'd research more ideas to make my open house a success."

"Aren't you staying with your mother and me tonight?"

"No, Dad. I have my cottage to stay in."

He squinted. "I thought you were renting the cottage out for the week. Didn't the real estate agent call you?"

"Yes, Maureen called me, and I told her that I could lend her the guest house."

His eyes popped. "Isn't that unfinished? It's not to code and we don't have an occupancy permit."

"I didn't say I'd *charge* anyone, Dad. It's a favor for a friend. Besides, it's my property to do with as I see fit. You shouldn't have made a commitment to Maureen without first discussing it with me."

Her father scowled at her, but she noticed that he wasn't arguing.

"Will you be present at my open house or not?" she asked calmly.

He ranted about liabilities and risks, before picking up his motorcycle keys. "There's a helmet for you under the front desk. Put it on and come with me to the sandcastle competition. I need to count official ballots, and since you don't have anything else planned, you might as well meet some of the organizers from out of town and see how everything works so you can decide if working here is what you really want."

A Saturday night with her father. Somehow, this was not what she'd had in mind when she'd asked him to come to the law offices to talk about her open house.

"I know that working here is what I want," she said quietly.

"Then you won't mind taking the ride with me." He passed her the helmet.

Why did she still get the feeling that she wasn't being taken seriously?

A thick gloom settled over her, and it stayed there as she rode with him out of the village and headed over the breezy causeway at the entrance to the beach. There they followed a train of other motorcycles weaving down the middle of four lanes of crawling traffic. Gasoline fumes filled her sinuses, and heat rose from the pavement in waves, but the occasional gust of sea breeze cooled her arms and shoulders.

Late afternoon shadows lengthened over the sand, where couples and families were packing up their towels and chairs, headed to their cars to join the mass exodus as the seagulls stalked the shore, looking for crumbs.

But a new crowd was coming in for the evening as well, lovers on dates, and groups of friends meeting up for the night, and she and her father were part of that wave, too. To Natalie's mind, there were few things that said "summer night" more than a drive to the strip, with its old-fashioned ballroom, quaint arcade and modern pavilion where visiting rock bands performed.

But not with her dad. And here she sat on his Harley,

hugging her daredevil father around his chubby waist and leaning her cheek against his back. How pathetic was she?

When they got to the platform where the sandcastle competition judges were gathered, her father pulled in to let Natalie off before parking near the police station. Crowds filled the sidewalks on both sides of the strip and the crosswalk between.

Her phone vibrated in her pocket. Natalie checked the number and blinked at the Florida area code, shocked to her sandals. Bruce. Who else would it be?

She had a few minutes before her father would be back, so she ducked under an awning between a buttery-smelling fried dough shop and a kiosk that sold pretty beach-glass jewelry.

"Hello?" she said, putting the phone to one ear and blocking the other with her hand.

"Is this a good time for you?" Bruce asked.

"Why?" she asked cautiously. "Is everything okay?"

"Ah, I had a legal thing I wanted to ask you about. But that's not really why I called."

"Why did you call, then?"

He paused.

"Bruce?"

"I'm…well, would it be hokey if I asked you out to dinner?"

Her heart thudded hard. Had she heard him correctly? But she must have— What else could he have said? Inside her, a self she hadn't heard from in over a decade was hollering, *Bruce! He called me! Yay!* and jumping up and down, clapping like an excited teen.

"Natalie? I'm sorry, is it difficult for you to hear me over the phone?"

"I hear you great. Thank you for asking." He had been good to her on that count, and she didn't want him to think otherwise. "Actually it's not hokey for you to ask me out. That's a…lovely thing, and I appreciate it very much."

"So…you'll go?" He sounded unsure of himself.

She smiled, thinking back to high school. Bruce had been the popular one. She had been the dork. Even all these years later, it felt like a small victory here on a summer night by the strip, feeling the ocean breeze blow on her bare shoulders and watching the lights slowly flicker on. "What did you have in mind?"

He didn't hesitate. "A boat. The ocean. Maine lobster. And live music. With you, of course."

"Live music?" she asked.

"Yeah. Of all the things I miss about summer here, that's right up there on the list."

He missed summer here? But he'd never been back. She glanced at the ballroom behind her. A band with a string of hits in the eighties was listed on the arcade. Maybe that's what he'd meant.

"Is…that okay with you?" he asked.

Again, there was that uncharacteristic note of uncertainty. Something had upset him—something to do with a legal issue.

Well, legal issue or not, she was upset, too. Their one-sided truce couldn't stand as it was, and she needed to tell him.

"Do you want to pick me up now?" she asked. "I've never driven the strip in a hot sports car before."

His deep voice chuckled over the phone. So male, so Bruce.

Her heart skipped. This is what it must have felt like to be one of the girlfriends in Bruce's gang. They'd always dated the girls that everybody knew and liked, who were connected to the social fabric of their seaside town. That hadn't been her, though she'd wanted it to be.

"Ah, me, neither," he joked. "Except when I was parking cars at the hotel, and I uh, borrowed the occasional hot rod…"

His voice trailed off, and her heart sank.

Brian had "borrowed" one of Bruce's valet-parked cars the night he died. Bruce had been accused of passing Brian the keys. Bruce had been investigated, and though the police and the insurance companies had found no criminal wrongdoing, Brian's parents had still sued him in civil court. Her father had represented Frederick and Bunny Faulkner.

And now she'd agreed to go out with him. What would Bruce do when he found out who her father was?

She could tell Bruce that she knew he hadn't done it and that she thought it wasn't fair what he had gone through. She could tell him that she'd always felt guilty about not telling her father about letting him into the funeral home, and that based on what she'd seen there, she believed Bruce was innocent.

Or, she could change the subject and drop it, as they had originally agreed, and as she was normally apt to do.

She took a breath. Hadn't she just vowed to be more assertive in her life?

"Where are you?" he asked more quietly. He was changing his own subject.

Maybe it was better for them to discuss this in person.

"I'm…where the sandcastle competition is being judged. I caught a ride here."

"I wouldn't mind checking that out," he said.

"Why don't you meet me here?"

Immediately she winced. She didn't want to risk him bumping into her father. Not before she'd talked to Bruce. Not yet. He still didn't know she was Asa Kimball's daughter, and she didn't want him to know until she'd told him her story in person.

"On second thought, it's crowded here. Why don't we meet at the pavilion instead?" The pavilion was a hundred yards farther up the beach, and the crowds would be thinner there.

"Sure," he said. "The traffic is heavy, so I'll walk. Then I'll walk back with you to the cottage. I need to take a shower before we leave, anyway."

"I'm sorry I didn't leave you a key to my place."

"Not a problem, Natalie. Besides, I miss walking the beach. And I'd…welcome talking to you."

*About what?* She paused. Something was definitely wrong. "Is everything okay? Will the crowds bother you?"

"Yeah, everything's fine. And I live near a beach town. Trust me, I'm used to crowds."

"Maureen said you live in Fort Lauderdale."

"Technically I live on a boat moored in the marina."

He did? "She also said she's going on a sailing honeymoon in Florida. Is she using your boat?"

"She is." He chuckled again, that low, deep rumble

that never failed to thrill her. "I told her I doubled up my insurance before I let her take it. She can be crazy."

In high school, Maureen had spent her summers surfing, sailing and working on a tourist fishing day boat as a snack girl in hot pants. "She used to be on the water all the time. She'll do great."

"How about you?" he asked. "Do you sail?"

She found herself unconsciously touching her left ear. "I had to stay away from the water so often when I was a kid that I'm afraid I don't swim well."

"Why did you have to stay away?"

"If I get water in my middle ear, I'm inviting another infection. My ear can't drain properly."

"That sucks. The whole fun of growing up near the ocean is the water sports."

"Yeah." And it sucked that she enjoyed talking to him so much, too. Because he wasn't going to like it once she broke their truce.

Bruce waited until Natalie disconnected before he also put down his phone. After talking to her, he felt jazzed to keep going—which was what he'd been hoping for when he called her. Before he put the phone away, he keyed in a new contact for her in his phone. He typed in Natalie—her real name—not standard operating procedure for him. Then he set her ring tone to the lowest, softest one possible, like her voice. If she ever called him, he'd know immediately who she was, and it would make him smile.

He pulled down his sunglasses and walked along the sand as the beach curved west, and he headed slightly into the glare. From here, he could see the crowd in front of the ballroom where the sandcastles likely were. A mob scene. He lowered his baseball cap and quickened his pace.

NATALIE PHONED HER FATHER to let him know she was busy after all then she headed toward the pavilion. Careful to stay on the sidewalk, she walked beside the arcade. Still, it was slow going. She shuffled along, in the flow of foot traffic. The crush of cars in the street was so thick and heavy, especially with tall SUVs and pickup trucks, that it was hard to see across. But after a few minutes, over the top of a compact car, she saw him.

Bruce wore ear buds, an iPod cord dangling around his neck. In his cargo shorts, T-shirt, a low baseball cap and dark, aviator shades he looked laid-back, like a celebrity going incognito.

"Bruce!" she called out, waving.

But he didn't hear her.

# CHAPTER EIGHT

CROWDS BLOCKED BRUCE'S VIEW. Tourists walked four and five abreast—families, college kids, teenage couples, young moms and little kids, elder statesmen, even soldiers on leave…all of them a swollen mass of humanity, walking, skating, shuffling, running, cruising on the sidewalk. The road was worse—a backed-up traffic jam, the smell of gasoline and the shimmering vapors and puffs of smoke from old beaters.

This was what he remembered of the boardwalk on a Saturday night. Stands for French fries, saltwater taffy and pizza by the slice. Across the road was the main beach, honky-tonk, hot and sweaty. A bandstand was erected. Behind that, he assumed, was where the sandcastle people were set up. He didn't know for sure, the crowds were too thick. It wasn't dark yet, though the sun had settled west behind the buildings. The beach was cast in shadows. Seagulls trolled looking for French fries and discarded potato chips. And the waves were incessant. Crashing. Not high, because it wasn't yet hurricane season down in the Caribbean, and so the water would be low and icy cold.

It was a strange feeling, coming back to a place that had once meant everything to him. And then his illusions had been shattered, so that he'd thought he could never return.

But now he was here, and it was doing things to his chest, to his heart—maybe even his soul, if he still had one. His mind may have forgotten, but the rest of him certainly hadn't.

He didn't know what to do about it, if anything. It didn't help that he was listening to his favorite band from his youth. A "best of" album, with songs that had been significant to him when he'd been the young man who had lived here and been affected by this place.

Everything was stirred up again. The feelings. The memories.

He sucked in a breath of sea air.

And then he saw Natalie. The lyrics on his headphones reminded him of her. She was sweet. Dressed like summer, in the skirt and top that had enticed him earlier, with her long arms bare and her sweater cut in a V so he could see a hint of cleavage.

Of really nice cleavage.

He pushed through the crowd and strode toward her.

She saw him. Smiled and waved. And stepped off the curb into the crosswalk, blocked by cars, and not hearing the motorcycle that whizzed past the stalled traffic.

"Natalie!" And only because she was looking at him and could read his shouts and gestures did she jump backward, just in time.

But Fate was a bitch and sent Natalie back into harm's way. Bruce watched, horrified, as she tripped and fell. On the way down, she hit her temple against one of the ballroom poles, hard enough that he imagined he could hear it even through the music still playing in his ears.

"No!" Shouting her name, pushing, running on autopilot, he plowed into the crowd and was the first to crouch beside her.

Afraid to move her in case she'd hurt her spine, all he could do was shelter her with his body hovering over her. "Natalie?"

But she was out cold, and his alarm increased. His first instinct was call up his long-ago emergency training, which told him to check that she was breathing okay and that her air passages were clear. She was, and they were.

He smoothed back her hair—long, shiny, light brown hair streaked with gold highlights. Up close, she wasn't exactly a blonde, but not brunette, either. She made him think of…gold. A golden summer princess. Tall and thin with slight shoulders.

But she was unconscious, and not coming to. This was bad, very bad. And the blood…it was sticky on his fingers, flowing from her temple and matting in her hair.

"Hey—" A uniformed police officer leaned over him. "Did you see what happened?"

"Yes, I did. She fell and hit her head. Call an ambulance, now," Bruce ordered him.

But his voice was lost by a blast from the radio, echoing against the building, cars, the suddenly silent crowd circled around Bruce and Natalie. "Hang in there, Natty," he said, stripping off his T-shirt and pressing it to the gash on her forehead, stemming the bleeding.

Her eyelids fluttered open. "Don't call me that," she mumbled, touching the hand that held the T-shirt.

*Thank you,* he thought. She was coming to. How long had she been out—a few seconds, less than a minute?

"Why can't I call you Natty?" He pressed his other

hand on top of her hand. Squeezed it. *Keep her talking,* he told himself.

"My parents call me Natty," she mumbled, squeezing him back.

That was good. "You're right," he said lightly, "I can't call you Natty, then."

"You look really, really great without a shirt on," she whispered.

Ah…that was nice she thought so, but…

"What do you like people to call you?" he asked.

Her gaze wandered. Was she confused? Forgetful?

"Natalie," she said finally, which relieved him.

"Well, I can't call you that now, either."

She sat up, giving him a quizzical look. One hand was on her head, the other rested on his bare chest, cool and soothing. "Why not?" she asked.

"Uh, because I need to call you something that nobody else calls you. Something that nobody has ever called anybody else in the history of the world."

A loopy grin spread over her face. Both hands went to his chest, soft hands, lightly caressing. He and Natalie were crouched so close—him pressing his T-shirt to the cut on her temple, and her just…holding on to him. If he wasn't so scared for her, he'd take more time to think about it, but…

And then the sirens blasted, almost on top of them, echoing through his bones. He saw the huge fire truck pull up. Then the emergency services van. Finally a black-and-white police cruiser, blue lights flashing brightly.

He glanced at Natalie, and she was wincing, both hands covering her eyes.

No, no, no. She really was hurt. "Help her," he called to the cop. "The lady has a head injury and she needs to go to a hospital."

"Coming through," one of the emergency guys said brusquely to Bruce. Bruce stepped aside and gave them access to Natalie as they checked her vital signs and bandaged her cut. One of them gave Bruce back his T-shirt, which he held, stupidly. The other gazed into Natalie's pupils and asked, "What did you have for breakfast?"

She smirked, the silly woman. "Him." She pointed to Bruce.

"Don't joke around with this stuff," he told her.

"Why? I'm fine," she said. "And I like to joke."

The paramedics were loading her onto a board to transport her. Bruce felt so helpless.

"Are you family?" the second paramedic asked him.

"Yeah," Bruce said. Because if he told him no, they wouldn't let him take the ambulance ride with her. And he wasn't leaving her alone. No way. No way in hell. "Is she gonna be okay? She hit her temple against that pole." He pointed to it, as if it made any difference which pole it had been.

"How did it happen?" the officer asked him. He grasped Bruce's arm. "Sir, I'm going to ask you to step back. Can you tell me what happened?"

"She fell off the curb. Now I'm going with her in the ambulance," Bruce said, jerking free. He stepped over to the vehicle where they were loading Natalie, and he hopped in beside her.

"You're her family?" the first paramedic asked.

"I said I was," Bruce said. The other paramedic was securing her to the board with straps.

"I'm fine," Natalie was saying to the paramedic. "Truly, I'd like to refuse to be transported."

"That's your right, but you'll need to sign a waiver," the paramedic said.

"Forget it," Bruce told Natalie. He remembered something he'd read. "You need to get checked out by a doctor, now, because the first hour after the accident is most important. After that, it can get real dicey, real fast. Remember the actress who died because she waited too long to go to the hospital?"

He felt sick mentioning the tragedy. He couldn't lose Natalie. Not now. *Not again.*

"Do you have medical training?" the paramedic asked him.

"U.S. Navy," Bruce muttered. For the second time this weekend, he was giving away information he rarely admitted to, though he did feel grateful for the courses in emergency medicine they'd made him take. "How are her vitals?"

"She's stable, but we won't know much more until we get her to the hospital and run some tests." The first paramedic slammed the door and jogged to the front of the cab. He was also their driver.

"Well," Natalie cracked at Bruce and the other paramedic, from her position prone on the stabilizing board, her neck in a collar and her eyes staring straight up at them, "It *is* an old lawyer canard to always take the ambulance ride..."

"She's not a lawyer, is she?" the paramedic asked him.

"Oh, yeah," Bruce said. "This is your lucky day."

"...and, if you're stopped for a driving-under-the-influence citation," Natalie continued, "it's also a good rule to refuse the on-the-scene sobriety test. Don't blow into the tube until you've talked with your attorney."

"Please tell me she doesn't specialize in ambulance-chasing," the paramedic muttered.

Bruce didn't know what she specialized in. "There's a first time for everything," he said.

The paramedic sighed and picked up a pen, concentrating on his report.

The ambulance steered into traffic, and the driver turned on the siren, a piercing, constant scream that sent lightning bolts up Bruce's spine and made him cringe. He reached for Natalie's hand. He was really nervous for her. She'd hit her head hard, in a vulnerable spot on the skull, and there had been a lot of blood. She'd even lost consciousness. The danger of the situation was sinking in again. Just because she seemed lucid and was joking with them, didn't mean that she was safe yet.

The siren seemed to bother her, because she closed her eyes and gave up the bantering.

"Does she have any medical issues we should know about?" the paramedic asked Bruce. He also tossed Bruce the top to a pair of hospital scrubs, which Bruce tugged over his head.

"Thanks. And, uh, not that I know of."

The paramedic looked sharply at him.

Oh, hell. "She has a hearing impairment," he murmured, lowering his voice and averting his face so Natalie couldn't catch it. "But that's privileged information, so don't put it in your report."

"What kind of impairment? Is there a device implanted?"

"No. She had a lot of…middle ear surgery when she was young. Mastoids, I think."

The paramedic nodded. "That shouldn't be a problem. How about allergies or medications?"

"I'm…not sure."

"Okay." The paramedic looked up. "We're here."

The ambulance came to a stop, and he opened the doors. The two paramedics whisked Natalie out and set her up on a stretcher. Her eyes were still closed, and her head bobbed slightly as they wheeled her inside. Bruce felt sick to his gut to see it. And the blood that still seeped through a wide bandage plastered across her head.

Unwillingly he flashed back to Brian. He'd worn a bandage that had flattened his forehead and covered his blond hair, under the sheet inside that sickening morgue, downstairs in the cellar of the town's only funeral home.

Where a scared, skinny, fifteen-year-old girl had found a key to let him inside. Because he'd needed to say goodbye to his friend, his own way.

Yeah, of course he remembered Natalie. He'd been lying to her when he told her he hadn't, just because he didn't want to go back to that night. But maybe he had to. Maybe having her in his life now was a sign.

Back then, he hadn't known her name, just that she'd been quiet and kind, though not self-composed like the woman she was now. As a girl, she hadn't had a clue as to how to handle the situation. Neither had he.

*Damn it, Natalie, I am not saying goodbye to you yet. I am not.*

Someone pushed him from behind. "You're family? We need you."

Bruce jolted back to the present. "Wait a minute, which hospital are we at?"

"This is Wallis Point Regional Hospital."

Oh, God, no. He'd come here first, looking for Brian after word had filtered back to the beach that somebody had heard Brian's name on the police scanner.

"Don't worry," Natalie said to him from the stretcher. "Bunny Faulkner is retired. She doesn't work here anymore."

"Why would I care about that?" he snapped. "I wasn't thinking about her."

But Natalie smiled. And he knew why. Because *she* wanted to protect *him*. She was injured, and she'd been worried about him.

NATALIE GATHERED HER BEARINGS as a nurse wheeled her down a quiet corridor on a stretcher. The hospital was white and beige on every surface and smelled like antiseptic. A tight, scratchy bandage pulled at the skin on her forehead, hurting her slightly. She still wore her own skirt, but her top had been removed in favor of a hospital gown instead. On top of that was a warm blanket that only made her feel sleepy.

As she was wheeled into a large room cut into sections by blue curtains that hung from the ceiling, she heard Bruce speaking from behind one of the four curtains. She could hear his deep, low voice but the way it echoed off the tiled floor made it impossible for her to pinpoint exactly where he was. "You're her father?" he was asking.

"Yes—why did you tell these people that *you're* her

family?" her father asked. There was no mistaking the accusation in his tone, even with her damaged ears.

*Oh, no.* Natalie bolted upright, her palms bunching the flimsy blanket into her fist.

"If I hadn't," Bruce said to her father, "then they wouldn't have let me in the ambulance and your daughter would have been alone."

She let that thought register. Bruce had said she was her family. It felt...well, it felt nice. Even though it was a blatant lie, it was sweet of him to be so concerned for her. It would have been easy for him to have left her on her own to struggle through this embarrassing accident herself, but he hadn't. Instead he'd stayed with her.

The nurse wheeling her on the stretcher left through a gap in the curtains. Natalie leaned over to glance through it.

"Who are you?" her father was demanding of Bruce.

This was very bad news. If each figured out whom the other was, this could be disastrous.

"My name is Bruce Cole, sir. I'm pleased to meet you."

"Cole? Did you say Cole?" her father asked.

"I did, sir," Bruce said. Natalie knew what it cost him to stand up and say that.

"Did you grow up around here?" her father asked.

*Now.* She had to stop this *now.* Natalie jumped to her feet, barging through the curtain.

It was time to take charge.

## CHAPTER NINE

"WHAT ARE YOU DOING on your feet?" Bruce demanded.

"Yes, Natty, what are you doing up?" her father echoed.

So they were agreed on one topic, at least. That was good, wasn't it?

"I'm fine," Natalie insisted, trying her best to look dignified in a ragged hospital gown and her now-wrinkled skirt. She lifted her chin and looked from Bruce to her father. Bruce wore the top to a pair of blue hospital scrubs. It reminded her that he'd stripped off his shirt to make a bandage for her. If it weren't so important that she step between them now, she would have loved to dwell on that vision again, thank you very much. The guy had a body that just drove her insane. "I'm going to be okay," she said. "You don't have to worry about me anymore."

But they were staring at the bandage on her forehead. She touched it, feeling self-conscious. "All right, the side of my head is scraped, but it didn't need stitches and the bleeding has stopped. I don't have a headache, dizziness or memory loss, so that's good news."

They were listening intently to her, so she took heart. At least she'd come out before either of them had exploded. "The doctor told me that as soon as I have a CT scan to make sure there's no bleeding or swelling inside my brain, I can go home." She gave them her most brilliant smile. "So you see, all is well. Neither of you need to stay and babysit me anymore."

"It's not babysitting," Bruce said. "Head wounds are nothing to joke about."

"He's right, Natty, head wounds are serious," her father said.

Okay, even better. Maybe she had a shot at smoothing this over after all.

"Go lie down," her father ordered her.

"In a moment," she said, shifting on her bare feet, suddenly self-conscious about the flimsy hospital gown. She crossed her arms over her chest. "Ah, I really need to introduce you two."

She glanced to her handsome rescuer, his soulful eyes seeming to caress her, and something fluttered inside her. She couldn't help giving him a big, goofy grin. By all rights, he should have bolted from her, but he hadn't. *He'd* called *her.* He could've asked anybody out, but he'd chosen her.

She cleared her throat and turned to her father, whose head was swiveling from her to Bruce. *Now or never,* she thought. "Dad, this is Bruce Cole. He's Maureen Cole's brother. He's staying in the guest house at my place."

Her father nodded as if that explained everything. Even Bruce seemed calm on the surface. But underneath, she knew he was wary.

She reassured him of her support by smiling at him. Was she crazy that despite the circumstances, she would still give anything to lean over and touch him again?

She shook the thought away. "Bruce, this is my father, the attorney Asa Kimball. I'm working in his law offices."

Bruce's eyes widened. It obviously hadn't occurred to him at all that she was related to Asa. She looked nothing like her father; with his leather jacket and his motorcycle helmet tucked under his arm, he appeared more of an overweight biker than a respected attorney.

He was also heavier, his hair grayer than in the old days, especially since his father—her granddad—had passed away last year. After that had happened, something in her dad had seemed to snap. It was as though he didn't want to be a lawyer anymore; he seemed to find so little joy in it. Instead of embracing his sole proprietorship, he acted like he'd rather be free.

But Bruce didn't know that. And years ago, her dad had reveled in being a powerful man in town. Natalie watched Bruce studying Asa, recognizing who he was, the emotions running over Bruce's face. Sometimes it seemed like Bruce had shut himself down, turned himself into a stoic—if charming—shell of himself. Now was not one of those times. Bruce was angry, his jaw clenched tight. With a single breath, his posture went ramrod straight, as a Marine set to march. His gaze flicked toward the exit.

*Please don't leave.* "Bruce, I'm sorry I didn't tell you about my father earlier. But I honestly thought the two of you would never meet. I thought it wouldn't be an issue."

"And why would it be an issue?" Bruce asked tersely.

She exhaled. She *had* promised never to discuss the circumstances with Brian's accident, and they were in public. "You're right." She nodded, feeling miserable. "There is no problem."

It was a whopping lie, and they both knew it.

"Why would there be a problem?" her father repeated, glancing from her to Bruce. Natalie girded herself. Here came his bull-in-the-china-shop response. "Bruce and I know each other," Asa said, "from when I interviewed him down in Annapolis."

"*You* went to Annapolis?" Natalie blurted. She hadn't known that her father had traveled hundreds of miles down to the Naval Academy in order to question Bruce about the accident because of the lawsuit against him.

This was worse than she'd thought.

Her father grabbed Bruce's hand from his side and pumped it with a smile. "Yes, I did, and Bruce and I are already well acquainted, aren't we?"

Bruce jerked his hand away from her father. A vein in Bruce's neck throbbed, and his normally warm brown eyes were burning. If her hearing were better, she was sure she would catch his teeth grinding, too.

"You're kidding," Bruce spit out. It was the first time Natalie had seen him be honest about something that bothered him, and strangely, it heartened her.

But Asa looked confused by Bruce's response. "You're not stuck on that, are you? It was a long time ago, and you got off in the end, didn't you?"

Bruce stared at him incredulously, his mouth open. Apparently this was too much. "You sued me, you sued my boss and you questioned my sister and my grand-parents. If that wasn't enough, you spoke with my Commandant at the Naval Academy, which jeopardized my whole future. I was lucky to be allowed to stay."

Her father shrugged. "Without my notes, I don't recall all the details of past cases."

"Then let me remind you," Bruce said through clenched teeth. Natalie knew she could step in, but this confrontation seemed cathartic to Bruce. Maybe it was best he got it off his chest. Heaven knew, her father didn't mind angry words. He was used to them.

"You grilled me," Bruce continued, "in that deposition as if I was the enemy. That wasn't…nothing was as bad as Brian dying, but I did not steal those car keys, or give them to him, or tell him to take that car. Encouraging his parents to believe that was a kick in the teeth on top of an already hellacious summer. Worst of all, it was disrespectful to Brian's memory."

Her father shook his head. "Son, I was hired by the parents to represent them, and that's what I did. It's what attorneys do. You need to understand it's nothing personal."

"Nothing *personal?*" Bruce spat.

Her father looked quizzically at him. He genuinely didn't see how the routine procedures he took in the name of their profession weren't traumatic to the people who had to live through them. "Of course not."

"You don't care that I'm back in town?"

"Why would I?" Asa asked. "You helped my daughter today and I appreciate that. It's all I care about, frankly."

"And what about the Faulkners?" Bruce asked. "How do *they* feel?"

Natalie listened with special interest to this part. She needed to know, too.

Her father shrugged carefully. "The matter is closed, as far as everyone is concerned." Bunny Faulkner was an active client. He had to tread carefully, Natalie knew this.

Bruce seemed skeptical. The matter wasn't closed, not to him. He'd told her before that it was, but it obviously wasn't.

It broke her heart, but at least it helped her understand him. She went to Bruce and touched the hem of the surgical scrubs. Oh, God, she had failed miserably at smoothing over this meeting. How could she make him feel at peace?

He glanced at her as if waking from a trance. "I shouldn't have done that. You're hurt," he said clearly, as if more worried about protecting her than himself. "Stuff like this isn't good for you. You need to heal and get better."

"People in town don't blame you, Bruce. They know you were unfairly treated."

He let out his breath. "I respect what you're doing," he said quietly. "But it's best that we drop it."

"I know you didn't take those keys. You understand how I know that, don't you?" She glanced at her father. She couldn't go into this with him here. Her apology was private, for Bruce only. "And I know you stay away from Wallis Point because you want to make life easier for your family. I can imagine how horrible that time was for you and your family. I knew Maureen during that time, and I saw how much it hurt her."

"I'm *fine,*" Bruce repeated. "It's water under the bridge."

"Of course." It wasn't fair for her to talk about that now with her father standing there. "I didn't mean to insinuate otherwise."

She turned to her father and smiled. "Maybe you should call Mom and let her know I'm okay. She'll be upset if she hears about the accident from somebody else."

Her father looked at her long and hard. "You're right," he said finally. "About everything you said." He dropped his voice. "But I hope you're not forgetting that Bunny Faulkner is still our client." And then he pulled out his phone.

SHE REALLY IS A NATURAL-BORN *diplomat,* Bruce thought.

She couldn't help considering all points of view, and he admired that about her, he really did. But he hated that Kimball-the-ball-busting-attorney was her father. How had he not anticipated that?

This guy had been like Satan to him when he'd been eighteen. Bruce had been terrified of him back then, because Asa Kimball had possessed the power to ruin his life. And yet, even then, Bruce had almost *hoped* he would ruin his life—because a part of him had thought he deserved to get kicked out of the Academy.

And the irony was, not a single deposition had gotten close to the real truth—he *was* responsible for Brian's death. Not in the literal sense, that he'd given Brian the keys, but because figuratively, he had set him off.

Bruce had been trying to help him, ironically enough. He'd spent the afternoon attempting to talk him into going to his parents, telling them that he didn't want to go to the Naval Academy for Plebe Summer, that it was their dream for him to be a midshipman, not his.

But Bruce had only succeeded in riling Brian up. The last time Bruce had seen him, that night at the valet stand when Brian had stopped by, drunk, to visit him, Bruce had taunted him. "Go ahead and run away from the responsibility." Those had been Bruce's last words to the only best friend he'd ever had.

He turned away from the curtain he'd been staring at. Unclenched the fists he hadn't consciously realized he'd formed. Natalie was nibbling her lip, concerned, and every protective instinct he had to wrap her close and keep her safe kicked in.

*She has a head injury. She doesn't need this stress.*

He hated that she'd been hurt. Looking thin and frail in her giant bandage, he was seized by the urge to smack down anyone who threatened her.

*Wow.* Where was all this anger coming from?

Releasing the shaky breath he'd held, he offered his hand to Asa. "You're right, the matter is closed. We've all moved on." *And I don't feel a thing about it. I'm numb. I'm an island.*

Asa reached out and shook his hand. "An excellent attitude," Asa boomed. The lawyer was rounder and grayer than Bruce remembered from fifteen years earlier, but he still had a voice like a boxing announcer. He beamed at Bruce. "And now that that's settled, can we expect you at Natty's open house on Tuesday night? At 4:00 p.m. sharp, at the law offices. We're introducing her to Wallis Point—everyone in town is invited. Hope you decide to be there."

WHAT HAD JUST HAPPENED?

Bruce pushed a tray along a steel counter in the hospital cafeteria, feeling shell-shocked.

Nothing had turned out like he'd expected. Instead of a romantic meal and a pleasurable, distracting evening out with hot, sweet Natalie, he was scrounging up hospital food, while she—the woman he should have been more careful with—was getting a CT scan.

And the lawyer he'd been so terrified of all those years ago—her *father*—not only didn't mind that Bruce was with his daughter tonight, but he wanted Bruce to go and meet everyone in town again?

Why? Besides his family, who were in Florida at the moment, Bruce only cared about one person in town, and that was Gramps. And Gramps didn't even know who Bruce was.

He paused before the premade salads. So what was he doing here, wondering if Natalie liked Caesar salad better than garden salad. Or did she prefer Cobb? Did she even eat meat or eggs? He knew so little about her, and yet, the only decent part of his night had been when she'd stood with him back there. She could have— should have—stayed quietly in bed and concentrated on feeling better. Her head had to be hurting her.

But no, she'd jumped out from that curtain like a guardian angel, more concerned with smoothing the way for him than with anything else. Even now she'd insisted she wasn't hungry and didn't need food and that he could leave—she would find her own way home. Bull. He knew what she was doing—she was trying to downplay her injury and get him to not worry about her.

Not likely. He was involved with this accident of hers, too. And he was staying until he knew she was okay. She needed to let him help her through it, in his own way.

He pulled off his cap and tossed it on the tray beside the plastic utensils and the bottles of water. He was well aware that Natalie was someone he should be steering clear of if he wanted to avoid opening all the old wounds.

And yet, he was just so damn drawn to her. On too many levels.

"I HAVE TO ADMIT," Asa said to Natalie, "you have more steel in your spine than I thought."

The nurses were getting ready to wheel her down to the radiology department—finally, the CT scan machine was open. She looked up at her father from the wheelchair they insisted she ride in. "I'm your daughter," she said simply. "How could you think I didn't have backbone?"

"Mmph," he grunted, smirking at the chair. "Now, there's a point."

They were actually laughing together. A very rare thing. They weren't exactly the closest daddy-daughter duo in town. But that was partly her fault, because she'd always been so afraid of expressing her thoughts to him and then discovering that it was the wrong thing to say.

"You know you made it hard for Bruce," she said, "inviting him to the open house like that."

"Why are you so worried about other people?" he asked cheerfully. "If he wants to come, he'll come. If he doesn't, he won't. If I were you, I'd worry about yourself. Make your open house the best it can be, because your ability to keep a law practice open depends completely on revenue." He slapped the armrest, startling the nurse who pushed behind her. "Make rain, Natty! Go out there and shake some trees!"

"Oh, I'm shaking trees, all right," Natalie said. "And afterward, you'll bring me in as a partner, correct?"

Her father rolled his eyes. "We're a long way from that decision. But yes, if you can shake trees and get people—viable people—into the offices, then I'll hold off on the meeting with the Portsmouth group."

"What meeting?"

"Don't get excited, Natty." He glanced at her. "What have you done for advertising?"

Plenty, but she was always worried that she hadn't done enough, that there was one more step she could take. Talk about digging herself a deeper hole. She fiddled with the sheet draped over her lap, which was silly. It wasn't as if she was going into surgery or anything.

"I'm fine," she said aloud.

"Of course you're fine." He coughed. "Are you set with Bunny Faulkner, though? It bears repeating that our dealings with her are confidential."

"I know that." She looked at her father, and since they were being honest, she decided to ask him the one thing that had always bugged her. "Why did you take that case against Bruce?"

"Frankly, it was a legitimate moneymaker. When the insurance company offered to settle—as I knew they would—I convinced the Faulkners to take it. Frederick was ill, and it's what was best, what he wanted."

"And Bunny?"

He shook his head. "She's never gotten over the accident. She's a recluse. If you want to get anything done with those scholarship applications, you'll need to go to her." He glanced sharply at her. "And if you want my advice, you'll be careful to keep your priorities in order. Personal feelings can get messy."

He was talking about her and Bruce. She rolled her eyes. "He's only staying in Wallis Point for a short time, Dad. You don't have to worry about a conflict of interest with me."

"That's good, Natty. Because you'll find that being

a small-town lawyer isn't always what it's cracked up to be. Sometimes you have to make the hard choices."

"ALL RIGHT. You've heard of dim sum? Or tapas? Well, behold. We've got Greek salad, we've got garden salad and we've got Cobb salad. There's a turkey sub with mustard, and a vegetable and hummus on pita sandwich."

*He did this for me?* Natalie looked at all the dishes Bruce had displayed over the tray-table beside the hospital bed she'd been brought to after her scan. Talk about surprised. And happy. "Our first date," she joked.

"Nope, not a date. I'm a perpetual bachelor."

Her former boss, the ancient, honorable Judge John J. Madison, Jr. had been a perpetual bachelor. Perpetual bachelors didn't ask their landlords out to dinner. They didn't sit beside them in hospitals. They didn't dance at weddings with their nieces, and they didn't bring salads to temporary invalids on Saturday nights.

She inhaled the scent of the fresh olive oil and goat cheese, and sighed happily. "Of course you are."

"I am," he said, his mouth full with turkey. "I'm a rock. An island."

Sure. That was why, even after her father had left, he was still sitting with her in the emergency room while she waited for the on-call doctor to review the results of her CT scan, to tell her she was fine and let her go home.

"Then you're a romantic island," Natalie said, stretching out on the bed and grinning at him.

He raised his eyebrow at her, but it was true. From somewhere, he'd found a single red carnation in a vase, and he'd placed it on the tray for her. It also looked like he'd bought everything left in the cafeteria, because the nurse had told them it was too late to order her a hot meal from kitchen, and it was no telling how long it would be until her tests would be read.

"Sorry," she said to Bruce, "but you can't escape it."

"Maybe I want to take you to bed."

She put her hand on her heart in a pose of feigned shock, even though he'd painted a picture in her head that made her pulse speed up. "And me in my wounded condition."

"All the better." He nonchalantly opened a bag of potato chips. "You won't be able to resist."

She laughed. He was so laconic and amused, sitting sprawled in a leather easy chair he'd found God-knew-where, his elbows perched on the arms, his legs crossed in front of him.

Despite all the good reasons they had for not being together still, here he was. And she also noticed that though the curtain was drawn around him, he made no effort to lower his voice, or hide his face beneath the brim of that ever-present baseball cap. Currently it was tossed on the end of the bed with his sunglasses.

"You're not nervous you'll bump into somebody you don't want to see?" she asked in all seriousness.

"Why should I? You've shown you'll stand up to bat for me."

She felt a glow. "You were there for me tonight and it really helped me." Because if she heard better, then maybe things like this would stop happening to her.

He shrugged. "I'm a fixer. It's what I do."

She passed him the Cobb salad. "And here I'd thought we'd agreed not to fix each other."

"We did agree to that in a sense, didn't we?" He ate some of her salad from the plastic container with his own fork. "But you didn't hear that motorcycle coming at you," he pointed out. "Of course that concerns me."

And it concerned her that she was getting used to enjoying his presence. "Maybe I should be more careful about running across the street to greet you in future."

"I liked that part."

"And I liked that you tore off your shirt to staunch my wound."

That made him smile.

She leaned closer, teasing. "Though you know you were thinking about Bunny Faulkner working here, once we got to the hospital. Admit it."

"If I had, it would have been for good reason. She's the one who banned me from coming to Brian's funeral."

The breath stilled in Natalie's throat. Bruce paused, too.

"I wish I'd known," she said. "I'm really sorry she did that."

He obviously hadn't meant to say that. His brow furrowing, he rubbed his palm across the day's beard growth at his jaw. Wow, he looked sexy.

Better than that, he had *told* her something about himself. They weren't so one-sided now. He shrugged and gave her one of his sheepish grins. He could deny it all he wanted, but she knew that his confiding in her meant something.

"It's old news," he said, "but you're the only person on earth besides me who knows that. I'm counting on you not to repeat it, okay?" He glanced at her. "Are you all right?"

No, she felt teary. "Thank you for telling me that. I mean it, Bruce."

His gaze lowered, and he removed the wax paper holding the remnants of the turkey sandwich from his lap. "Don't read meaning into anything I say," he said, brushing his hands. "I'm a mercenary." He stood and stretched, and she saw a sliver of skin between his waistband and the hem of the borrowed surgical scrubs. "Maybe I'm telling you this because I'd like your opinion on something as a lawyer. Another deal of sorts with you."

He could deflect her, but she knew better than to believe it. She cleared away her plate and utensils, too. "All right, but I warn you, I charge top dollar," she said lightly.

He looked at her, and there was no laughter in his steady brown eyes. "I have some paperwork I reviewed earlier, which I'd like you to take a look at. You see, I need to get my grandfather out of the rest home he's in, just for the afternoon, but they're making me wait until Tuesday. If you could help me convince them to do it tomorrow, then I'll help you however you want. Maybe I could find you another specialist for your ears? Someone really top-notch this time. Seriously, Natalia."

"Natalia?"

He looked sheepish. "Sorry. It's a silly habit. I call my siblings by foreign versions of their names. Mikhael. Marcus. Moe—well, she's just Moe."

Did that mean he thought of her as a sister? She was so confused. And she really, truly hoped not. Then again, he was giving her a nickname—an endearment—

that no one had ever called her before, just as he had promised.

"Natalia." She tested the name on her tongue, and it felt nice. "Yes, I'll take a look at your paperwork. I do elder-care work, so it's right up my alley. But I'm telling you, a visit to another ear doctor is out of the question."

"Something you'll push back on. I like that." He paced to the end of the bed and back. "I've got it. How about if I help you with your house renovations?"

"No, thank you, I have a contractor for that." Though the thought that Bruce was handy enough to lay tile or hang kitchen cabinets made him appeal to Natalie even more.

He snapped his fingers. "Your open house. Do you need any computer work done for it?"

"Don't you have work of your own to do instead?"

"On the long weekend? I have tonight and the next two days free." He suddenly stopped and looked down at her.

"What?"

He shook his head. "Nothing."

"No, really. What?" She sat up on her elbows.

She was mere inches from him. From his face. From his mouth. And suddenly, she wasn't the only one looking at lips—he couldn't seem to stop staring at hers. The breath seemed to have gone out of him. He made a small noise and dipped his head to her.

She shouldn't do this. He was leaving and she was staying. But she wanted to, badly.

She raised her chin and lifted herself from the bed to meet him.

He gave her a light kiss then quickly moved away.

She had a fleeting taste of olive oil and the sensation of...Bruce. His skimming touch felt so nice, so easy and natural, it sent warmth to her abdomen and tingles to her breasts.

He drew back. Disappointed, she caught her fingers in his belt loops. *Please kiss me again.*

But he was tearing his hands through his hair. "Damn it. Pretend I didn't do that. I'm not staying in town long, Natalia."

*I know, and I don't care,* she wanted to say, but the doctor came in. He pushed aside the curtain with a loud scrape of metal on metal. The fluorescent lighting changed, flooded them instead of casting them in shadows.

"The scan is clean," the doctor announced, "no signs of brain injury." But she could barely concentrate on what he was saying.

"Is she okay?" Bruce asked him. "What can I do to help her?"

"You'll want to monitor her for the next day or so," the doctor answered. "Watch for any change in the signs—headaches, dizziness, nausea." He smiled at her. "And don't you go break dancing. Or bodysurfing."

"I don't swim," she murmured.

The doctor glanced at Bruce. "You'll check on her tonight?"

*No. He did not just say that to Bruce.*

"Sure," Bruce said with that deceptively casual smile. "I'm the perfect guy for the job. I never sleep."

# CHAPTER TEN

IF SHE THOUGHT the night was going to be a repeating loop of their hospital kiss, Natalie was sadly mistaken.

"Tell me about your open house," Bruce said.

They were buckled into the backseat of a taxi, on their way back to her cottage. The dome light was on, and Natalie could see the words form on Bruce's lips, though she felt deflated by his choice of topic. She would much rather talk about what had happened between them on that hospital bed.

Then again, the driver could hear every word, so maybe it was better to keep the conversation neutral.

Where to start? "To make it as a solo lawyer, I need to earn money to pay my bills, and to earn money, I need clients," she said.

He nodded. "No different from what I do. The only difference is that I typically work through a subcontractor to place me at a client. You have to draw yours in yourself."

"My biggest problem," she admitted. "I'm not used to promoting myself."

Now there was an understatement.

He was thoughtful for a moment, drumming his fingers against the seat between them, and looking out the window at the lights from homes and streetlamps.

"An open house is a good idea. Did you contact everyone you know? All your family and friends and acquaintances?"

She hesitated. His question was guileless. But how could he know that she wasn't like him…or at least, how he'd been in high school? She had few family and friends to contact. "Why don't we talk about your grandfather's paperwork instead?"

He chuckled in that low tone she'd always found so sexy. "Tomorrow we'll visit my grandfather. Tonight we're fixing your problem."

"I don't have a problem. My open house is perfectly under control."

"Did you advertise?" he asked.

What was it with men and advertising? "Of course, Bruce. I put a notice in the local newspaper. I also sent invitations to all our present clients, plus a few that I want to target."

"How about your social media accounts?"

"I…don't do that."

"Why not?" he asked.

This was so embarrassing. Did she have to admit to him she'd never seen the point of signing up for any because she didn't have massive numbers of friends?

She turned toward him with a sigh, the seat belt cutting across her shoulder. "Do you get good results from social networking?"

"Me?" He smiled faintly. "It's not necessary in my line of business."

"Don't you use it to keep up with your friends?"

He stared blankly at her. "I told you, I don't need it."

What was he saying? "You mean…a guy like you,

a social guy…you're not on Facebook or Twitter. Any of that stuff?"

"No need." He was staring right at her, warning her to back off.

She bit her lip and looked out the window. The taxi was turning onto the beach road. A full moon shone overhead, and it looked beautiful over the water. She wanted to keep pressing, to dig into the layers he kept hidden from people. He was a walking contradiction. Of all the people in their high school, Bruce Cole was the one destined to be king of the "friends lists." Everybody had known him, everyone had loved him.

She watched him, leaning back in his seat, eyes closed. He was easily the hottest guy in any room he entered, at least in Wallis Point. Any woman would be drawn to Bruce.

"If your head feels okay, I'll get you started," he said, noticing her staring at him. "It's easy enough to set up the accounts, and you should stay awake tonight anyway. I don't want anything to happen to you."

That was…nice. His warm eyes made her insides melt.

"Do you have a laptop computer?" he asked.

"I…have a computer in the office in town."

He shook his head. "Nothing at home?" His gaze caressed her face. She couldn't concentrate.

"Y-yes." She caught herself. "I mean, no."

"That's okay, we can use mine if you want." Considering her, he laced his hands behind his head, drawing her attention to his biceps. This guy was one hundred percent male. When she was younger, she'd been awkward at dating. Even though she was fascinated by men, her good grades in school had scared them off. Her poor hearing had been a factor, too, truthfully. She misunderstood them or didn't hear them, and, like Bruce said, they probably thought she was a snob. Or weird.

"Out of curiosity, how do you look things up on the internet without a computer at home?" he asked.

"I use my smartphone. Or my iPad."

He nodded. "Then the iPad it is. Tonight we'll get you plugged-in to the wonderful world of social media. Or as one of my sisters-in-law says, 'Welcome to Addiction.'"

She laughed. "No danger of that happening to me." She wasn't feeling hopeful about this. How did collecting online friends and broadcasting her every, banal thought to the internet at large fit her personality? Even if she took a risk and decided to create a profile somewhere, how would this help her grow a business?

She thought back to the marketing course she'd taken in law school. To the articles she'd read in her legal trade magazines. Until Bruce had mentioned it, she hadn't given an online presence serious consideration.

"My father was never on Facebook," she said aloud.

Bruce said something, but she missed what it was. He noticed her looking at him belatedly then repeated it. "Your father grew up in the last century."

She sighed. She liked the last century. She was a genealogist by hobby, after all. "Lucky him."

Bruce smiled at her. He was sprawled out, completely relaxed. It was dark now, as they drove along the beach road. She had no idea how much time Bruce's computer work would take, but regardless, they would be up late together. Alone in her cottage. The house on one side of her was a multimillionaire's second or third home, and he wasn't present. The home on her other side was owned by a New Yorker whose college-aged kids sometimes spent the weekend hosting late, loud parties, but they weren't in town this month, either. She knew because the owner, Jock, had called and asked her to put out his trash for him.

That meant the neighborhood would be quiet. The beach would be quiet, with nothing to interrupt them.

"If you're worrying, don't," Bruce said, "because it will be a simple working session tonight."

A real business transaction, he was saying.

"And tomorrow I'll be helping you with your grandfather as payment," she said. "Is that the idea?"

He nodded. "A fair trade, I'd say." Then he glanced sideways at her. "But we don't deal with my grandfather tonight. Tonight, we fix your problem."

"Except I don't have a problem. Not really."

He grinned. "And neither do I."

Right. Point taken. They were both in denial. About everything.

The problem was, she knew the extent of it. But she doubted he did.

NATALIE LISTENED TO THE WATER running in her bathroom, suffering through the torture of imagining Bruce naked in her shower. He had asked to use her shampoo, so she was sure he would smell like her. Afterward, her towels would touch his bare skin.

*Stop.* Pushing him from her mind, she instead bustled about the cottage, picking up her breakfast dishes and putting away the laundry basket. She opened the door to the porch and checked for her neighbor's cat, but Otis wasn't there. She quickly changed her clothes. Should she open a bottle of wine, or was that too dangerous?

But when Bruce came out, dressed in a pair of jeans and a fresh T-shirt, his hair toweled dry and tousled, he grinned at her as if he was completely relaxed and comfortable. As if this was something he did every day. "Got anything with caffeine in it?" he asked. She assumed that meant the night was still all about work. Mentally she put away that bottle of wine.

Ten minutes later, she'd poured them some iced tea, and they were set up in her living room, shoulder to shoulder on her small couch. Outside were the full moon and a sea breeze. It was high tide; she could see the waves breaking and foaming against the sand. As much as she told herself not to think of the night as romantic, her breathing was light and fluttery, shallow in her chest as she watched Bruce work.

His fingers flew over the keyboard. He had brought over his own laptop and it was perched on his thighs; she was curled up beside him with her tablet computer. But she wasn't paying attention to her own screen, she was studying him. His hands fascinated her. What would they feel like, skittering over her bare skin?

She looked up at him, at the silhouette of his cheek and lips against the lamplight. And was imagining those lips brushing hers again.

A shudder went through her body. She was dressed in a loose cotton sweat suit—yoga pants and a zip top. Beneath, she wore just panties. She felt so daring without a bra. The fabric was soft and sensuous against her skin. She wanted his hands against her.

From his concentration, he nudged her with his

elbow. "You're not listening to me, Natalia. What password do you want to use?"

She pushed herself back into reality. "Make one up for me."

His eyes crinkled and his mouth curved up on one side. Those fascinating fingers kept typing.

"What did you choose?" she asked.

He picked up the notebook that had all her passwords penciled inside—he'd rolled his eyes at this, but he was honoring her system, antiquated as it was.

Then he put the pencil down, and his hands were back on the keyboard.

She picked up her notebook. *Hotmama69* he'd written.

"Bruce!" she squealed. "What is this?"

The smile danced on his lips, and he laughed from deep in his chest. "Maybe next time you'll pay attention and choose your own password, Counselor."

"Sixty-nine? Really, Bruce?"

But even as she said it, her body was aching for him. Yearning, all over.

His mouth on her, there, would be so nice....

He glanced sideways at her. "A good computer password needs numbers in it. That's computer security 101."

So he was teasing her. She could tease back. She wasn't so dorky that she couldn't do that. "Is there a sixty-nine in your password, too?"

He tilted his head, thinking for a minute. His gaze slid to hers. A slow smile grew.

Uh-oh. Danger.

"Maybe tomorrow I'll add one," he said.

She swallowed. What did he mean by that?

But he shook his head, set aside his laptop and took her tablet from her. Began touching the screen. Boxes opened and closed.

"What are you doing now?" she asked.

"I need a photo of you."

Heat flooded her face. "Bruce!"

"Relax. I'm looking for headshots. For your account. That way, when we load you up with contacts, people can tell who you are from your picture."

"You're making me an avatar." She knew what that was. "But I don't have any professional portraits."

He'd stopped at a candid photo he'd found in her files. "I like this one," he said.

She leaned over his shoulder, prepared to go into defensive mode, to argue with him, but the protest died in her throat. He'd chosen a photo of her taken by her late boss, the honorable Judge Madison. She and the rest of the court clerks had been on a get-to-know-you mingling cruise in Boston Harbor. She'd been uptight, worried and nervous about not knowing anyone and about them discovering she couldn't hear well.

Natalie tugged the iPad closer, so she could see what he was doing on her screen. Bruce had isolated her from the scenery in the background of the photo. Then he zoomed in on her face.

"Wow, I look happy," she blurted.

"You look hot, too."

"Hot?" She frowned at him. "This isn't a dating site—this is for me to get clients."

"Okay, you look hot to me. But to the world at large, you'll look…naturally confident. But not standoffish. You know, how you really are."

"Should I be insulted?"

"No. Hell, no."

"Why do you think me hot, but the rest of the world won't?"

He only smiled. "Tell me when this photo was taken."

"The first week of my first job after I'd graduated law school. I was working for a judge in Boston. He took all of us on a whale-watching cruise out of Boston Harbor."

"For team-building," Bruce said.

"Is that what you call it? Well, in the legal world, it's called…I don't know, an out-of-office party."

"You liked your office, didn't you?"

"No." She'd been terrified, actually. "He—Judge Madison—had said that the first person to spot a whale would win privileges for their group. He was a wise man. Prior to him making that announcement, everybody was crowded around him, trying to suck up to him at the expense of everybody else." She smiled. "Lawyers can be very focused in our efforts."

"You're no brownnose, Natalia."

He was using her nickname again. That was a good sign, maybe. Maybe he considered her more than a business consultation. She gave him a smile. "It's hard to brownnose when you don't hear well."

He grinned back at her. Then, to her surprise, he put one arm around her shoulder and pulled her close.

"What was that for?" she asked.

"You know why I like this photo?" he said, holding up the iPad for her. "Because it's genuine. You saw something you truly liked. The photographer caught that split second when you let down your guard to show the real you. When your happiness came through."

"Do you think I'm usually a faker?"

"No, I think you really liked seeing that dolphin."

"Whale. And yes, I did."

"Whale," Bruce corrected himself. Then he pointed to the posters over her television. She'd decorated her walls with three blown-up photos that had been sent to her by her intrepid grandma before she'd passed away. The first was a colorful market in Turkey, then a labyrinth of shops in Venice by the Grand Canal, and last, a photo that looked like a picture of Christmas in Dickens's London, a street with lots of cheery people, shopping, laughing and intermingling.

"Do you really want to go to those places?" he asked. "Because I've been to all three. Would you like to get out of here someday and travel? Maybe find someplace new? Or are you going to be a person who ties herself to this town and never leaves again?"

He stared at her as if a lot rode on her answer. She knew how he wanted her to answer. If she lied and said yes, that she wanted to leave, then he would kiss her again.

His eyes were wild now; he looked so hopeful that she would admit to him that she didn't want to stay in Wallis Point, that she wanted his life, on the road, traveling from place to place and having adventures.

But as much as he thought he saw her—and maybe he did, somewhat—he had also misunderstood her. She hadn't been attracted to those images and chosen them for her wall because she wanted to go to Venice, or London, or wherever they were set. She'd chosen them because they represented a *feeling* to her. They were community. They were the connections with people that she wanted. And her grandma had given them to her.

They *were* Wallis Point, in a sense.

But she could never explain that. She could only hope to show him—maybe at the open house, if he decided to attend.

"I'm happy where I am," she said in all honesty. And as she'd expected, his expression closed up again. The fun, passionate Bruce left, and the polite but distant Bruce came back.

She sighed and picked up her iPad. "Let's finish the assignment."

BY THE END OF AN HOUR, Bruce had set up Natalie's Facebook and Twitter accounts.

He was back in his habitual groove now, all business. It had taken a while, but he'd finally been able to let go of the earlier energy, the *juice* that coursed through him every time he was with her.

It was mind-boggling, actually. Why else had he kissed her back in the emergency room? Natalie had a head injury, for one, and second, he'd meant what he'd said to her—he was leaving this town, preferably sooner rather than later. Now that he knew Natalie better, he saw that there was no way he should initiate a temporary fling with her. That wasn't who she was at heart. She'd introduced her father to him, for God's sake.

The only guy who should start something with her was someone who could stick around and help her with the dreams she had for herself in this town. He didn't have that in him.

And yet, he couldn't make himself stay completely

away from her, either. He *liked* being with her. There
was something about Natalie that made him feel good
about himself again. Sometimes he even felt…fun again.
Putting sixty-nine in her computer password—had he
gone crazy? But there was a quality about her that drew
him in, made him think about hanging around her, talking to her, joking with her. Kissing her.

No doubt about it, she was definitely one-of-a-kind.
There was a sweetness to her that he didn't often see in
people. He loved that, and he wanted to protect her from
people who would take advantage of it and destroy it.

Ironic, considering the main person who threatened
to take advantage of that sweetness was himself.

She shouldn't trust him. He had years of practice
with meaningless hookups. It was how he preferred his
women.

He didn't feel. And being with Natalie wasn't going
to change him, no matter how much her presence made
him forget to hate that he was still in Wallis Point.

He must have been frowning, because she nudged
him and made a funny face as she got up for a trip to the
kitchen. He laughed aloud. Good God. If he was halfway smart, he'd shut himself down again. He *should*
go back to that numb place. But it wasn't as reliable to
him as it once was. He kept yo-yoing in and out of it,
confusing them both.

He shook his head, grabbed one of her sofa pillows
and stuck it between him and where she would sit once
she got back in the room. Doubled down on the computer keyboard he held in his lap.

She strode back into the room from the kitchen, holding a glass of water. She wore a soft jersey outfit that

clung to her curves and drove him crazy, so he kept his eyes on the computer screen. "I'm giving you homework," he said. "See this profile? You're going to write a short biography for it."

She groaned, but he didn't dare look at her again, so he just held up his hand. "I know you think it seems like you're bragging, that it's not who you are because you're too polite to put yourself forward. But you have to do it. You need to attract clients, right? Well, this is a place where businesses maintain a presence and attract clients."

"Is it where your clients are?" she asked, sitting on the couch beside him with one leg tucked beneath her.

*Focus.* "My clients are other businesses, yours are individuals. Two different things. Back to you." He opened the window he wanted her to fill out. "You're going to enter the info here, tell people a bit about your business, where you are, what you specialize in. Then, every day for the next few weeks, you'll add people to your network. I recommend you search your college cohorts, to start. Tomorrow, add five of your undergraduate classmates." He pointed out the search function, but she was shaking her head as if there was a problem. "What's wrong?"

She crossed her arms. "I was studious in college, Bruce."

"Yeah? And I went to a military academy. They had us scheduled from five-thirty in the morning until eleven o'clock at night. Socializing wasn't high on the list there, either."

She took a sip of water, studying him with those big blue eyes. "Why did you leave the navy?"

*Don't go there.* "It turned out not to be the right place for me."

"That makes sense." She nodded. "Friends always were important to you."

He stared. "People change. I'm not that high school guy you knew."

"Isn't it interesting how I'm becoming more extroverted, and you're becoming more introverted? There is nothing good about being introverted, by the way."

There was a whole host of great reasons for a person to keep to themselves. Protection, for one.

But that word didn't seem to be in her vocabulary tonight.

NATALIE WAS DETERMINED to get him out of his funk.

"Don't you think it's funny that we're probably the only two people our age, on the entire East Coast seaboard, maybe even the country—maybe even the Western World…or the entire world…who aren't tied into social media in any way, shape or form?" she asked.

That made him crack a smile. "Now you're leaving me, and I'll be the only one not on social media."

"I think I'll write a profile for you, just so I'll have one person to be my friend."

"Don't even try it. Here…" He typed on the keyboard. "I'm giving you another job—find and follow a fellow lawyer, someone who does what you do, and does it well. They're going to be your role model in the advertising world, and you're going to learn from them from afar. Perfect for an introvert."

"You're very good at telling people what to do," she remarked.

"*Advising.* I advise businesses what to do. And yes, Natalia, it's a living."

"*I* would hire you."

"Okay," he said, typing some more. "Password time."

She'd been waiting for this. She grabbed the keyboard from him. *BruceCole69* she typed. Then handed it back to him with a perfectly straight face.

"What did you choose?"

"That's my personal secret," she declared.

"No, seriously," he said.

"Oh, seriously." She gave him her version of a Mona Lisa smile.

He was squirming. "Aren't you going to write it in your little black book?"

"No. This one, I will not forget."

He looked decidedly off balance, and that felt good.

She was about to ask if they were finished with the computer when he shook his head and brought up a new window.

"Show me your website," he demanded.

"Excuse me?"

"You're getting my best, gold-medal consulting. Show me the damn website."

He wasn't even facing her; he'd forgotten to be kind to her, and she'd had to lean around him to see what he was saying. Obviously she'd struck a nerve.

She picked up her iPad and typed in the address for her father's website. The familiar photo of their law firm's sign came up, and she felt a glow of happiness. That had been her photo, her idea.

She passed the iPad to Bruce. "The law firm has been

in my family for five generations. I'm the last Kimball in the line."

"So that's why you're doing this," he remarked.

"It's important to me, Bruce."

"Where's your personal website?"

"I don't need one."

"You do." He stared meaningfully at her. "What if you leave your father's firm?"

"That *will* not happen." She grabbed the tablet back.

"It could," he insisted.

*"Won't."* And it was hopeless, she felt more disconnected from him than ever.

"We need a website," he gently said, "to put on your social media profiles, where people will go for more information about you, to find more in-depth info about your practice specialties, your background, that sort of thing."

"I don't need it," she said.

"I'll reserve you a domain name."

"You'll be wasting your money."

"It's not an either-or thing, Natalie. You can keep both websites. That way, when you grow your firm, and you have lawyers working for you, then you can link your personal website to your law firm name." He showed her one by example.

She was floored. "You believe in me that much? You think I can be that successful?"

"I saw the way you handled your father and I saw the way you handled me, too—don't think I didn't notice that, by the way."

"I didn't handle you."

"Yeah, you did, Switzerland."

"I don't think I like that name."

He leaned close to her. "It's a compliment. Take it."

"I like Natalia better."

The look he gave her in return was so full of passion and approval that she felt swept away. Without quite knowing what she was doing, she leaned over the pillow between them, and kissed him full on the lips. She liked the feel of it so much she stayed there, with her lips pressed to his, both of them breathing. Desperate to devour each other, but not daring to. In her case, because she was afraid. In his case…well, he was afraid, too. He just wouldn't ever admit it to her.

He smelled and felt so good. And he *tasted* so good. With a slight moan, he parted his lips. His hand went to the back of her head, cradling her to him, his palm warm against the tender skin of her neck.

She could have cried. The strength and purpose of his hand, of those hands she'd been watching all evening, cupping her sensitive nerve endings…it made it feel like he was accepting her. As if he wanted her just as much as she wanted him.

A loud boom shattered their magic. They both jumped, turned to look out the window.

A spectacular flash of color lit up the heavens. "Fireworks," she marveled.

She grabbed Bruce's hand. "Come on!"

THIS WOMAN WAS ABSOLUTELY killing him.

They stood outside on the porch, the fireworks exploding around them in chaotic displays. Natalie had wrapped a shawl around her shoulders. Her feet were bare. A look of sublime wonder was on her face as she

watched the fireworks finale. It lasted for maybe fifteen minutes, and he didn't watch the sky much. Or at
least, he pretended to. But he was really looking at her.

He'd never wanted to take anyone to bed more. She'd
given him a tempting preview, and it was torment knowing he couldn't let her do it again.

She turned and smiled at him, her lips glistening in
the lamplight.

She had no idea how much he could hurt her.

He gripped the railing so tightly he risked splinters
in his palms. But it was preferable to touching her. Because he couldn't go further than a kiss. He couldn't run
his hands over her amazing body. He couldn't touch her
breasts. Couldn't taste her skin. Couldn't press his hand
between her legs, or make love with her until they were
both satisfied.

No matter how much they both wanted it.

AFTER THE FIREWORKS ENDED, a long moment of silence
spread along the beach. In the sky above, smoke was
clearing, like a battle ending. Natalie's pulse was high,
her body revved, as if her "fight" mechanism had kicked
in.

Never had she wanted a man to stay with her more. At
the wedding last night, Bruce had been almost predatory
in his approach to her, but she hadn't been interested.
She was more than interested now. Bruce would never
admit it, but they *clicked* together; they had a connection, and it went deeper and further back than just tonight. To her, it went all the way back to her childhood.

Bruce respected her and he took her goals seriously.
He saw the potential beneath her sometimes awkward

social demeanor, in a way that nobody else did. There wasn't that habitual struggle she always felt, of trying, and of missing the mark.

With Bruce, it wasn't a matter of trying. At any time tonight—and even before that, this afternoon—he could have jumped into his sports car and roared out of her driveway. There were plenty of options available to him besides her house. But he had stayed with her.

She loosened the shawl and it dropped to her waist. Under her shirt, her unbound breasts felt free in the night air. A slight breeze chilled her, but it was a good chill, a cooling off from the heat that burned inside. She glanced into his face, shadowed by the darkness. She knew the stubble lining his jaw, and she could see herself touching it. Touching him.

It would be easy for him to curl her into an embrace, if he wanted to. She stepped closer so her hip brushed his hand.

*Pull me to you. Kiss me again.*

He didn't move. Maybe it was wild on her part, but she turned, opening her body to him, so he would be sure to feel it, letting him know that this was an invitation.

He was gazing at her in the moonlight. His look was intense. Heated.

The breath left her throat.

*Now.* Would she sleep with him? She wanted to… Which was shocking.

Her whole life she'd been driven by the desire to fit in with people her age. Part of how people did that was by hooking up when hooking up was required. But she'd never liked it. And she'd stopped when she went into the work force, simply because she was busy and there was no time. She didn't miss what she'd never liked to begin with. It had left her with a sense of emptiness, that this was not what love was supposed to be. If she wanted to really connect with people, then she'd need to be authentic. So she had determined that she wouldn't do it again, not unless that connection was there.

Maybe she was betraying that determination now, because it was apparent Bruce didn't see her as completely as she wished, but…something was happening with her body. She'd never felt full-on…lust. A mad, direct urge to feel him inside her. Stroking inside her.

Everything that she'd never understood about the drive for sex, everything that the rest of her peer group, so saturated in sexual images and advertising and pornography, it now seemed so clear. Making love was so strong an urge. And now, to her, as well…

*I'm there,* she thought.

Why wasn't Bruce reacting?

And then she realized, that if she wanted him badly enough—wanted to make that connection—she needed to take matters into her own hands.

"Would you like to go inside with me tonight?" she asked.

## CHAPTER ELEVEN

BRUCE STOOD ROOTED like a tree on Natalie's back porch. It was a first in his life. The woman had invited him. All he had to do was fold her into his arms. He wanted to, with an urgency that rushed him like a wave. But he couldn't.

He didn't want to hate himself. He'd spent so long, so many years not being proud of himself. Feeling lousy with guilt and wanting to make that go away.

Now he was in Wallis Point, the place where that had all started, and it seemed important that he make the extra effort here. A strange sort of redemption.

He backed away from her. Gripped the wooden railing to keep from reaching for her. This sweet, beautiful, heartfelt, attractive woman shouldn't want him. She was mistaken in that.

"Bruce?" she whispered.

"You…need to get your sleep. Tomorrow is an early day."

Under the glow of the porch light, she frowned at him. "Tomorrow is Sunday."

"Right. But even so, I'm up at five-thirty. I jog." He'd kept the habit from his Academy days. He'd liked the routine because he was a poor sleeper, and because the exercise kept him in shape no matter how many terrible airport meals he consumed. "I was thinking I'd bring you breakfast at seven-thirty or eight. We could get going then."

She hugged her shawl tighter around her chest. "You want to work on your grandfather's paperwork on Sunday at 8:00 a.m.?"

What? "No. There really isn't anything to work on. The paperwork seems in order—it's some forms Moe filled out for the nursing home, and I was mainly hoping to have you—a lawyer—accompany me in case they gave me a hassle again. You know, like sometimes how a letter on a law firm's stationery...just the subtle threat of legal action can help sway a decision. That's what I'm talking about."

"Yes, I can do that." The light from the back porch bulb shone clearly on Natalie's face. She really was taking him seriously, God help her. He searched for a joke to crack, something to escape this feeling, but he couldn't come up with anything.

Well, maybe one thing. "I was thinking of stopping at this donut place, over the line in Massachusetts."

"Donuts on the Beach." She nodded. "It's still there."

"I'm glad. My grandfather loved that place." He rubbed his thumb along her porch railing again. Solid. Traditional. He needed a familiar place right now, something perhaps to take the sting out of Gramps not remembering him. The donut shop might do the trick. "How about if I pick up breakfast for all of us there? Will you be awake at eight?"

She didn't answer right away, so he said, "Shoot. Do you even eat donuts?"

"I love Donuts on the Beach donuts," she said softly. "And yes, eight o'clock is fine. But don't bring coffee—

I have a machine." She didn't sound disappointed, she had seemed to move on. Diplomatically. She was definitely being easy on him, smoothing the way for him and keeping the tension low.

Sweet Natalie. He felt overcome by an urge to pull her to him in a good-night kiss. But that would be wrong.

"I'll see you tomorrow, sweetheart," he mouthed to her. He didn't make a sound, but he knew she would hear him. Their special communication.

She smiled. Yeah, she got it. "Do you have your house key?" she asked.

"I'm set." She really was trying to help him. Which amazed him every time he thought of it.

Wait…he'd almost forgotten. "How is your head? Are you sure you'll be okay?" He glanced at the bandage she wore. *Damn it.* "I really shouldn't leave you alone tonight, should I?"

But she smiled gently and tightened her shawl around her shoulders. "My head is fine," she said. "I'll see you tomorrow."

And then she went inside. He stood there for a while, watching the waves roll in, feeling more empty and alone than he had at any point since he'd arrived in town.


DONUTS ON THE BEACH was exactly the way Bruce remembered it. The Sunday morning crowd filled the foyer of the tiny area landmark. Judging from the smell wafting through the early morning breeze, they still made their donuts, crullers and Boston Creams fresh on site, which was a rarity. Few places did that anymore.

Bruce slammed the car door and adjusted the visor

on his baseball cap. His sunglasses were dirty, so he squinted as he walked across parking lot, the gravel crunching under his feet. The familiar bells on the shop door tinkled as he entered.

In his house growing up, this place had been a Sunday morning tradition with Gramps. He and Moe had jumped from the backseat of the car and had clambered inside to pick out a variety box. They always bought dusted-sugar (his favorite), old-fashioned (his dad's), chocolate-covered (his gramps's) and jelly-filled (Maureen's).

Brian had liked honey-dipped.

Bruce slowed. There was an ache in his stomach.

Hunger pains, that was all it was.

And he'd promised Natalie donuts. He couldn't go back empty-handed, no matter how tempting it was to leave now.

He got into the long line and waited, shuffling forward until it was his turn at the counter. He placed his order, and was pleased when it arrived still warm from the fryer. Man, this brought back memories.

The smell alone...

He stuffed those memories away, opened the sack on his way back to the car and grabbed whatever was on top. Felt the sticky sugar on his fingers. Sank his teeth into a huge, deep bite.

Honey-dip.

Of course.

NATALIE ROLLED OVER, yawning, and immediately bumped into Otis. The big gray tomcat stood and stretched lazily, then jumped to the floor.

This was her fault. A previous owner had installed a cat door, and in a moment of weakness last night as Natalie had closed up, she'd unlocked the pet door in case he wanted to wander in.

Foolish of her, really. Besides, she knew it was Bruce she wanted to wander in, but he wasn't ready. She wasn't exactly sure what was going on with him, but all she could think of was her father's advice: *keep your priorities in order*.

Fine. She would do so. Her business was the most important thing to focus on.

Unfortunately, today's business also involved Bruce. She had to give him legal help—her end of the bargain. Drat.

She rubbed her eyes and sat up. How much time did she have? The cat had started meowing at her at around 3:00 or 4:00 a.m. She'd gone downstairs to the kitchen and had fed him, but couldn't get back to sleep again. Then, she'd gradually drifted off, only to feel his claw—one claw, opened slightly—poking into her cheek. A tomcat's wake-up call.

She yawned again and reached for the alarm clock, to shut it off. But somebody—who could only be Otis—had knocked it over.

Eight o'clock. Bruce was coming!

She leaped up, and immediately stubbed her toe. She was so not a morning person.

She was brushing her teeth when the doorbell rang. She'd installed a special, extra loud doorbell, and it was pitched to the low tone she heard best. Otis meowed and ran under the bed. The poor cat probably thought it was thunder.

"I'm coming!"

She entered the kitchen to find Bruce already inside. She'd forgotten he had the key.

"Uh, sorry…" He backed up, momentarily surprised.

With as much dignity as she could muster, she took the toothbrush from her mouth. "Good morning, Bruce."

"Damn." He looked her up and down. "Is that what you sleep in?"

"It's a nightgown," she said.

"It's…short. And see-through." He grinned. "I like it."

She rolled her eyes, then turned on her heel and marched upstairs to her closet. She grabbed her thick terry-cloth robe and pulled it on, belting it tight. She went back downstairs and moved past him toward the kitchen.

"Hey, don't feel bad." Bruce followed her. "I don't sleep in anything."

"Too much information," she said.

He winced. "Yeah, sorry, I didn't mean that." He sat on one of her kitchen chairs and put the distinctive white paper bag with the Donuts on the Beach logo on her table. Which, thankfully, was neat and tidy; she'd stayed up a bit late last night to pick up her place. Not everybody liked it "comfortably cluttered," the way she did.

He seemed quiet all of a sudden. She glanced at his face. Bruce was staring at the bag, oddly withdrawn.

She drew in her breath. Something had happened at the donut shop, but whether that was connected to the past or to his grandfather's current situation, she had no way of knowing. He wasn't trying to hide his sadness from her, which she supposed was progress.

She sat on the chair across from him, and pulled the bag toward her. It smelled good, freshly made and yummy. She drew out the donut on top.

Glazed, with one bite out of it. "May I?" she asked him.

When he nodded, she carefully put her mouth beside Bruce's bite mark and sank her teeth into it, her small vote of solidarity with him. The flavors of honey and butter and dough burst on her tongue. "Mmm." She sighed, chewing happily. "Honey-dip is my favorite."

"It was Brian Faulkner's favorite, too."

Her heart thudding, she put down the donut. This was significant.

She waited for him to continue.

But he didn't speak again. He just kept staring at the white bag.

"I'm sorry," she said. "I know how close you were to him."

That seemed to snap him out of his trance. He looked up at her and smiled that old devastating smile, except this time, it didn't quite reach his eyes. "We need to get this show on the road. Do you mind if I make some coffee?" he asked.

"Go ahead, make yourself at home. I have a single-cup machine." She pointed to it in on the counter. "There's regular, decaf and dark-brewed to choose from."

"Those things are great." He grinned at her, and this time it seemed genuine. "Did I tell you you're an angel?"

She was no angel. She swallowed. "Bruce, I sometimes wonder what would've changed if I'd told my dad how I saw you in the funeral home that night. Maybe if

I'd gone to him back then, if I'd made an effort to convince him to talk to the Faulkners on your behalf, then you wouldn't have had to go through the grief of Brian's death all on your own."

Bruce shook his head and stood. "You're not responsible. Don't think that way."

"What about you? Do you feel responsible?"

"The only thing I want to feel responsible for is this." He peered at her, studying her pupils, then the cut at her temple. He didn't touch her, though, as if he didn't want to get too close. She understood now, how keeping himself away from her had so much to do, at core, with his unresolved feelings about what had happened with Brian.

"If anything changes with your injury," he said, "any dizziness or pain, will you let me know?"

"I will." She lifted her chin. "Will you tell me what happened at the donut store to upset you today? Did someone say something to you?"

He laughed shortly. "Nothing happened. Most people probably don't even remember Brian anymore. It's just internal to me." He glanced at the clock on her wall. "We should get going. I'll get the coffee on the way out. Do you want to use the shower first, or should I?"

"You go ahead." She couldn't magically change him. He was going to open up to her—or not—at his own pace.

She tried not to feel sad about that. She got up and handed him a clean bath towel and a washcloth from her hallway linen closet. When he closed the door behind him, she went to her room to throw on a pair of sweats. The hard part was, she could get used to having him in her house.

His shower was a short one. Her cup of coffee had just finished brewing when he came into the kitchen dressed, his hair damp and combed. "Do you have a hamper?"

"Yes." She pointed to the wicker basket in her laundry room and he tossed the towels inside. He was neater than she was.

He smiled sheepishly. "I'm used to leaving them on the floor of hotel bathrooms. I had to catch myself today."

"This place isn't exactly maid clean."

"It's a home. I appreciate it." He glanced at her. "Do you want more coffee before I make some?"

"No, I'm set." But she couldn't tear her eyes away from him. It was so surreal seeing him just out of the shower and going through the motions of daily life with her, after her having had a crush on him for so long.

She sat back and watched him brush past her. He smelled great, like her shea butter soap and herbal shampoo. He hadn't shaved, which gave him a dangerous look. If she touched his chin, she would feel the coarseness of his stubble beneath her fingers.

But there would be no more touching, no matter how much his eyes strayed after her, or he'd stared at her in her nightgown. There was this force inside him that prevented him from wanting a relationship with her. No matter how much of a diplomat she was, there was nothing she could do to smooth that over and fix it.

The finality of that realization seemed to sit heavily with her.

He chose a flavor from the assortment on her coffee rack and then loaded the machine, the motor humming to life. Dark brewed coffee dripped into his mug. He walked to the refrigerator. "May I?" he asked. She got the feeling he was using politeness to overcompensate for the reluctance to talk to her about what really counted.

"There's milk on the door," she told him.

He nodded and poured some into his mug. He took a long swallow and then fixed his gaze on hers. "This is really good."

"I make better coffee than Donuts on the Beach."

"You do." He looked into his cup. "And...I should explain about my grandfather before we see him. He's... not himself."

The smile on his face turned to a frown. "He doesn't recognize me. I'm hoping he will soon. I promised Maureen I would spend two hours today visiting him."

So that was bothering him, too. And was this the reason he stayed in town?

"Of course I'll accompany you for as long as you want," she said quietly.

The relief showed plainly on his face. "Thanks. I mean it."

"I promised I would help you in return for your helping me with my business, remember?"

He leaned against her counter, oozing sex appeal, his dark eyes watching her over the rim of his mug as he downed his coffee. "Yeah, but I shouldn't have assumed you didn't have plans. It's a long weekend."

The truth was, she'd originally been planning to work on the guest house renovations. The added income once she was able to rent it would help repay her college loan debt. It was also her reserve fund, in case her father insisted she invest a chunk of money to buy into a partnership.

Still, he was right—it *was* a holiday weekend. And it was acutely embarrassing that she had so little of a personal life that she had nothing exciting going on.

"I do have plans later on," she said lightly. "A hot date tonight with a millionaire who's jetting me off to his private yacht in Monte Carlo. We'll spend the rest of the holiday gambling, shopping, getting to know one another..."

He stared at her.

"I'm kidding, Bruce." She took a sip of her coffee.

He smirked. "I was actually thinking that I could probably swing a pair of commercial first-class tickets, but definitely not the yacht."

She gaped at him.

He grinned back. "So. You don't want to travel as a lifestyle, but you do want to be whisked away for the weekend every now and then. Duly noted."

Was he hinting that he wanted to take her away for a weekend? "Maybe if you promise to keep sleeping naked," she cracked.

He pushed away from the counter, laughing. "You are one interesting lady."

Yeah, that was her, interesting. Just a wannabe small-town lawyer who wasn't having too much success establishing herself, or helping the people she'd most wanted to help.

She sighed, and watched him snag a sugar-dusted donut, then head for the door with a wink. Then again, he was genuinely smiling now, and she had done that. It was a start.

"I'll pick you up at ten, Natalia," he called.

Heartened, she called back, "Don't forget your hot sports car."

He poked his head around the corner. "I almost forgot—wear a bathing suit under your clothes."

"Why?" she asked.

"You'll find out why when we get there."

BRUCE PULLED OUT of the Surf, Cast, and Rod shop with three saltwater fishing poles disassembled in his trunk. He drove down the coast road on autopilot, not really seeing the scenery. A warm summer breeze blew his hair against his forehead, but he barely felt it.

If all went well, this would be his last day in Wallis Point. He'd been serious about asking Natalie to help him. He might have screwed up in his past where Brian was concerned, but he could still fix his relationship with Gramps. It, at least, was in the present.

But first, he needed Gramps to recognize him, and in his gut he knew this fishing expedition was the best tactic.

He turned into Natalie's driveway and parked beside her Toyota. He was lucky he still had her on his side. She was amazing to him. She was changing his impression of lawyers, that was for sure.

He was checking his glove compartment for the envelope Moe had given him when a rap sounded on the passenger window. It was Natalie, shocking him like a heart attack again.

She wore a peach-toned tank top that left little to the

imagination, and short white shorts. He blinked and lifted his shades. Her hair was piled on her head, showing off her long neck. Dimples lit up her face.

He quickly reached over and unlocked the door for her.

"Thank you." She slid into the seat gracefully. Hooking one thumb under the sleeve of her tank top, she pulled out her bra strap. Pink. "I'm dressed to code, Bruce. What's the occasion that we need a bathing suit for a visit to an old-age home?"

A *bathing suit?* This was a skimpy bikini. He stared, unable to think of a single word to say to her. She just... blew him away. She had a way of making him smile like nobody else did.

"Cat's got your tongue, huh?" She glanced at the dashboard odometer. "Wow, this is low mileage. It certainly has that new-car smell. Do you mind if I drive it later?"

Mutely, he nodded.

"Is that a yes, I can, or a no, I can't?"

It was a hell, yes. She could do anything she wanted as far as he was concerned.

Her brow crinkled. "Why are you not wearing a bathing suit? Did I hear you wrong? Did you say 'bring a martini' instead of 'wear a bikini'?"

Laughing, he found his voice. "I said 'bathing suit.' And mine's in the trunk. Maybe you can look at the papers for me before we get to the nursing home?" He passed her the envelope.

She opened the flap, slid out the contents and glanced at the pages. Her forehead creased, and her nostrils flared. She was still cute to him, but she looked...angry.

She continued to study the papers, shuffling them back and forth.

Bruce was getting a sinking feeling. "What's the verdict, Counselor? Am I allowed to take my grandfather out of that place for the day, or not?"

Natalie pressed her lips together. He caught a fleeting look of...hurt?

"When did Maureen have this document made up?" she asked.

*Oh, hell. What did you do, Maureen?* "I don't know."

"Never mind." She took a breath. "The date's right here." She tapped her finger on the page.

"Is something wrong with it?"

"No, everything is perfectly legal." She stuffed the papers into the envelope and plunked it on her lap. "This is a copy of Maureen's power of attorney document, along with the internal forms the nursing home had her fill out. For one week, Bruce, you're in charge, you can do whatever you want with your grandfather, and nobody can tell you otherwise."

"That's...good news." He peered at her. "Why do you look so mad?"

She nibbled her lip. Finally she sighed and gave up. "Maureen drove up the coast to Portsmouth two weeks ago to get the power of attorney made, rather than walk two minutes to my—to her bridesmaid's law office. And I *specialize* in this stuff."

"Oh." He could see her point. "Yeah, that sucks." He scratched his head. "Do you want me to talk to her when she gets back?"

"No, that's not necessary. This is my problem and I need to take care of it."

NATALIE WALKED LIKE A WOMAN with a purpose. Somehow, this nursing home agenda had taken on a life of its own, and a meaning deeper than what it appeared on the surface. She was tired of being dismissed, tired of being forgotten. Maureen must not have even thought of her for the legal work.

She stopped at the nurses' station and handed Bruce's forms to the attendant on duty. Natalie didn't particularly feel like being gentle or diplomatic. She was feeling uncharacteristically direct. "Hello, my name is Natalie Kimball. I'm an attorney, and I'm with Bruce Cole. We are taking his grandfather, William Cole, out for the afternoon, and here is the required paperwork."

Natalie turned to Bruce, who was looking at her like… Well, did it really matter? For once, she had reached her limit. She didn't care what anybody thought.

Then again, this was partly her fault, too. She made it too easy for people to overlook her and take her for granted. No more.

Natalie turned to the nurse, who had finished scanning the forms and was putting them back in her envelope. "Please bring us the sign-out sheet and in the meantime, we'll get William ready to leave," Natalie said.

"Certainly." The nurse nodded and headed for a back room. Bruce opened his mouth as if he wanted to say something to Natalie, but in the end he didn't. He remained quiet and trusted her to let her work. His restraint ranked right up there among the best things anyone had ever done for her.

The nurse returned, smiling at Natalie as she passed her a clipboard. "Okay," she said. "William is all yours."

BRUCE LET OUT HIS BREATH. *Thank God.*

True, they were facing a different nurse from yesterday—Gail, her name badge read—but still, Natalie, with her gentle but direct presence, had been able to accomplish what he couldn't. Gramps was officially cleared to leave with them.

He gave her full credit. He would be talking to Maureen about her, setting his sister straight as soon as she returned from her honeymoon. As a lawyer, Natalie was smart, direct and competent. It was foolish to overlook her. His sister should be dropping her old prejudice—because of him—regarding the Kimball Family Law Firm, and she should partner with Natalie when it made sense.

He leaned back, watching Natalie scan the small print on the form on the clipboard the nurse had passed her. Absently she tucked her purse strap over the tank top she wore, which only drew his attention to her breasts. She rocked that tank top and those short shorts. She had an amazing body, a pretty face and…and he was an idiot.

Every part of him wanted to take her by the waist and pull her close, even though this wasn't the time, and it certainly wasn't the place. They were here to pick up his grandfather. Why hadn't this realization hit him last night, or even this morning, when he could have done something about it? What had been stopping him?

So what if she lived and worked in Wallis Point? He could still be part of her life and support her agenda. He didn't have to be present here every single weekend; maybe she could fly out of town to meet him sometimes. They could make an arrangement like that work, if it came to that.

He took the pen Natalie handed him, then scrawled his signature. She already knew he traveled for a living. Weekends were…weekends, after all. Time for enjoyment. He could fly her to Florida with his points. They could go anywhere.

When he passed the clipboard back to her, their hands bumped, and he intertwined his fingers with hers. For a brief second she accepted him, and his pulse kicked up. But then she slid from his grasp, her expression distracted. "Excuse me," she said. "Why don't you get William ready to go? I need to do something first."

She strode off after the nurse. Bruce told himself to let it go. He had all day with her.

"HELLO?" NATALIE MARCHED into the room—it looked like a break room for the rest-home staff. This was totally on a whim, but she felt energized.

"Oh, hi," the nurse—Gail—said. "Is everything going okay with William?"

"Yes, and thank you again. I just wanted to mention that if you know anyone who needs an elder care lawyer, that's what I specialize in. My rates are affordable and I'm local." From her purse, Natalie pulled out a flyer.

"Here's an announcement for an open house I'm having on Tuesday." She pointed to the photo of her family's law office. "Here, right in the village." In future, she would add a photo of herself to the flyer, too—the one Bruce had found and cropped for her.

"Nice building," Gail said. "I know that place."

"We also do wills, real estate, estate planning, family law. Oh, and I'm a Notary Public," she finished up.

She glanced around the break room. "Would you mind if I tack this up somewhere?"

Gail pointed to a bulletin board. "I'll get you a staple gun."

Her handiwork front and center, Natalie walked down the hallway looking for Bruce, feeling like Wonder Woman.

She found him in the last room she looked in. A slight, confused-looking man wearing gray sweatpants and sneakers sat on the bed. In front of him was a walker. Bruce was beside him, bent over a chest of drawers.

"Keep looking!" the man who had to be William shouted. "I need my TV remote!"

Bruce knelt and rifled the bottom drawer. Just the sight of this big, strapping, physically fit, ex-navy guy, turning himself into knots for his grandpa, made her heart do a dip.

"Who are you?" William shouted to her.

Bruce looked up at her. And immediately banged his head on the drawer. He winced, and she knelt to check him.

"You should be arrested wearing those shorts and that outfit," he grumbled.

"It's hot outside." She turned to William and spoke loudly so he could hear her. "Hello, my name is Natalie. I'm Bruce's friend. Are you ready to go to the beach with us? Bruce is taking us fishing."

"Fishing?" William repeated. "Fishing?"

The elderly gentleman was obviously confused. She hoped the outing wasn't a bad idea.

But Bruce had that stubborn look on his face. Their

day at the beach was going to happen whether William wanted it or not. Natalie glanced at the pile Bruce had gathered on the bed: a hat, a baggie of medication, a tube of sunscreen, two adult diapers and a zip-up hoodie sweatshirt in case it was breezy by the sea. Something in her heart caught. Bruce was a good man to have thought of all this.

He touched her shoulder, and she turned. "What about the bracelet on his ankle?" he mouthed to her.

"Walk William to the elevator," she murmured. "The staff will disable the alarm for us."

Bruce led his elderly grandfather down the hall, taking careful steps to match William's gait and the slow progress of his walker.

Bruce was gentle with his grandfather, she noted. In the past weeks she'd seen two potential clients bring in elderly parents to the law firm in an attempt to legally get their parents' assets transferred to them prematurely. To her father's credit, he was ethical and turned such people away.

But Bruce wasn't like that. He genuinely loved his grandfather. He seemed attached to him.

The ache was in her heart again, but she pushed it away. "What beach are we taking him to today?"

"Doesn't Sunrise Beach have the easiest access for people on walkers?"

She nodded. "Does William like to fish?"

"I..." Bruce looked down, his face clouded. Had she imagined it, or had his voice caught, too? He cleared his throat. "I need him to remember me. I can't leave Wallis Point until he remembers me."

William had early stage Alzheimer's disease, Natalie

recalled from the forms. He might never remember who Bruce was, and that was sad. She hoped she could help Bruce somehow, no matter what happened.

When they got to the elevator, William hesitated. With a gleam in his eye, he inched forward until the alarm went off. Then he backed up quickly.

Another resident came out of her room, and shuffled over to the elevator to investigate the source of the blaring alarm. When the nurse came upon the scene, she scolded the second resident. William smiled like an angel.

"We'll have to watch out for him," she whispered to Bruce. "Your grandfather is a rascal."

"He is, isn't he?" Bruce mused. He grinned. "I always loved that about him."

The nurse deactivated William's alarm and he beamed like a man given his freedom. When they all three piled into the elevator, William patted her wrist with his gnarled hand. She smiled at him.

"Natalie," he said.

THE LITTLE HIDDEN FISHING INLET was quieter than usual, given that the second day of the sandcastle competition was in progress farther down the beach.

Gramps was too frail to walk unaided, and it turned out that the Cadillac of walkers—and Bruce had had a hell of a time shoving that huge thing into his car trunk—didn't work well on the short stretch of sand near the parking area, but that was easily solved by Bruce picking him up and carrying him to a folding chair Natalie set up on the promontory for him. He helped Gramps take off his shirt, slather on sunscreen and push up the pant legs of his elastic sweatpants to the tops of his knees. Bruce hadn't been able to find a swimsuit in the chest of drawers—apparently no one had thought he'd need one after moving to the nursing home. But Gramps was happy. He wore an old navy cap Bruce had once given him for Christmas, and he sat on a camp chair Bruce had picked up at a beach store, along with a swimsuit for himself and other stuff he needed, plus a carton of bait, a cooler of drinks and sandwiches, and a few oversize towels.

Natalie was stretched out, sunning herself beside them. Since Gramps wasn't a talker when he fished— in truth, they rarely said a word to each other—Bruce was content to kick back, drink his soda and gaze at Natalie in her bathing suit.

He doubted there was another woman on earth he could take on a day like this. But this outing meant more to him than anything else he could do. He *needed* Gramps to remember him. He had to.

Gramps had remembered Natalie's name from her introduction, and that gave Bruce hope. Maybe Gramps was screwing with him. Playing mind games, the way he did with the nurses and the elevator alarm. Making Bruce stay because he liked Bruce's company.

He certainly enjoyed the fishing. They were in the groove of it, as always.

Natalie sat up suddenly, turning to smile at Bruce. "This day is perfect," she murmured.

"Yeah," he said. They could talk because Gramps couldn't hear them talking. It disturbed the fish, he always claimed.

To his shock—considering they'd often spent mornings catching nothing but crabs or seaweed—Bruce got a tug on his line. Since Gramps was too frail to hold a rod, Bruce was doing the fishing for both of them while Gramps watched intently. He stood from the chair, waving his arms and giving Bruce the same directions he'd given him as a kid, as Bruce reeled in the striped bass.

"A striper!" Gramps said. "Good size, too."

It was only a matter of time before Gramps remembered him.

NATALIE GATHERED THE TOWELS and shook out the sand. Too bad their day at the beach had to end. Bruce was actually starting to get back some of the old, carefree personality she'd remembered. The only hard part was that his grandfather hadn't called him by his name, or given an indication that he even knew who he was.

William called her Natalie. That had to mean something. Didn't it?

But William was starting to doze off. They returned him safely to the home—bundled him into the car, then out of it and ushered him up the elevator, none of which were simple, quick tasks. Once on his floor, the nurse reattached his ankle bracelet, and William didn't complain.

"I'm tired," he simply said.

"We'll see you later, William."

"Yup," William said. And then he rolled over on his bed and went to sleep.

Natalie stepped aside to let Bruce have some privacy, but he left, too. On the way out, he seemed to shake himself. Some of his happiness had worn off.

"I can't believe he went downhill so fast," Bruce said when they were buckled into their seats.

"When did your parents move him there?" she asked.

"I don't actually know," he said in a soft voice.

"They didn't tell you?"

He frowned into the rearview mirror as they pulled into traffic. "I found out at the wedding on Friday." He glanced at her, hope blooming on his face. "You were with Moe for all the preparations. What did she say about it?"

Natalie shook her head. "Nothing. It was a surprise to me, too." She curled her body toward him, the better to see his lips as he drove. "I knew Maureen in high school, but I didn't see her again until recently."

She paused, but he was listening intently, saying nothing. She took that as a signal to keep talking. "When I came back to town a few weeks ago, my father asked me to talk with her, to see if we could convince her to throw some business our way." She looked at him, but Bruce was silent. Those ever present shades covered what he was feeling, if indeed he felt anything. She took a breath.

"It ended up that she asked me to be her bridesmaid, but she never really included me in her confidences, and as you saw, she didn't think of me for her legal needs."

She looked at him again. Still silent. "I was…" *Hurt,* she thought. But she didn't say it.

"Anyway," she said, filling in his silence with her babbling, "you should probably know that the only reason she asked me to be in her wedding was that in addition to needing a fourth bridesmaid, she knew that I'd always liked you. She thought it would be a good idea to pair me with you. I think she thought it would help you."

He stared at her. "What?"

She could feel her cheeks burning. Telling him this was a mistake. They were home now, and the beach sand felt comforting and familiar underfoot as they walked the path to her cottage. Bruce followed behind her, and she hoped they could sort this out together, as they'd been doing all weekend. She climbed the porch, opening her bag as she looked for her house key.

His hand touched her bare arm, stopping her and making her look up. His face was completely closed off, as if a storm front had descended. The keys dropped from her hand to the jumble in her purse. "Bruce?"

"I can't do this."

"Do what?" she asked.

"I'm not good company tonight," he said.

What was he talking about?

"You've been a good friend to me these past couple days. Better than I've had in a long time…." He looked down.

*I'm losing him,* she thought.

Beside the door, there was the box she'd been waiting for. The shower stall for her guest house renovations. She was supposed to call her contractor when it arrived. For now, she leaned on the box for balance. "You don't have to say anything," she said. "I understand you're upset about William. Anybody would be."

"I can't do this," he repeated. "I thought I could, but it's too much."

She didn't know what to say. She tried to smile pleasantly at him, ever the diplomat, but her smile faltered.

What had he called her—Switzerland? She was a lousy Switzerland. Didn't want to do it anymore. "What's too much?" she asked.

"She shouldn't have paired me with you. I don't…I can't…feel this. I don't want to feel this." He looked at a spot above her head. "Every hour that I spend with you, I want you so badly. When I was looking for just sex, it was easier." His Adam's apple bobbed as he swallowed. "But now that I know you, and I like you, and I see what you expect and deserve, I can't…"

"You can't what?" she pressed.

"I can't feel like a normal person." He shook his head. "I can't invest myself in a close relationship. It ends up like…"

"Bruce—"

"I've got to go." He backed away, and she turned helplessly to watch him.

"I'm leaving after this week," he called. "When Maureen returns."

"I know that," she called back.

He shook his head. And suddenly she knew that it didn't matter what she did. Because Bruce couldn't feel. What could *make* him feel?

In desperation, she blurted, "Tomorrow is the Memorial Day holiday. I'm going with my mother and my two aunts to the cemetery to lay wreaths on the family graves. You can come with us if you want to."

He blanched. Literally blanched.

Immediately she put her hand to her mouth. She'd only made it worse.

Without anything left to say, she went into the house and softly shut the door behind her.

Once inside, she leaned her back against the door, breathing heavily. But she needed to know what he was doing, so she glanced back out the window.

Bruce was still standing on the walkway, staring at the spot where she'd been. As she watched, he stuffed his hands into his pockets and walked away.

# CHAPTER TWELVE

Monday morning, Bruce's car was gone from the driveway. He didn't come in to use Natalie's shower, either.

She went to the cemetery with her mom and her aunts. This was their tradition. Every year they laid geraniums at the graves of both sets of her grandparents. One of her grandfathers had fought in World War II, so they arranged that he had a flag and a veteran's medallion planted beside his headstone. The day was mild, and the lawn was a brilliant green, which made her feel hopeful.

On the way back to her car, she saw two of her genealogy students, so she stopped to say hello. Genealogists were often found in graveyards; Margery Whiting's daughter, Lil, was busy snapping photos of the memorials, and Margery slowly recorded the names and dates into a data collection program on Lil's phone app.

Lil had printed out a map she'd made of the eastern end of the cemetery, the older section. "I'm loading it onto the internet for other family researchers," she told Natalie proudly. Natalie flipped through the pages until she came to the Fs. Faulkner. They had a longtime family plot on the northern edge.

While her mom was busy talking with her friend Jeannette from the Town Clerk's Office and her aunts were resting on a bench at the cemetery's entrance, Natalie headed for the Faulkner plot. She made three passes up and down the freshly mown rows until she found it. Brian shared a stone with his father. Two urns were filled with red geraniums, just like the ones she had planted on her grandparents' plot. Natalie spread her long skirt and sat on the ground. She wondered if Bunny Faulkner had come to leave the plants there earlier.

She traced the inscription on the stone with her finger. Brian had been eighteen years old. It was still so very sad, and always would be. She noticed that Brian's father had passed on two years after Brian. Natalie had heard her father once claim that he had died of a broken heart, and she believed it.

She sighed. Lawyers dealt in death every week, on an abstract level. Wills, probates, death certificates—those were tools of their trade. Her father, and his father before him, had made it a point to attend the funeral of everyone in town. She would be doing the same. It was part of life, part of the fabric of her job and the traditions of the people she hoped to serve.

At the moment, though, all she wanted was for Bruce to acknowledge how that date—right there chiseled on Brian's tombstone—had affected him. She'd seen the raw emotion he'd felt that day. Bruce had cried. That tough, military guy had broken down and sobbed in a way she'd never seen anyone do before or since.

Maybe he had used up a lifetime of emotions on that one night. She supposed it happened.

But it was still a shame.

She held her head in her hands. Bruce was right—he had changed. As long as he continued to hold himself back, he wouldn't be able to connect with anyone. He wouldn't set down roots, and he wouldn't enjoy being part of his family's life.

"Goodbye, Brian. Rest in peace," she whispered. She stood, her heels sinking into the soft ground, and lightly touched his stone. She went down the hill and found her mother.

BRUCE RAN THE LENGTH of the beach and back, twice, but that didn't get the turmoil out of his system. Then he swam in the ocean, frigid enough to numb his heart. With a sort of equilibrium finally achieved, he toweled off and dressed to go visit his grandfather.

It was more of the same. This time, though, the nurses said hello to him. He sat in that beat-up leatherette chair beside Gramps's bed with the fleece blanket covered in cat hairs, and watched *Wheel of Fortune* and *Family Feud* on the game show channel, turned up extra loud.

Gramps had no idea who Bruce was. He also seemed to have no memory of going fishing yesterday. He was a lot farther gone than Bruce had realized. It was no use.

But he sat for the two full hours out of a perverse sense of stubbornness and willpower. The day ahead might pummel him with one hit after another, but he wasn't lying down or giving up.

He couldn't, however, discipline his mind against drifting to thoughts of Natalie. So it was no big surprise when he found himself at noon, pointing his car into the heart of the village of Wallis Point. Natalie had done a lot for him—she'd given up her day for him and Gramps yesterday, and how had he repaid her? By taking her for granted the way Maureen had taken her for granted.

He didn't want to be a guy who hurt people, especially not her. He wanted to make it up to her. Unfortunately he needed to do it in a way that didn't actually require him to interact with her.

He stepped on the brake for the stop sign at Crabapple Lane, where Gramps's old house was. He continued on, hung a left at the old dump road and traveled to the end, passing new cul-de-sac developments everywhere. Twice as many houses were stuffed in as when he'd grown up and it had been woods they'd played in, during the Golden Age of being a kid.

He drove to a small ranch-style house still owned by the former dump-keeper's family, judging by the old bike parts and the abandoned car chassis in the front and side yards. As always, the reality show junk-pickers would have a field day in his hometown. He backed the rental Mercedes into the overlarge driveway, between a commercial tow truck and a rusted pickup truck with a snowplow still attached to the front. He smelled barbecue and heard the telltale shrieks and splashes from a pool party in the back, so he headed around the house. For the first time since he'd been in town, he was actually hoping that someone would recognize him. Surely Moon Buzzell wouldn't have forgotten him over the years.

"Bruuuuuceeeee!" one Buzzell brother started, and then the other two joined in with the call. *Yes, I am home,* Bruce thought. Somebody heaved a football at him and he had no choice but to catch it against his solar plexus with an *oomph.* For a moment, he couldn't breathe.

"The former all-state quarterback is out of practice!" Moon shouted. And it was definitely Moon, his nickname given because his face was as round as a full moon.

"Yeah, yeah." Bruce coughed and recovered himself, handing off the football to one of Moon's rug rats, who was hovering beside him.

"Man, I cannot wait to tell everyone who's back in town." Moon was grinning as he held up his hot-dog-turning fork. Bruce saw he was at a backyard get-together. Some kids running around, jumping into an aboveground pool, a few guys holding beer bottles, some women on lounge chairs. Standard holiday fare. But besides Moon and his two brothers—one older, one younger—Bruce didn't recognize any of them. Fifteen years was a long time to be away.

"Do you want to grab a plate and a brew and join us, old buddy?" Moon asked him.

"No, I stopped by to ask for a quick favor."

"A favor for Bruce Cole. Legendary!" Moon said.

"Can you keep it quiet that you saw me? The truth is, I'm not in town long."

Moon opened a beer for him. "Sit and stay for a few minutes. Talk sports."

Bruce wasn't one to drink and drive, but he accepted the offered drink and sat beside Moon in a camp chair and held the bottle in two hands. He kept his voice low, so Moon had to lean forward to hear him. "Look, I saw from the delivery label on a shower stall that you've been doing work on Natalie Kimball's place at the beach."

Moon grinned. "Yeah. She's something, isn't she?"

"Are you married, Moon?"

"Nope. These are all my brothers' kids."

"Great." Bruce looked on the bright side. "Then I can borrow you for a half hour today?"

Moon laughed at him. "It's a holiday."

"Hooking up a shower is a ten-minute job," Bruce said.

"Nothing is a ten-minute job."

"With my help you'll be in and out."

Moon scratched his chin. "Is she home?"

Bruce hoped not. He was only doing this because he'd been racking his brain for a way he could help her. Getting Moon Buzzell to install her guest-house shower was something he could do. Moon had earned his diploma mainly because Bruce had babysat him through high school, riding him hard to make grades in order to keep him eligible for football, basketball and baseball seasons. Moon was a great asset to those teams. He just wasn't the most self-motivated guy in the world. Most times, Moon needed a kick in the pants to get going.

Bruce sighed. He couldn't think of any other way to make it up to her. "Listen, Moon, I didn't want to say this, but, ah, Natalie…I want to do her a favor."

Moon blinked at him. "You're seeing her?"

Of course he wasn't. But Moon didn't need to know that. Especially since Bruce was getting the sneaking suspicion that Moon might be interested in Natalie. "Yeah," he lied, "you could say that."

"You want me to get the word out to everybody?"

"No!" Bruce said quickly. "I mean, this is a surprise for her. The shower stall and all, to make her happy." God, this was worse than he'd anticipated.

Moon squinted. "Did Natalie tell you about the tile?"

"What tile?"

"The tile that I'm going to teach her how to install next week." Moon winked at him.

"Oh, hell, no," Bruce spit out. "Forget it. I know you…you're a dog with women."

"Are you forbidding me to lay your girlfriend's tile?"

"Yes! I mean, where is this tile, and where does she want it installed? Hell, I'll do it myself."

But it wasn't until he was on his way to Natalie's house, with Moon in the front seat of the Mercedes and his toolbox in the back, that Bruce realized he'd opened himself up to scrutiny. He just kept digging himself deeper and deeper with no end in sight.

Then again, he mused, as he pulled into the driveway, thankful that Natalie hadn't returned yet, Moon had done one remarkable thing that Bruce hadn't expected at all.

He hadn't said one word about Brian Faulkner, their teammate and friend.

WHAT IF NOBODY CAME to her open house?

Tuesday morning, Natalie woke with a churning stomach. Last night, she'd gone over to her parents' house for a cookout—steak tips with her father's special sauce and her mother's homemade strawberry shortcake with locally picked berries—but instead of enjoying herself, she'd been preoccupied with worrying.

What if her party was a flop?

Besides work, she was worried about Bruce, too. When was he leaving town? It was inevitable. He'd avoided her all day yesterday, and he hadn't come into her cottage to use the shower this morning, either. That showed how much he wanted to stay away from her.

She could only hope that other people in town didn't feel the same way.

Grabbing her batch of freshly printed flyers and her briefcase, she stepped outside, thankful, at least, that it was clear and sunny, with no rain. She tossed everything in the car, opening the door gingerly because Bruce's Mercedes was parked beside her. At least she knew he was home. She found a pen and scribbled a note on the back of one of her flyers. "Thanks for the help with the marketing advice. If you're home this afternoon, I'd love for you to stop by. –N."

She hurried down the walkway to the guest house, and stuck the folded flyer inside his screen door. She paused with her hand poised to knock, so tempted to see him again. She had an ache inside for missing him. A small ache, but she couldn't deny it was there.

Who was she kidding? It had been a big ache. She was crazy about him. The night at the hospital and the day at the beach with his grandfather had sealed it.

When Bruce let his guard down, they had a really great connection. The problem was, he never let it down long enough.

Maybe the flyer would help him along. It was all she could do. The rest was up to him.

She was backing out of her parking space when she realized that her shower stall was missing from the walkway. Very odd. If she'd noticed before, she would have had a great excuse to talk to Bruce. As it was… well, she had an open house to prepare for.

Inside the law office, her father's door was closed; most likely, he was on the phone. Zena, their receptionist, was in the kitchen cleaning out the coffeepot. Natalie had deliberately kept her calendar clear; there was only one thing she had to do, and now was the time.

She needed to push herself. Get out there and shake some trees.

She dropped off her briefcase, then, clutching her flyers, she exited the law firm for the street. Outside, she touched the familiar stenciled lettering on the glass for good luck. If all went well and she was able to prove herself to her father's satisfaction, then her name would be added to the door, too. But she was getting ahead of herself. Tightening her grip on her flyers, she visited every small business on the north side of the busy main street. She smiled and introduced herself to every owner and employee, passing out flyers and reiterating that sandwiches and refreshments would be available. In less than an hour, she stopped in at a dry cleaner, a family restaurant, a florist, the library, a hardware store and a dog grooming shop. If nothing else, she'd met more people in one morning than she had in the six weeks since she'd been home.

Then she started with the businesses on the south side. The guys in her father's favorite Italian deli asked her who was catering the party. When she told them honestly that no one was, that she would be picking something up at the supermarket, they surprised her by offering a calzone tray. It looked so good, she ordered an assorted sandwich tray from them, too. Then she retraced her steps to the family restaurant and picked up some homemade pies.

The same thing happened to her in the cheese shop. And all three proprietors were eager to attend, they told her. They had never actually been inside the law firm.

It turned out that law offices scared some people. They thought lawyers were expensive and snobby, and you only visited one when you were in trouble with the law.

Who knew?

Feeling energized by her morning of improvised public relations, Natalie sank into her desk chair when she returned to her office. Was that what marketing people called a Meet and Greet? If so, she'd liked it. Face-to-face with these business owners, her hearing hadn't been a problem. She felt more confident than she could remember. Maybe she was a "people person" after all. What a shock.

While she was still on a high, she turned on her computer and checked her social media accounts. She'd been keeping up with the homework Bruce had given her, so she had added a few friends—a very few, but her network was slowly building.

She'd received three replies to the event notice she'd posted: two RSVPs stating "yes," and a private message from Maureen.

How is Bruce doing? it read.

Natalie paused. He'd retreated from her, that's how he was doing. But she would never betray the feelings he'd confided in her. "He's doing great," she typed. A total lie.

But she couldn't think about Maureen now. She positioned her computer mouse and clicked on the icon that told her she had new friend requests. One was from an owner of the cheese shop she'd just met on her Meet and Greet. No one had been in the shop at the moment, and he'd been eager to talk. He'd been three years ahead of her in school, and she'd only known him by name, but he'd seemed nice enough today. She accepted his request.

Almost immediately, he sent her a message. I heard Bruce Cole is back in town.

Her hand hovered over the computer keyboard. The cursor was blinking; he was waiting for a reply. He is, she typed.

Another message popped up on the screen, rapid-fire. I can't find any contact info for him anywhere, but Moon Buzzell says he's staying at your place.

Her heart seemed to still in her chest. Moon Buzzell. Oh, God, he'd stopped by to install the shower in the guest house after all, and had bumped into Bruce. That's what must have happened. "Yes," she typed. She wouldn't lie, but she wouldn't say anything to betray him, either. There was a reason Bruce avoided Facebook and didn't keep in touch with all his old friends.

She got another reply. Cool, I'll spread the word. You might need another cheese tray or two. Don't worry, I'll take care of it. Nick.

Natalie jumped to her feet, the backs of her knees bumping her chair. Bruce didn't *want* anyone to "spread the word"—he wasn't ready.

He was still in his self-imposed exile, and the only person who could nudge Bruce out of it was Bruce.

IT WAS A BEAUTIFUL DAY to be holed up in a beach house.

Bruce had set up his laptop and was working on requirements for the next project phase with a team of three other people, all at different remote locations. But Bruce was sure he was the only consultant sitting in jeans and bare feet, digging his toes in sand and enjoying a commanding view of the Atlantic Ocean.

He leaned back and laced his hands behind his head. The truth was, he could do his job almost anywhere. He traveled every week to the client site only because he volunteered to do so. Some of the people he worked with only flew out every third or fourth week, in order to save on expenses. As long as the client didn't mind, that was their call.

Natalie's place was the best office Bruce had worked from in a long time. As usual, he'd been up early and had jogged the beach as far as the sandcastle competition. Yesterday, the professional sculptures had been judged, and they were amazing—huge and varied in their designs, as if they'd been statues sculpted from marble. The artists had sprayed some kind of solution onto the sand that kept the sculptures intact in the elements, at least for the next few days, and so he'd been able to enjoy the show without the crowds.

Still, he couldn't let himself forget that leaving was his ultimate goal. He would hunker down in the guest house, get his work done and visit Gramps, who would probably never know who he was, pulling out the stops, trying day after day until one time, just once—Gramps said his name the way he'd said Natalie's.

Yeah, she was under his skin. He couldn't give her the pairing she wanted from him, and yet, he couldn't forget her, either.

What was she doing now? Who was she hanging out with?

It drove him crazy. Last night, every small noise and light on in her house had kept him awake, wondering. When he was walking back to the house this morning, cooling down from his early morning run, he'd seen her for the first time since Sunday night.

He'd stopped and stared at her, his T-shirt bunched in his fist and sweat running down his face.

She'd looked so beautiful. Dressed in a nice suit—her lawyer clothes—she was stepping into her car and leaving for work. The big gray tomcat had been perched on the rail fence, watching her. Bruce had been observing the creature coming and going from a cat door. Lucky creature probably got to share her bed, too.

He planted his feet on the ground; he really needed to get back to work. He was staring at the computer screen, not paying enough attention to it, when a knock sounded. He jumped, expecting Natalie, but it was the guys delivering the bathroom tile. He held the door open for them while they tromped inside, their arms full with the heavy boxes.

He noticed a flyer on the ground, which he picked up and read.

Aw, hell. Sweet Natalie had taken his advice and done some advertising. She'd also written him a personal note on the back, inviting him to her open house.

The paper fluttered in the breeze as he stared at it. He felt…something, a pressure in his chest. Everyone else had let him isolate himself in exile. His family hadn't pushed him all that hard. Friends had never tracked him down. The navy had let him drift away.

But Natalie hadn't given up on him.

He traced the graceful lines of her signature with his finger.

He really, truly needed to see her.

Now, that was a change.

So much was at stake.

Natalie glanced at her father, but he was happily engrossed in a conversation with two of his oldest clients. That was a good sign, she hoped. She had taken a chance, and without checking with her father, had called their client list and personally followed up on the invitations she'd already sent, reminding each of them to drop by. The only person she hadn't phoned was Bunny Faulkner. Ever since Bruce had told her that Brian's mother had banned him from Brian's funeral, she'd had a bad feeling about Bunny. A person didn't do something like that unless there was blame and bitterness involved.

That would be all Bruce needed, if he showed up. She was holding out hope that he would come by, along with many others as well. She didn't know how successful her efforts would be, but her future was worth the try.

She glanced at the freshly cleaned foyer, hardwood floors shining, street-front windows gleaming, and hoped for the best. So far, it was just after 4:00 p.m. and only four people had shown up. She met them, greeted them, and was on her way to giving them an impromptu tour and a quick pitch, when the door opened, and two more guests brought the smell of early summer inside with them: the nail salon owner and Jimmy's assistant at Wallis Point PC.

"I hear you've been decorating the place," Jimmy's assistant said. "My sister works in the frame shop. She told me about your collection, and I really wanted to see it."

Networking was never straightforward, Natalie reflected. That was the beauty and the magic of it. "Sure, let me show you what I've got." She led him to the wait-

ing area where she'd hung her memorabilia. Several
people crowded closer to hear her speak.

She pointed out the antique postcards of Wallis Point
that she'd been purchasing online over the years. Two
of the older women admired the artifacts from the high
school that no longer existed, since their town school
merged with the new regional system. That had been before Natalie's time, but she was fascinated by the history.

Watching the women's faces light up as they remi-
nisced about days gone by, Natalie realized that without intending it, she'd hit on something key to hook her
desired demographic. Definitely, she would grow and
highlight this collection in the office. Maybe the ladies
would spread the word, and that could help her build her
elder care and estate planning business, as well.

Feeling bolder, Natalie disengaged herself and went
to the entrance to meet more arriving guests. She was
cornered by her former first-grade teacher and her husband. She was hunting for a pen on Zena's desk to take
down their address when she saw them—Bruce's old
gang. Five or six of his closest high school buddies
were gathered around the calzone tray. The guy from
the cheese shop was in the center of the group, which
seemed to be growing by the moment. Word had gotten out.

Cutting her off before she could greet them, her father
stopped by her side, holding a plate of strawberry pie
in one hand. She held her breath as his gaze met hers.
*Please say that it's going well.*

He pointed with his fork toward the diverse people
gathered in their reception area. "You did all this?" he

asked. Lucky thing she could read lips, because the noise of chatter and laughter was getting louder.

"Yes, I did," she said.

He grunted. With a nod to her, he glanced over her head and called out to another friend he spotted in the crowd. She waited for him to finish.

"You're on the right track, Natty. In my grandfather's day, he hosted lecturers and influential people. You could make it a regular program for us."

That was the best possible thing he could have said to her, and she smiled inside. Yes, she was convincing him! "I'll consider that," she said as calmly as she could. "It's a good idea."

She left him to pencil in an appointment for a gentleman who wanted a consultation about resolving a dispute with his condominium association. Her father moved on with a contented expression as he surveyed his kingdom.

She knew exactly how he felt. When a longtime dream clicked into place, it was the best feeling ever. She made small talk with the gentleman and handed out her business card to two more people who asked for it.

Excitement, gratitude, relief...it was all building in her, making her feel euphoric. With a lull in the demands on her attention, Natalie stood back for a moment and took a breath, just to imprint the image of the night into her memory forever. Zena, bless her, was also snapping photos of the event. "Your debut," Zena had called it, and Natalie was sure she was right. It was the proudest day she could remember in a while.

*Home. I'm really home.*

Only one more thing would make the day perfect. She

found herself scanning the room for a tall, broad-chested guy with dark hair and laughing brown eyes. Obviously she hadn't gotten Bruce out of her system yet. Fanning herself, she tugged on the hem of her tight-fitting jacket and smoothed her skirt. Bruce had made himself clear: he wasn't interested in her.

*Move on.*

And then she turned around, and he was right there, standing in her doorway. Through the crowd she caught a glimpse of his sun-kissed face, and her heart leaped.

Did this mean there was still hope?

Her heart pounding, she decided to find out. Someone said hello to her, but she excused herself to go to Bruce. As she made her way closer, she saw that he was with his grandfather, who pushed his walker and looked happy to be out for the day. He wore a collared polo shirt and what looked like dressier sweatpants. His hair was combed and slicked back. Instinctively she knew that Bruce had done that for him.

Natalie approached his grandfather first, and held out her hand. "William, it was good of you to come see me."

"Yes." William shook her outstretched hand. "Hello, Natalie. You're very…pretty…tonight." He spoke slowly, but she was patient.

"Thank you." She pulled out a chair near of group of people closer to his age. Maybe he might know some of them. "Would you like to take a seat, William?"

"Yes." William left his walker where it stood and shuffled toward the chair. "I think…I'll have…some pie."

He seemed better today, more lucid. Natalie exchanged a signal with Zena, who went off to fetch William his pie. As Natalie held William's arm, lowering him to the seat, she was aware of Bruce's quiet presence behind her.

Had William recognized him yet? She hoped so.

"You're here tonight with your grandson?" she prompted William.

"No." William shook his head and looked with interest at the table beside him, where somebody had left a full plate holding a deli sandwich and a pile of potato chips. He smiled and began to dig in.

Intending to apologize for the question she'd asked, she turned to Bruce. But he didn't appear to be affected by it. He was gazing at her. To see him there, entranced by her, it was like…a shot of pure joy to her heart. He had dressed up for her, in a collared dress shirt and a blazer over a nice pair of jeans. His hair was combed back like his grandfather's, and he had shaved. He was rugged, and devastating, and he made her knees go weak.

He was looking her up and down, too, drinking her in. She took big gulps of air to try to calm her racing heart. When he locked eyes with her, she couldn't find words to speak. Her hand drifted to her chest.

He moved around the walker, and dipped his head to her. "Natalie," he said in a raw voice, as if he hadn't spoken in a while. He leaned in to kiss her on the cheek, and she met him halfway.

His touch on her skin was like electricity.

"Thank you for coming," she whispered. She knew it was a choice he had made. It would have been easier and so much more self-protective to continue to stay away from her entirely.

"You did great tonight," he mouthed so that only she could tell what he was saying. "So many people came."

"Thank you. I'm humbled by everyone supporting me like this."

He glanced around at her workplace. He was tall, so he could see everyone in the room. She braced herself for him to notice his former friends. Would he blame her for inviting them? Would he shut down and leave once he saw them?

But he turned to her, smiling. Completely unconcerned about himself. "Show me where you work every day," he said in that deep voice that always affected her so much. "I want to know what you do."

Since he wasn't worried, she decided not to, either.

She gave him a tour, and it was a pleasure to watch his face as he studied the prints and documents and photos she'd framed. He listened intently as she brought him into her office in the back and showed him where she sat, and related who had worked there before her. He questioned her about the jobs she did, and she explained to him as best she could. It only took ten minutes, but it passed too quickly. It felt good that he was genuinely interested in what she did every day. His interest in her wasn't just about sex. Maybe he could find that anywhere, if that's what he wanted.

He sighed and glanced at his watch. "I've monopolized you enough, Natalia. People are going to be looking for you. After I drop William back home, can I meet you later?"

"You want to be with me tonight?" she asked.

His smile curved. "Moon Buzzell already thinks

you're my girlfriend, and I'm sure he's told the whole town, so…"

His dark gaze brushed over her as if he wanted to touch her, but this was absolutely the wrong time and place.

Her mouth felt dry, and she licked her lips. She suddenly wanted every barrier out of their way. Yes, it was good he had seen Moon. But she wanted more from Bruce than his careful, emotional distance.

If he couldn't understand that, she couldn't sweep it under the rug and be agreeable to whatever he wanted anymore. That wasn't good for her.

She dug her nails into her palms, hoping that what she had to say wouldn't end disastrously. Even if it did, it was better to know now. He may not have wanted more, but *she* did.

"Bruce…" She shut the door for privacy, and then squared her shoulders. "What changed your mind about me from Sunday night?"

He grinned as if to lighten the mood. "You left that flyer in my door."

"That's all?"

"It's everything, Natalia. You stood by me. You didn't give up." With a longing look to his eyes, he leaned down and kissed her. A lingering kiss that wrapped her whole body in tremors.

When he straightened, he gazed at her, his hand smoothing her hair from her face.

Her heart was thumping wildly, and she put her fingers to her lips. The last time she'd seen Bruce, he had told her that he hadn't wanted to feel. That he couldn't feel.

But right now, she could see in his face that he cared about her. Deeply. That expression wasn't the charming smile he pushed the world away with, or the enthusiastic grin he'd always given to his friends in school. That look was romantic. That look was…*special.* For her only.

He wasn't so afraid of being close to her now. Maybe that fact was enough to know. Maybe the *why* of the situation didn't matter?

Her hands shaking, she rose on tiptoe to kiss him again. She was so in trouble.

He groaned, pulling her to him and kissing her mouth, her chin, her hair. He seemed to be breaking down some sort of internal barrier. "God, I missed you…"

And then they were making out in her place of work. Their tongues melding, stroking, thrusting as she let out little moans and gasps of desire. For about ten seconds, she allowed herself to enjoy it, ignoring that tonight was a big event for her future career, and that she was foolish to jeopardize that.

Finally she pulled away. "Bruce, I have to go." She looked into his dark eyes, hooded with desire, promising her all sorts of decadent pleasures.

She swallowed, rubbing the telltale pink lipstick off his mouth with her fingers.

"We'll finish this tonight," he said.

## CHAPTER THIRTEEN

BRUCE STOOD IN THE FAR CORNER, absently watching who was coming and going from the open house, but mainly thinking of Natalie.

He hadn't intended to kiss her like that. Not in her office, anyway. When he'd seen her standing there, working her heart out to make progress in her life, to make something of herself, a longing for her had smacked him in the chest. Wanting her wasn't purely physical. Lately, though, the physical was overpowering everything else, dissolving his natural caution and smashing his "code" to pieces.

Taking care of Gramps was supposed to be his main job this week.

Bruce made his way through the throng and found his grandfather still seated where they'd left him, but now he was with two of his friends who used to walk the beach with him, looking for treasure. None of three was talking much, but they were obviously old cohorts.

His grandfather remembered everybody he met *except* for Bruce. Would he never make up for the fact that he hadn't been there for Gramps all these years? He didn't see how he could.

Mr. Whiting, the man who'd danced with Natalie at Maureen's wedding, came over and stood beside him. "We'd like to visit Bill sometime," Mr. Whiting said.

Being with his friends did seem to give Gramps a new kick to his stride. "That would be great," Bruce said. "I was going to take him back to the home, but being here with his buddies seems to help him."

Mr. Whiting leaned in closer. "It's the Alzheimer's, isn't it?"

"That's what they say."

"It's an epidemic," Mr. Whiting whispered. "They either get the Alzheimer's, or if not the Alzheimer's, they get the cancer." He looked grim.

"How are you doing?" Bruce asked.

"Can't complain." He patted Bruce's arm. "Don't get old, son."

Honestly, if Bruce had to get as sick as Gramps, he would rather be amongst old friends than alone in Florida. But Bruce didn't have companions from childhood like Gramps did. And it was no use wishing that things had turned out differently. It was better not to think of it at all. "I appreciate you coming to see him."

Mr. Whiting cocked his head. "Is tomorrow okay? Margery keeps the schedule." He nodded toward his wife. "We've got a morning dentist cleaning, and then Marge has an appointment at the podiatrist." He whispered to Bruce. "The diabetes, you know. Enjoy your life while you're still young."

Bruce planned to. He thought of Natalie. That woman had a way of shaking up his life and completely derailing his plans.

"Tomorrow morning would be fine," Bruce said.

"Rest assured, we won't cut in on your time with him."

It probably didn't make a difference to Gramps

whether Bruce visited him or not, but he would play along with Mr. Whiting's concern. "I'll be stopping by at lunch to take him to an MRI appointment. Maybe I'll see you on the way out?"

"No, no." Mr. Whiting waved his hand. "Margery likes to leave early. That noontime traffic can be awful. I like to get a jump on it."

"Good thinking."

Mr. Whiting patted Bruce's shoulder. "We need to be going. Margery likes to watch the six o'clock news."

"See you later." The crowd was thinning out. Bruce had positioned himself in a far corner. A bunch of guys exited a conference room where, judging by the crush of people, it looked like the food had been set up. One of the men reminded Bruce of Matt "Guzzy" Guldezian, the strongest link in his high school offensive line. The guy had those distinctive shoulders built like a brick wall.

If it was Guzzy, he'd gained a bunch of weight and had lost most of his hair. He had shaved his head and wore dark sunglasses. His T-shirt read Guldezian Paving. Guzzy's dad's company. Yeah, that had to be him.

Bruce paused, crossing his arms. He had no idea what to expect if they made eye contact. Moon Buzzell was in the group. Also Joey Bevilaqua and Keith Olsen and Garrett Kennedy.

Mother of God—that was his snake pit! *His* guys. *His* offensive line.

By rote, he strode toward them. For a moment he forgot that maybe they didn't want to see him, that everything had changed once that stolen white Mercedes had wrapped around that oak tree fifteen years ago. Because Brian, the center to his quarterback, had been an integral part of their "snake pit"—he'd even been the one who'd made up the group's name.

Bruce stopped in his tracks. Would his old friends even recognize him? It had been a long time.

But they weren't the ones who noticed him standing there like a freshman wary of approaching the senior lunch table. Natalie did. And it pained him to see his old teammates looking at her with pure male appreciation. She looked damn good tonight. She wore a skirt that hit just above her knee and a pair of high heels that showed off her great legs. Even her jacket top was cut close to her body, highlighting her curves.

Guzzy wrapped Natalie in a bone-crunching hug.

Bruce hated that. *He* hadn't even held her that close when he'd kissed her in her office. Yet here was Guzzy, getting the full-dose feel of Natalie's, *his* Natalie's breasts against his chest.

Bruce was walking across the polished hardwood flooring even before he knew what he was doing.

"Hey!" He stopped in front of Guzzy. From this close, he could see the gray peppering Guzzy's stubble. When had they all gotten so old?

"Brucey?" Guzzy asked, peering at him.

"Yeah."

And then Guzzy was transferring his hug from Natalie to him. All in one smooth motion, without thought or hesitation.

"Oomph," Bruce said. At age fifteen, Guzzy could bench-press the equivalent of a small car. Even back then, before all the additional weight he'd packed on in his gut, Guzzy would have made a great Sumo wrestler.

"Brucey, how ya been?"

And then, to his shock, Bruce was shaking hands with the rest of his remaining snake pit. They were slapping his back and grinning at him if nothing had changed.

TWO HOURS LATER, Bruce broke away from the open house after-party in order to take his grandfather home. It took twenty minutes to unload Gramps's walker from the trunk, assist him from the car and get him settled in his room. It took another ten minutes to get Gramps's security bracelet reactivated.

"Nobody else goes through the trouble of taking William offsite for outings," the nurse said. "You've helped him. He truly appreciates you." Bruce didn't know about that. But he did see that, as before, Gramps was asleep before his head hit the pillow. Bruce wished he shared that skill.

By the time he drove past the law firm again, the place was dark. A group had stayed behind to help Natalie clean up, but he couldn't join them because he'd been responsible for Gramps. Frowning, he wished he'd brought her with him. They had unfinished business as far as he was concerned. But his friends had been insistent.

They'd taken to Natalie, accepting her as one of them. That had been fine, at first, until Bruce had remembered that they all lived in Wallis Point, while he wasn't staying long. He didn't think he liked that they would have the advantage of him with Natalie. It burned him, in fact. A hot rope of jealousy sat in his gut and twisted and grew the longer he thought about it.

He needed to stay cool. He drove down to the main beach, then around the labyrinth of streets until he found parking, and then killed the engine. He left his jacket in the car and rolled up his shirtsleeves as he headed inside the beach bar.

Loud music pulsed from overhead speakers. This was the place he'd passed on the evening of Moe's wedding. Even on a Tuesday night, it was packed with both vacationers and locals. He scanned the pub and saw Natalie, sitting on a barstool near his friends. Some women had joined them; Guzzy had said he was married, and maybe the others were, too. Bruce could only hope.

When Natalie saw him, relief flooded her features. He quickly saw why. It was so noisy that, in order to talk, people were ducking their heads and shouting into each other's ears. It couldn't be easy for her to follow the conversation.

He headed over and stood protectively beside her, wedging himself between her barstool and her neighbor's. Her knees brushed his thighs, and he caught them, his hand resting on her bare legs, feeling the soft skin from where her skirt had ridden up slightly.

"I'm glad you're here," she shouted into his ear, letting his hands stay on her legs. She took a sip from a glass of soda. He watched, fascinated, as her tongue licked off a bead of cola from her lips.

Somebody handed him a bottle of beer, and he drank from it, the cold, familiar lager helping him relax.

"How did you make out tonight?" he mouthed to her.

She smiled, pleased she could understand him. "I cleaned up," she said. "A dozen scheduled consultations with the potential for a lot more."

"Any tomorrow?" He wondered if he could get her to stay over with him. Maybe he could put off that 8:00 a.m. conference call he had scheduled.

Her brow creased. "No, but I have my first ever court appearance in the morning." She smiled. "Before a judge, though, not a jury."

Then they had better get going. "Let's walk out to my car. I'm parked down the beach." And before she could say anything, he held up a penlight. "I borrowed this from William because he had an extra. That way, when you and I are walking in the dark, or riding in the car with no lights on, you can shine it on me whenever you need to see my mouth, okay?"

She blinked, her eyes looking misty. And then she hopped off the barstool and threw her arms around him. He closed his arms around her waist. This was their first time they'd been body to body, her breasts against his chest, her hips pressed to his.

It felt like heaven.

He buried his nose in her hair, inhaling her scent. He scraped her hair away from her cheeks and let it slide through his fingers like silk.

"Bruce, talk to me with your mouth behind my ear. You'll be surprised how well I can hear you when your mouth is touching my skull, right there."

"Are you sure?"

"There's something about the low tone of your voice…I hear you better than I hear most people."

Gratefully, feeling like he was home, he lowered his head and brushed his lips against her skin, tasting it. "Like this?" he spoke against her.

She shivered in his arms. "It feels like you're part of

me when you do that. Like you're inside me and I can hear everything you're saying perfectly."

She could have everything from him. He slid his hands from the small of her back to her bottom, grazing the sides, wanting to give to her but not to ruin it or make a mistake. "Come home with me tonight," he breathed.

She shifted her head so her mouth found his, and she was kissing him. Once, twice, three times, and then finally, melding with his lips, as if they were lovers already. Here, in public, with anybody to see and everybody to know. And it felt good. Damn good. He tightened his embrace around her waist, not wanting to let her go.

"This was the best day of my life," she whispered into his ear.

He could not resist this woman. That should have scared the hell out of him, but right now, it didn't.

He pulled out his wallet, tossed some bills on the bar and said a quick goodbye to his guys. Guzzy leaned over and hugged him again.

Bruce wished Brian was there. Brian always punched Guzzy, laughing at him when Guzzy did that, usually when he drank too much, which they weren't supposed to do as teenagers, but had sometimes done anyway. A choke burst out of Bruce's throat, but it was so loud in the bar, nobody heard him. Maybe if he had stopped him...

But who could stop Brian when he got like that? Who had wanted to? He made everyone feel alive.

Bruce slapped Guzzy on his large, slightly damp shoulder, and told him to "rock on." Brian would approve. *No regrets,* he used to holler to the guys in the snake pit. *Go, go to your girl.*

Brian had always been the one who'd had girls. "My girl," was big with Brian. He was too loud, too passionate and he lived too large for his own good.

Near the door, Natalie was looking at him with bright eyes, waiting. He lifted his hand to her. "I'm coming," he mouthed.

He escorted her outside.

"My car isn't here," she said. "I dropped it off and then caught a ride with your friends."

"Good. I want you to come home with me." He opened his car door and settled her into the passenger seat like she was a precious object, because to him she was precious, and he drove her home.

"Take the long way," she begged him. For too long he'd been taking the long way, in a figurative sense. But if she wanted to see the waves crashing on the rocks in the moonlight on what had been the best day of her life, he wasn't going to ruin that.

When he finally parked beside her car in her familiar driveway, he told her to wait, and then jogged around and opened her door. Struck by something crazy—Brian's influence?—he picked her up and carried her, past her own door, down the pathway and to the guest house where he'd been sleeping for the past four nights.

He carried her over the threshold and set her down, gently. He turned on the lights. She looked around. It was his space now; his computer, his clothes, his food, it was all there for her to see.

But the room smelled like tile grout. He had forgotten that.

Her nose twitching, she walked past the air mattress with his tangled sheets and the pillows he had fluffed and refluffed but still could not get comfortable on, and opened the door to where he'd spent a few hours that afternoon, largely on his knees.

He heard her gasp, and walked in to find her with her hand over her mouth, staring at what he'd done.

"I meant to tile half and then finish the second half with you, so you could learn how to do it, too," he explained. *Please don't be mad at me for taking over. I'm trying to do something good for you....*

Tears streamed down her face. Was that good or bad? He tried to look at it through her eyes. A tiny bathroom with a modern shower stall tucked in the corner, and shiny, new blue tile, the color of her eyes, set halfway up the most difficult wall, the one with the fixtures that needed to be cut around.

He turned to her. "Did I screw up? I twisted Moon's arm to get your design plans and I..."

She shook her head, laughing through her tears. "It's perfect. You're perfect."

"I'm not."

"You're perfect to *me*. I see how you care about people, and I don't misunderstand you."

She did understand him, and she'd been patient. Not pushing him. Not blaming.

"I can't...promise you anything."

"I know." She touched his face with her gentle fingers. "I know you, Bruce."

His throat felt raw. She did. He could not comprehend the trust she was placing in him. "Natalie, I've fallen for you, head over heels. It's crazy in so short a time, but it's real."

And then they were together, like magnets and filings. She pressed herself to him as he reached for her, kissing her cheeks, her lips, her open mouth. She moaned and strained against his erection, which forced the breath out of him.

Any more of this, and he'd have her on the floor in a heartbeat. *Slow down,* he told himself. But it felt so urgent that he didn't want to mess this up, like he'd messed up so many things. This was their first time, and she deserved better.

He pushed back and gazed into her eyes, slowly undressing her, unbuttoning the oversize buttons of her form-fitting jacket. When the two sides fell away, he looked down, and the breath left him again. He had seen her in a bathing suit and had loved every second of that, but this view wasn't nearly the same. Her white lace bra was scooped low, the edges covering rose-budded nipples. He couldn't stop himself; he skimmed his hands up her stomach to just under the fullness of her breasts, everywhere he could touch.

She tilted her head back and whispered an encouragement. "More," she said, so he lowered his head and with his tongue, pushed away the scratchy fabric and circled first one, and then the other.

"That's so nice," she sighed. She stretched against him, her fingers combing through his hair, feeling erotic against his scalp. "Please let me touch you, Bruce." She fumbled for his zipper, but he lifted his mouth from her breast and caught her in a deep, soul-bearing kiss, his tongue intertwining with hers.

Oh, God, he was lost. That only encouraged her to lift her knee to his hip and grind herself against the length of him, feeling his hardness and his heat. "I need you," she said against his neck, whispered in a way that seemed to echo through him. "I need you inside me. I don't want to wait anymore." She dug her hands down the back of his pants, kneading his flesh.

He couldn't take this. He could not. He pushed up her skirt and, with his thumb, traced a circle around her heat, her center. She wore soft cotton panties, and she was ready for him. He brushed her opening with his fingertips and she gasped, tugging down his zipper and pleading with him, "Now."

"Are you sure?" he asked in a guttural voice.

"We need a condom," she suddenly said.

Ah, stupid of him. How could he have forgotten?

Berating himself, he reached on the shelf for the baggie he was using for a toiletry bag. Shoving his hand inside, he rifled through it by feel until he found one ragged condom that had been bumping around inside his suitcase for months. The wrapper felt bent and worn, but it was all he had, so he closed his palm around it and turned to her.

Her hair was tousled and her lips looked swollen. She was smiling at him as if he meant everything to her, and they were about to share something special and rare.

His heart went out to her. He wanted to protect her and keep her safe. He wanted it to work with her, unlike with everything else, where he'd failed.

He glanced around. Should he carry her out to the air mattress for their first time, or should they stay here? Which would start them off right?

College kids and transients slept on air mattresses. At least here, beside the tile he'd laid and then carefully cleaned with water and sponge, and beside the box of tile she was going to install with him, later…he supposed that meant something to them. A reminder of the future they were building.

He stepped up to her and kissed her as gently as he possibly could.

But staying gentle wasn't easy when he was with *Hotmama69*.

AFTERWARD, NATALIE felt boneless.

"Natalia," Bruce murmured against her ear. And oh, when he hit that tone in just the right place, she heard his voice as clear as a bell. Deep and strong, it beckoned to her. It caressed her. It covered her in his regard.

She was lying languidly on his air mattress, her naked back pressed against his chest and groin, one of his strong arms—interspersed with dark, masculine hair that tickled her senses—crossed over her chest.

Natalie sighed and wriggled closer to him. She felt full and complete. After they'd made love standing up against the new tile, smooth and calming against the hot skin on her back, they had leaned there for a long while, their naked bodies still fused, their hearts racing in unison.

She'd always been looking for a connection. In all her years, that was the most honest and true connection she'd found. He'd stroked into her slowly and gently, and then passionately, with abandon. They'd both been completely naked, not a strip of clothing on them, not an iota of shame. It was pure love. She didn't see how any two people could possibly get any closer.

She rolled over and kissed Bruce, nuzzling his cheek, scratchy with stubble. He kissed her deeply, his hand roaming idly down her back and skimming over her behind...

She sighed happily again. There was no better place on earth, no better feeling than this. She wanted to grab the moment and keep it close to her forever. She sat up on her elbow to look at Bruce. She wished she could imprint the memory of his naked body, tangled up with hers, inside her heart. She'd already seen his bare chest, that evening when she'd hit her head, but now she saw all of him: legs and bottom, solid with muscles from running. A dark patch of hair, all man, and the most beautiful male body she could ever imagine.

No doubt, he would make a perfect sculptor's model. But how he looked was window dressing to her; in no way did it make him the man that she loved and wanted.

*Everything has changed,* she thought. There was no going back.

She knew what it felt like to make love with him now. She could never forget that; never go back to the way she was before. She had outright told him how she'd felt about him before they'd had sex, and that had been a risk. But if her statement had been a jump into the deep end of a pool, then this...this crossing from friendship to physical intimacy was like casting herself onto a flimsy raft in the middle of the sea.

She traced his hard jaw, sandpapery with stubble. He took her hand and kissed her fingers, one by one. It had been so easy to be with him. So easy loving him. It had a destined quality, and that was even scarier. Despite how into her he seemed now, she had no guarantee that once the erotic haze wore off he would remain that way tomorrow, or next week, or next month.

He was still so…raw about coming home to Wallis Point and confronting his feelings from Brian's death. It had shaken him up even more than she had realized.

He had pushed it aside for all these years. Until this week, she doubted he'd thought of it once. And she was doing something incredibly risky, too. She was handing him her heart on a silver platter. She honestly didn't know what he would do with it now.

No conversation could answer that question for her, not truly. She had to wait and see. Hold her breath and be agreeable to him. Not say a word about Brian, and see that all was well…

She turned to him, but his breathing had grown steady. His arm was draped across her waist like a sleeping man's, as if he was eminently comfortable and meant for her to stay with him, too. He wasn't kicking her out of bed…that was for sure. And even if he wanted to, he was sound asleep. Smiling to herself, she dozed off with him, inside his embrace. She meant to enjoy every moment. All of it.

Suddenly he bolted upright. "What's that?"

She jumped, too, but not hearing anything. He reached over her and lifted her skirt off the floor. Beneath it, on the old floorboards, her cell phone was vibrating crazily.

She blinked. It never rang this late—it beeped with incoming texts from her father, but not this. A ringing phone meant there was an emergency. She leaned over to grab it. "I'm so sorry," she said to Bruce.

"Who is it?"

She didn't recognize the number on the caller ID. But that didn't mean anything. "Hello?" she said as she picked up the call.

"Natalie? It's Moon." His voice sounded slurred. "You're my one phone call."

Inwardly she groaned. She glanced to Bruce, who was propped on his elbow, looking concerned. "Where are you?" she asked Moon.

"At the Wallis Point police station. I need…an attorney." He was saying the words carefully, as if they took all his concentration. She thought back. How much had he been drinking tonight?

"Moon, hang tight," she said. "I'll be right there. Don't make any statements or answer any questions until you see me, okay?" She hung up and faced Bruce, who looked alarmed.

"Is he okay?" Bruce asked. "He's not hurt, is he?"

"If he was, they'd have taken him to a hospital. I don't know if anyone else is hurt, though." She shivered. She could only imagine the emotions running through Bruce. "My guess is he got picked up for DWI. I have to go to the police station and take care of it."

"I'm coming with you."

"Thanks for understanding. Because why did I host an open house if I'm not going to be reliable?" She stood up, hunting for her clothes.

"I didn't know you handled criminal cases," he said, getting up and tugging his jeans over his legs.

"Not usually ones like this. But Wallis Point is a small town, and I'll do what's necessary." She pulled on her panties and stepped into her skirt. She hated to end the evening this way, but what choice did she have? "If the situation is bad, if Moon has priors and agrees to hire a specialist, then I'll refer him for whatever he needs. But I have to go find that out."

"Yeah, I get it. I just hate that it's Moon…damn it, I should have noticed if he was drinking too much." Bruce tossed on a T-shirt and over that, a dark blue zip-up jacket.

She appreciated that he hadn't objected to her leaving—that he accepted what she had to do. And that he naturally wanted to help his friend—that was good, too, wasn't it?

Even though it was so close to what had happened to Brian…

She tensed. They were going to the police station. God, what he must have gone through there, that night.

What was he going to do?

"Bruce, you really don't have to come…"

"Yeah, I do," he said, pocketing his wallet and picking up his house key, "for you and for Moon. Damn it, Natalie, you think I'd let you go there yourself? It's dangerous. It's one thing to be writing wills for people, it's another thing entirely to be hanging out at the police station at midnight. Because that's how long you'll be there—if you're lucky. They'll make you wait and wait and wait." He stared at her, looking angry and helpless. "Do you know the kinds of people that you'll see?"

"We'll be okay." She held out her hand.

"You're talking about the Wallis Point police station." He had a harsh look to his mouth.

"I'm sorry." If he was going to close down and leave her, then now would be the time.

BRUCE WAS SPUTTERING with anger. Those jerks at WPPD had interrogated him for hours, without notifying his parents or his grandparents, and he'd only been seventeen years old at the time. He would never forget, or forgive, the crappy way they'd treated him after Brian's death.

But he looked into Natalie's eyes, the woman he was falling for so much it scared him, and he knew that he would cross the Sahara desert without water for her if she needed him to.

He grabbed his car keys from the counter and locked the door behind them. Then he followed her down the lit pathway to the driveway, pointing his remote to unlock the doors.

"You're mad at me," she said, rubbing her arms in the moonlight.

"I'm not mad at you. "

"This is bringing up bad memories, isn't it?"

He let out his breath. "You have to work with them, don't you?" he asked. "Those cops."

She nodded.

There would be many other calls, on many other nights.

"If you stay with me," she said. "If you and I get closer…"

He crossed his arms, bracing himself for what she'd say.

He had *slept* with her. *He* had taken it to the next level. There was no going back to the way they'd been before.

"It's…it's important that I get established in this town," she was saying. And he understood that, too.

"The thing is, Bruce," she continued, "I need my practice, and I need you to be comfortable with me interacting with people in Wallis Point, even people you don't like. We'll both have to be comfortable with it, at times like this."

He didn't see how he would ever be part of the fabric of this place. Then again, he worked four or five days a week, on the road. Maybe he could use that as a shield.

He felt himself relaxing. Maybe it could work for him. "Climb into the Mercedes, sweetheart," he said.

She held out her hand, and her keys were inside. "I'm driving my own car."

"I only had one sip of beer, Natalie."

She dipped her head as if embarrassed. "Actually, I should have said this earlier, and Moon's arrest verifies it. But if you're pulled over, Bruce, and it's established that you were seen drinking beer at Moroney's Pub, then they won't make it easy for you."

"Yeah, I get it." He put away his car keys.

NATALIE WAS IN AND OUT of the police station in under an hour, with a chastened Moon Buzzell beside her. Bruce opened the Toyota's back door so that Moon could climb inside. Immediately his old teammate buckled himself in and closed his eyes.

"Is everything okay?" Bruce mouthed to Natalie as she climbed into the driver's seat.

She nodded and smiled, closing the door and buckling her seat belt. But she said nothing to him about Moon. Attorney-client privilege—he had better get used to it.

"Was anybody hurt?" Mentally Bruce girded himself. If there had been another accident...

Natalie's eyes widened. "Nobody is hurt," she quickly reassured him.

"Good." He shut off the dashboard light and settled back, letting her drive in peace.

Actually, the time she'd been gone had been good for him. He'd been able to clear his mind and better process where he stood, especially after everything that had happened tonight.

He had never thought about it before, but the truth was, nobody had poured that beer down Brian's throat. Nobody had pressed the keys into his friend's hands and told him to drive like a maniac.

Brian was eighteen, legally a man. And if Brian was feeling conflicted about his life, about not wanting to leave for the Naval Academy, then stealing a car from Bruce's valet stand—Bruce's responsibility—even if done in frustration, as a way of acting out, was not what a person should have done to a friend.

Yes, it had been a reckless, stupid, spur-of-the-moment mistake. It shouldn't have ended the way it did. Brian shouldn't have died. Bruce's family shouldn't have been blamed or shunned for it. The Faulkners shouldn't have persecuted Bruce, not through their connections, their lawyer, or their influence with the police department.

By not thinking about any of these things for so long, he'd thought he'd been protecting himself. By simply staying away from Wallis Point, he thought he'd been helping his family, protecting them from being reminded of other people's judgments. Maybe it was for the best that he'd done so, especially at first, until all the bad feelings had mellowed with time. Because until now, all these years later, he hadn't been able to see the events clearly.

He felt…anger toward the Faulkners, not the shame and sadness he had initially felt after the accident, before he had taught himself to go numb. He didn't see how he could ever *be* numb again. And maybe that was good. He liked seeing his friends again. He liked being close to Natalie. He wasn't thrilled she would be so open and available to other people back in Wallis Point when he wouldn't be here. Bailing Moon out after Bruce and she had made love for the first time and should be together…well, it did grate on him. Not because it was her job, but because it burned him that his friends would be here, seeing her face all the time, hearing her voice, and he would not.

Bruce had gone into the twenty-four-hour store across from the police station and he'd bought a box of condoms for them for the rest of the week, because he wanted Natalie close to him, as often as possible. He wanted her in his bed and in his life with ferociousness he'd never dreamed possible. He wanted to *feel*.

Natalie had been the person who'd broken him open to the rawness inside. She saw in him what nobody else did. And in her, he liked to think he saw what nobody else appreciated. By God, he would keep her protected. He would not let anyone hurt her, or take advantage of her, or make her sad.

But, he was jumping ahead of himself. For now, he and Natalie had a limited number of days together until his family trouped home, relieving him of his nursing home duties. Even if Gramps acknowledged him tomorrow—and Bruce did need to spend the whole afternoon with him tomorrow since there was an MRI scheduled at the hospital—his priorities had shifted.

He was staying for the whole week because he wanted to be with Natalie.

# CHAPTER FOURTEEN

ON FRIDAY MORNING, the last day of the work week, Natalie sat in her office chair, swinging her feet. She had a glow inside her that wouldn't quit.

After she and Bruce had returned from the police station on Tuesday night, they had moved his things into her bedroom in the cottage. Otis the cat had not been pleased; they'd found him sleeping on her coverlet by himself in the dark, but Bruce had scooped up the gray tabby cat and told him he could either go outside or stay downstairs on the couch, but nobody was sharing a bed with Natalie other than him.

She laughed to think of it, ignoring the bank form that she was supposed to be completing. She didn't think she'd had such complete happiness, ever. She and Bruce made love before she went to work. They made love at her lunch hour, when she drove back to see him at the guest house. They made love after work, and once he'd taken her into the ocean at midnight, though she'd been careful to wear her earplugs.

He was amazing. Inventive. Attentive. And he was all hers.

Her father came into her office and shut the door behind him.

"You look tired, Natty."

Wonderfully tired, yes. The kind of tired that came

from crawling inside another person's skin and not wanting to leave, even to sleep. Bruce was always the one who drifted to sleep first. She smiled, picturing how the cat had snuck back into the bedroom last night after Bruce was snoring softly.

But she shouldn't be thinking of that now. She needed to focus her father on the business at hand.

"Are you ready to discuss our partnership?" Natalie asked.

Her father took a seat in the chair facing her desk. Ever since the open house, he'd treated her more like a colleague than a daughter when they were in the office together. That she would be made a partner and successor to the Kimball Family Law Firm seemed almost a foregone conclusion. She just needed him to say so.

"How are the scholarship applications going with Bunny Faulkner?" he asked.

She put down her pen. She hadn't called Bunny yet. Bruce was leaving for his next job assignment tomorrow, after Maureen returned home. Then, next weekend, they'd made plans to meet again at her guest house. She was looking forward to seeing how he would react to both her and her family.

Their growing relationship had been all she could think about. Even though she hadn't known him very long, she was becoming more attached to Bruce than she was to anybody else.

"Natty?"

She jerked back to the moment. "Sorry. I'll call her on Monday."

"Why not today?"

Because she and Bruce had come to an agreement

of sorts, inside their bubble of "living in the moment." Neither of them rocked the boat. In essence, they were back to their original agreement of keeping quiet about their sore spots. Why risk spoiling that by contacting Bunny while Bruce was in town?

"I didn't see the urgency," she said.

Her father stared at her. "I told you to call her a week ago. Now the high school is getting anxious. They need Bunny's decision so they can send their graduation programs to the printer."

She opened her drawer and reached for the file with the applications. "I'll get right on it."

Her father was peering at her. "You called all my clients the day of your open house. Why didn't you call Bunny? She's always home. She always answers her phone."

Slowly Natalie leaned back in her chair. "It must have been an oversight."

He shook his head, clearly disappointed in her. "This has to do with Bruce, doesn't it?"

It did. She thought she'd been balancing her growing relationship with the career she wanted so badly. There had to be a way to do both. "Let me give Bunny a call now. It's not too late."

She reached for her phone, but her father stopped her.

"Bunny's not an easy person deal with," he said. "She's stuck in the past, and she's deeply unhappy. She'll lash out if she thinks your allegiances lean more to Bruce than to her."

"I'll handle her."

"I don't know if I want you to handle her." He drummed

his fingers. "Bunny's relationship is important to this firm. It's important to the *value* of this firm."

Natalie paused. "What are you saying?"

Asa leaned forward. "Do you know how much I'd rather be touring the country with your mother in an RV right now?"

"Mom wants to tour in an RV?"

"Yes, she does. We both do. Do you think you're the only person with a dream?" He thumped the desk with his palm. "This firm is my retirement plan. If I offer you a stake, then I'm trusting in an income stream that might not happen."

"It will happen! I've shown you—"

"You've shown me you're having problems with your priorities," he interrupted. "It hurts me to say this, but how can I offer you a stake when you're not prepared to handle the difficult decisions and personalities that come attached to this job? Trust me, Natty, organizing an open house is a cakewalk compared to fielding phone calls from disgruntled clients."

"I said I'll handle her!"

"Natty," he said kindly, "it's not necessary for you to compromise yourself. I'll negotiate a position for you working in whichever firm buys this one. I'm sure they'll let you work out of the building, if that's what's important to you. Take my offer. That could be a very pleasant living for you."

"What about the Kimball Family Law Firm?" she asked. "What about Granddad Asa and all the generations of Kimballs?"

"Granddad Asa doesn't own the firm any longer," her father said, his tone cold. "I do. And I'm doing you a favor by selling it. Do you know what I would have given to not have had all those expectations for what I was supposed to do with my life? I'm giving you that gift. The world is your oyster. Take it."

She thought she had been when she'd returned home to work with him.

She sat, reeling. Her father obviously didn't share her vision of what the firm meant to the connection between past and future. He didn't see the great things they could do for the community that mattered so deeply to her. Working for an outsider wouldn't achieve the same results.

Shakily, she stood. He thought that he understood her, but he was so far from the truth, it disturbed her. She slammed her palm on the desk.

Her father jumped. His gaze jerked to hers.

"Do I have your attention now?" she asked. "I'm telling you, I can handle Bunny Faulkner's concerns. I can handle your income stream and I can handle whatever difficult choices and priorities come my way. I'm not going to back down."

"How long," he asked quietly, "do you think it will take Bunny to figure out that Bruce is back in town on weekends and living in your cottage?"

Her father *knew?* She thought she and Bruce had been discreet. Maybe her father was only guessing?

*Bunny won't hear about it,* she decided. But that wasn't realistic, and certainly not honest. It wasn't what Natalie wanted from her relationships.

Hadn't she come back to town to be a different kind of lawyer? A helper, not an adversary.

"I watched you with Bruce," he said, "that night at

the hospital. You rushed to protect him from me. That lawsuit Bunny asked me to file is still a sore point with him. If he's still angry, how do you think Bunny feels? The woman lost her son."

"I'll help her," Natalie said.

"How?" He snorted. "By turning back the clock fifteen years? Because that's what she wants, and that's not possible."

Why not? "What if I talked to Bruce, and to Bunny, separately, and then I worked to set up a meeting between them?"

Her father burst out laughing. "The top mediator in the world couldn't make a meeting happen between those two."

"What if I bet you I can? I may not know Bunny yet, but I know Bruce."

"For one week?" he asked. "You'd risk a bet on someone you've known for only one week?"

*Yes!* her gut screamed. Her gut *adored* this man. Okay, so maybe her head told her it wasn't such a good idea to count on someone who couldn't discuss a future commitment beyond a weekend meet-up here or there.

And she'd be risking a lot with this idea. She risked losing the option of convincing her father to entrust the law firm to her in any other way. She also risked scaring Bruce away and losing him altogether.

Her knees shook. The promise she was making was not to be taken lightly. If a meeting between Bruce and Bunny didn't happen, or was unsuccessful, then Natalie would lose both things that made her so happy.

But she had to try. The risk of not convincing her father and having him sell the firm from beneath her was too much to contemplate. She had to put herself on the line.

"I'll do it, Dad," she said. "It's the best thing for them. If I can broker a sit-down with Bunny and Bruce, then that could help both of them. Bunny, because maybe it would help her feel less hurt. And Bruce…"

She let that part hang. Bruce was hurting, too, though she would never betray his confidences or his vulnerabilities to anyone, including her father.

Besides, the meeting would benefit her, too. Wasn't Bruce's secret pain about the accident, at heart, one of the main reasons keeping him from committing to putting down roots in Wallis Point with her?

"Very well." Her father rose. "I'm sorry I don't have much hope for success. I'll make sure you have a fallback."

"I don't need a fallback."

He crossed his arms and shook his head at her. "Be careful, Natty. You need to make sure that the choices you make are the choices you can live with."

NATALIE DROVE HOME at the lunch hour, feeling shaken. It was starting to sink in that Bruce wouldn't like what she had to say at all. Not at first, anyway.

Slamming her car door, she took off her heels so she was in her bare feet, and then walked around the side of the cottage to the guest house. She peered in the front window, but Bruce wasn't inside. It was a nice day, balmy and sunny with fat white clouds that looked like animal shapes, so she found him where she expected, facing the beach on the back patio.

Bruce was pacing and speaking forcefully on the

phone, the way he often did when he was engrossed in his work. But a telltale white plastic bag was on the table; at some point, he'd taken a break to walk to the gourmet deli in their beach neighborhood to pick up turkey and cheese sandwiches, potato chips and her favorite iced tea. *Oh, Bruce,* she thought. Their life together had been so great.

He turned in her direction, still holding the phone to his ear, and she caught the phrase, "tasks needed to be done to complete the upcoming deliverables."

When he saw her standing there, he broke out in a smile that lit up his face. He gave her a quick kiss and mouthed that he'd be done in a minute, so she walked to the edge of the patio facing the ocean.

William was a few yards down the beach, sitting in a sturdy, old-fashioned folding lawn chair. Some of his friends were with him, old men who stood around him chatting, wearing caps and carrying bulky metal detectors. From where she stood, she couldn't hear what was happening, but one of the men bent to pick something up out of the sand. It was hard to tell from his expression whether he'd found a coin, a piece of jewelry or a tin can.

What was Bruce's and her long-term future: Jewelry or a tin can?

They'd known each other again only for a week and he hadn't even said he loved her. In practical terms, it was foolish to place their budding relationship on equal footing with their careers.

And yet, here she was.

She rubbed her arms, the sea breeze even cooler than she'd anticipated. Were they solid enough that they could pull this off?

It hit her how much she was truly risking. What would Bruce do when she told him she wanted him to consider meeting with her and Bunny Faulkner?

Yes, he accepted that she worked with all kinds of people in Wallis Point that he might not want to see. He'd gone to the police station with her to prove it. Since then, though, there had been no more talk in that direction—there had been lovemaking. Twisted sheets. Long showers. Late nights.

He didn't let her keep her phone under the pillow anymore; he said he would be "her ears," and that had made her cry, she was so touched. She felt as if she'd been blessed by good luck, for once in her life.

If she backed down and didn't tell Bruce now, then she was showing her father—and herself, to be honest—that she was too timid to get what she wanted. She didn't want to back away from speaking up when she should. Not anymore.

She'd been given that lesson at fifteen, when she'd seen the ramifications of failing to tell her father what had happened at the funeral parlor. If she'd spoken up that night, then maybe Bunny would have known about Bruce's pain. Bunny might have thought differently about him had she known.

If only a healing of sorts could happen now.

"Hey." Bruce came up behind her, his embrace closing over her waist, his kiss lingering on her ear. She closed her eyes, enjoying the sensations. "How was your morning?" he asked her, as always, and genuinely waited for her answer.

She opened her eyes. The moment had presented itself, and it was time to tell him. She knew this with sureness in her heart that made her feel peace.

She pushed a windblown lock of hair behind her ear, and turned to face him. "I need to call Bunny Faulkner today. And I would very much like you to talk to her, too."

"What?" He laughed, assuming she was joking with him.

Natalie traced the collar on his T-shirt with her finger. "I'm helping Bunny choose a scholarship recipient for the Brian Faulkner Memorial Scholarship Fund."

His smile flatlined.

She took a breath. *Keep going.* "I'd like to know how you feel about that."

"I don't think anything," he said. "You go do your job without me." And then he turned to the table. "I got your iced tea. They were out of green tea, so I got the white you like."

He held it out to her, but she didn't want to accept his deflections anymore.

Bruce put it down and crossed his arms; he knew something was up, knew she wasn't backing down. She too often backed down. When he put up his defenses, she sidestepped away, offering soothing words instead.

But there could be no more sidestepping the truth she didn't want to face because it bothered her.

"Bruce, I *saw* you in the funeral home that night with Brian. You were honest when you were talking to him. Why can't you show me that part of yourself, too?"

He smiled, trying to joke with her to make her stop. "You're breaking the deal we made that first day, Natalia."

"Yes," she said, "I am. But I want you to be able to give me those emotions, too, the ones I saw you give Brian. That's why I'm pushing you."

Bruce seemed to waver. He knew she was hurt. He knew she had drawn a line in the sand.

Did he care about her enough to break down the fences he'd put up? Or would he go on the offensive as usual, in order to keep her away?

Bruce's expression seemed to harden and she knew she had her answer. "I don't see you telling people about your hearing loss," he told her bluntly.

She blinked. This wasn't about her; it was about him. "If you don't talk about it," she said, doubling down, "then there will always be this barrier between us, and that scares me."

"Does it scare you to talk about your hearing?" he insisted. "Show me you can talk openly about that with other people, and then maybe I'll talk to you about Bunny Faulkner."

The moment hung in the air between them. Did she dare? Were her efforts at healing a sham, as long as she got to take the easy road? Or did she have the guts to create the better life she wanted?

Natalie whipped her phone from her pocket. Before she could think, she punched in Bunny's phone number from the contact card her father had given her.

The call was answered on the first ring. "Hello?" Bunny sounded like a lifelong smoker, and one tough cookie.

Natalie's pulse was racing, and a thin line of sweat was trickling down her spine. But she didn't back down, or avoid what she knew she had to do. "Hello, Bunny.

My name is Natalie Kimball. I'm Asa Kimball's daughter. I'd like to schedule an appointment with you to review the scholarship applications for the high school graduation next month. We can meet either at my firm or at your house…it's entirely up to you."

Bunny was silent on her end of the phone.

Natalie looked up at Bruce. He was staring at the ground. His lips had thinned and his face was flushed. A muscle was twitching in his jaw.

She blew out a long breath. Whatever fear she had left in her, she cast off, imagined throwing it into the wind, into the sea.

"There is one thing you need to know about me first," Natalie said clearly to Bunny. "I am hearing impaired. If you and I are face-to-face, then I'm usually fine with conversation. But if my back is turned, or we're on the phone and I miss something you say, then please understand that you might need to repeat yourself. It doesn't mean I'm ignoring you."

She glanced at Bruce. His eyes were wide; he was staring at her in horror. And she felt…

Quite frankly, Natalie felt free.

"My Frederick wore hearing aids for most of his life," Bunny Faulkner said in that rough, tough voice that had suddenly ratcheted down a notch. "I know exactly how to talk to you. Why don't you come to my house, dear, and we'll look at those applications together. Any time this afternoon will be fine."

Natalie sat down on the step of the patio, suddenly light-headed. "I would like that very much. Thank you. I'll see you soon."

Somehow she disconnected. And then she found herself blinking. Tears stung her eyes, then dribbled down her face like waterworks, but they were happy waterworks.

It felt so good not to have to hide anymore.

Bruce saw her tears, and he put his arms around her. "I'm sorry, sweetheart. I shouldn't have said that to you. I didn't mean for you to call her and say that—"

"I'm glad I did." She laughed through her tears. "I feel really great right now. I feel…" She pointed toward his grandfather, sitting in his lawn chair beside the old men and the seagulls, instead of sitting in his nursing home and staring at a TV set alone. "I feel like William, out in the fresh air with the people he loves. Don't you see, I'm part of the world, finally. And I'm not going back to how it was before."


BRUCE SHADOWED HIS EYES from the glare of the sun as Natalie walked down the beach to William. He didn't understand her at all. Why had she admitted her weakness to Bunny Faulkner, of all people?

The more he thought about it, the more infuriated he became on her behalf. Didn't Natalie realize that if she didn't protect herself, then the world would destroy her? Where was her survival instinct?

He followed her to where she was sitting beside William, drinking her iced tea, her shoes off, digging her toes into the sand, wiggling them and watching the sand filter through. He sat down beside her.

"I trusted Brian with things about myself, too," he said, picking up smooth rounded stones and tossing them down the beach. "I told him things that nobody else knew."

He didn't want to admit any of this, but Natalie needed to see what she risked. He couldn't help her otherwise.

His chest and throat suddenly felt tight and were stinging him; it was too hard to talk. So he faced her, glad he could mouth the cautionary story and she would still understand it.

"I told him where I kept the keys at the valet parking stand," he said in barely a whisper. "And how one night on a stupid whim, I borrowed a Corvette without telling anybody, just for the thrill of it."

This was the heart of his problem; he *had* been responsible for this aspect of what Brian had done. And he'd never admitted this part. Not even when he'd been called before the commandant at the Naval Academy.

He pushed his hands into the soft sand to stop them from shaking. "I told Brian about what I'd done. He must have told his parents, and they became obsessed with it. It was the cornerstone of their lawsuit, but they got the facts wrong. They thought that I'd taken Brian along with me and that I'd done it more than once."

He blew out the betrayal the memory was stirring up. But he had to warn Natalie of the harm that trusting the wrong people could cause. "During the depositions, it killed me not to admit fully what I'd done. The Academy has an honor code, and so do I." He tossed another set of stones, not knowing what he could do to show her, to shake some sense into her, because all she looked was sorry for him. "Don't make the mistake of trusting people so much, Natalie. It will only come back to bite you if you do. You know that's why I'm cautious about getting too close to people."

"I'm asking you to get close to *me,* Bruce."

He sucked in his breath. He thought they *were* close. In truth, he was closer to Natalie than he was to himself.

"You know," she murmured, taking his hand in hers and tracing his fingers and his palm with her gentle touch. "My father told me something very wise today."

"Did he?"

"Mmm-hmm." She nodded. "He told me to make sure I could live with the choices I make."

What did that mean? Bruce was sure it wasn't good. He braced himself.

"If I were the lawyer the Faulkners had consulted," Natalie said, "asking me to sue you, I would have refused. That's the choice I would have made, and I would have taken the fallout that came from it."

"I believe that," Bruce said.

"And I'll also make the choice to say this to you, Bruce," she said, suddenly taking his hand and placing it in his lap, away from her, "with all the fallout that will come. Whatever excuse you're using to stay away from here and to stay disconnected from us—from *me* at some level—then I don't think I can live with that."

She looked him straight in the eye.

Everything seemed to still within him. "Are you telling me you don't want me to travel? It's my job."

"I know," she said.

He felt relieved. She wasn't forcing a choice on him.

She stood, wiping sand from her hands. She picked up her shoes.

"Where are you going?" he asked.

She smiled gently at him. And that's what hurt the most. "In case I haven't told you, this has been the happiest week I can ever remember. And it's all because of you. I love you so much that I can't..." Her voice faltered, and he reached for her, but she stepped back.

"I don't want you to keep me at arm's length," she said. "That's the truth. You can do what you want, but I can't handle tiptoeing around Bunny Faulkner for you, or even flying to Florida to see you for one or two weekends a month because you'd rather avoid being close." She held up her hand. "I know you're going to say it's your job, and believe me, I understand that, but it's too disconnected for me. And I'm not going to help you use your transitory lifestyle as your wall of protection to keep from getting too close to me."

"So come with me," he said fiercely. "Get out of this town. Start your own firm anywhere else in the world."

She gave him a long hug, her forehead buried in his chest. He squeezed her to him as tightly as he could. He wouldn't let go of her. He couldn't.

"I love you, Bruce," she whispered. "But I'm where I want to be."

"Please don't do this," he said.

"Then come with me to see Bunny."

"I'll come back to see you next weekend," he said. "Right here, in your guest house. The same as before."

"You don't understand," she said softly. "I can't go back to before."

THAT AFTERNOON, after Natalie returned to the office, Bruce decided to escape to the road. A late-evening flight, the same as always. He'd pulled his end of the bargain: Moe and the family were coming back into town first thing tomorrow morning. He'd done everything they had asked. He had sat with Gramps every day. He'd even taken Gramps fishing and to meet his old friends.

He drove Gramps back to the home and helped him and his walker up the elevator and into his room. "I'm leaving," he said to his grandfather, sitting in his chair before the TV and watching the hometown team losing to New York, two to nothing. "I'm going back to Florida to do laundry and get my stuff together tomorrow before I fly out on Sunday for the client site, the same as always."

But Gramps was silent.

"Do you remember me, Gramps?"

Gramps closed his eyes. He took the ball cap he was wearing and tilted it to shade his face.

*I failed.* But what could Bruce do? Life was what it was. Brian was gone. Gramps didn't know him anymore. Natalie wanted more from Bruce than he could give.

Bruce could come back next week, but he knew it wouldn't be the same.

He couldn't fool Natalie anymore. He couldn't fool himself.

The urge to escape was too strong.

NATALIE PULLED INTO THE DRIVEWAY of her cottage, the afternoon sun low in the sky, and immediately, she *knew.*

*He's leaving early. He's falling back into his old routine.*

Bruce's rental car was still in the driveway, but the trunk was open and his suitcase was sitting on the pavement, the handle extended as if he'd just wheeled it there.

Her hand over her mouth, trying not to cry, she walked down the path to the guest house. The inside door was open, so she looked through the screen. He was kneeling on the floor, zipping his laptop bag closed.

She must have made a noise because he looked up. But everything was blurry because tears were streaming down her face. She didn't even try to stop them.

She'd always known, and he'd always told her in a hundred different ways that he was never leaving the road, never changing, so don't even try to make him. Still, actually seeing the zipped suitcase hit her like a physical blow.

He stood, staring at her from across the crazy, half-finished room, with its exposed wall studs and the whiff of fresh tile grouting. He wouldn't help her build the new, beautiful room, and she wouldn't stop here to have lunch with him anymore, either.

Bruce didn't say anything. But there was wetness in his eyes that even he couldn't control. Leaving her *did* affect him. Maybe he hadn't expected Natalie to walk down the path and watch him go, to confront him and not to shy away.

He took a deep breath. She honestly didn't know what he was going to do.

BRUCE HAD TO LEAVE. They both knew he had to leave. But that didn't stop it from ripping his heart out.

He hefted the laptop bag and walked over to her. He wanted to kiss her. He wanted to wipe the tears from her face and keep her from ever crying again.

And she wondered why he'd numbed himself to block off his heart? This was why. Because it hurt too damn much.

But they had a standoff with no resolution. He

couldn't give her the access to his internal feelings that she expected. She couldn't let him stay locked behind his wall.

He walked to the door and paused before her, then bent his head to kiss her. He meant for it to be quick. An easy escape.

As he got closer, her scent brought back the memory of them in bed together. All that they'd shared in the past week.

"I love you," she said against his lips.

"Please don't," he replied.

It was the wrong thing to say. What had she called it? *Your wall of protection.* Instantly he felt her intake of breath against his cheek. The shift in air as she stepped back.

Her hand went to her mouth, and she silently shook her head.

"I'll be back now and again," he said. "I intend to visit my family more often." But the breezy promise wasn't enough, and he knew it this time.

On his way out of town, Bruce turned down the dump road. He hadn't planned it, but when he'd seen the turn-off, he was hit by a mix of regret and nostalgia, and the next thing he knew he was at Moon's front door, pressing the doorbell.

But it was Friday, and Moon was at Moroney's Pub. So Bruce drove back to the strip. Inside the popular gathering place, his old buddies had met after work. The snake pit were at the far corner, playing pool, a few of them with their wives and girlfriends. Moon was in the corner alone, drinking from a can of cola. Fallout from his arrest the other night, no doubt. Bruce wished he could stick around and help somehow. He went over to his friend and shook his hand, wondering how he could make things better for him now that he was leaving.

"Everything okay?" Bruce asked Moon.

"Yeah. Your girlfriend referred me to a lawyer. He thinks we can fight it."

Bruce nodded. "That's good." He shuffled side to side, not knowing what to say. He knew Moon needed his driver's license in order to keep working in his contractor business.

"It was stupid," Moon said to him. He leaned closer, as if to take Bruce into his confidence. "You're cool…I know you won't repeat it, so I'll tell you. I hit a parked police car. I was talking on the phone and I wasn't paying attention. It was stupid." Moon drank from the cola can. "Still, I took the arrest as a sign, you know? I'm a big believer in signs. Somebody up there is giving me a message." He pointed to the ceiling. "I gotta cut back, you know?"

"That's real good. I'm proud of you," Bruce said. An urge hit him, as if he wanted to stay and encourage Moon in his resolution, help to keep him on track, so to speak. Like in high school, when he'd kept Moon from flunking out. "Tell you what, I'll give you my cell phone number. Call me anytime you want to talk. I mean it—don't hesitate."

He took Moon's phone and plugged in his number. But even as he did so, he knew it wasn't the same as being here in person. The way he hadn't been here for Maureen, either, all these years. She would call him when he was on the road, and he would talk to her, yeah, but even he knew that it was the bare minimum. It wasn't a commitment.

Speaking of commitment…

He handed Moon his phone back. "One more thing. When you work on Natalie's house, could you maybe do an extra good job, go above and beyond for her? Send any extra bills to me—I'll take care of them."

Moon nodded. Getting that commitment from Moon was all Bruce could do for Natalie, and it felt so insignificant, but he didn't have anything else. Moon gave Bruce a bear hug, slapping his back, and Bruce said goodbye to the rest of them, too. Guzzy actually had tears in his eyes. "We only just got you back, man."

With a lump in his throat, Bruce turned. *Go. Now. Get out before you weaken.*

He'd almost made it to the door before Moon cut him off.

"I'm on my way to the airport, Moon. I mean it. I'm not staying."

"Yeah, I know, Brucey. I want to tell you something." Moon crushed his empty cola can in his hand. He furtively glanced to see who was around them before he continued. "You should have come back before this, you know? Everybody knew Brian didn't die because of you, Bruce. It was just…Brian being Brian."

Bruce sucked in his breath. He'd thought there was nothing more to say or to think about Brian and that night, but he found himself strangely grateful for Moon's vote of confidence. "Thank you," he said quietly.

"He was on his way to your house that night. He said he wanted to take your sister out for a spin."

"*My* sister?"

"Yeah. She might not have known, but we all did. We were drinking that night at the beach. He…well… he said he was going to drive down to the hotel to borrow a better car from your valet stand. We were trying to talk him out of it, but we couldn't."

Wait. So they knew Brian was impaired, too? And they let him go, too?

Moon and he shared a moment of silence. "He got mad at us," Moon finally said. "He raced off before we could stop him."

"It wasn't your fault," Bruce said quietly. *Mine, either.*

Moon hung his head. "Yeah, I know. The whole thing just…sucked. I felt horrible. I always kind of wondered if your sister knew and felt horrible, too. She never said anything, though. She's tough."

With a soft, vulnerable center, like him. Bruce balled his hands into fists. If Moe had ever gotten into that car with Brian… It turned him inside out thinking about it.

Moon nodded. "Anyway, it's over. You'll come back and visit us now, won't you?"

Bruce honestly didn't know. For his family, he might now and then. But he was pretty sure that Natalie wouldn't see him if he did, and to come back to town without her to go to… He took off his cap and faced the beach.

It was another heartbreakingly beautiful day on the coast of New Hampshire. He pushed back his sunglasses and wiped his eyes.

It must have been the setting sun.

## CHAPTER FIFTEEN

BUNNY FAULKNER WAS A SMALL, thin woman with deeply lined skin and an air of perpetual sadness.

But she seemed to have taken a shine to Natalie. She showed Natalie a box of old photos of her son, Brian, and of her husband, Frederick. When Bunny exhausted that box, she brought out another album of her parents from her childhood. They never actually reviewed the scholarship applications, but Natalie sat with Bunny for an hour in the formal living room, drinking coffee and talking about all the ways Wallis Point had changed since Natalie was a child.

*She's lonely,* Natalie realized. The woman had no one to talk to, no one to take care of except for her two standard poodles, a white female named Lady and a black male called Tramp. Tramp sat at Natalie's feet for most of the visit, and Natalie rubbed his furry head. Otis would be furious with her for this betrayal, but Natalie decided that admiring her clients' pets was part of the job. And she liked Tramp. He had sad eyes that reflected how Natalie felt in the hour since Bruce had left for the airport. And she didn't know what else to do to make herself feel better.

She missed him already, missed him with an ache deep in her chest. She wished Bruce was whole, healed and ready to love her, but until he was willing to face everything that had happened that night, she didn't see how that could happen.

"This is a picture of my Brian with a neighbor boy," Bunny said, passing Natalie a photograph of two boys at about age seven or eight. They were in their bathing suits and looked as if they had just come out of a backyard pool. Immediately Natalie recognized that the neighbor boy was Bruce. He was slight, with a big, guarded smile that showed no teeth, and inquisitive dark eyes that seemed too big for his face.

He was adorable. She clutched the photo, and it made her heart cry all the more. "May I make a copy of this for myself?" Natalie asked.

Bunny Faulkner blinked at her. "Did you know my son?"

"I knew him by sight from watching him at school, but I never met him personally," Natalie admitted. "Though I have come to know this boy—this man." She showed Bunny the photo. "This is Bruce Cole, and he was your Brian's best friend. And I can tell you that he's...that Bruce has never been the same since your son's accident. I hope you'll show some compassion for him, even if only for Brian's sake." Natalie smoothed her thumb over the edge of the snapshot. "From what I remember of your son, I don't think he'd want Bruce to suffer anymore."

Bunny looked at Natalie with rounded eyes. For the first time since their visit began, she had nothing to say.

BRUCE FINALLY MADE his escape from Wallis Point. He gunned the Mercedes out of town the way he'd wanted to since he'd first crossed the state line for Maureen's wedding.

He blew past the Welcome to Wallis Point billboard, pushing the sports car as it was made to be run. He turned up the radio until rock music blared over the speakers, the bass vibrating through his bones.

This was what he'd been dreaming about all week. He was on his way back to his real life.

But a half mile out of town, he blew right past the spot where Brian had crashed a stolen Mercedes on a hot summer night.

On a whim, Bruce circled back and made a detour. He'd never actually visited this spot. But when he came to a grassy knoll with a large oak tree that had a base as wide as a small car and tree branches that seemed to be tangled in the overhead telephone lines, he pulled over. That overgrown tree still held up its branches. Mother Nature kept on growing, no matter what had happened here.

Bruce sat in the car, the radio turned up loud, wanting to feel nothing, but he couldn't do that anymore. He felt…terrible.

This accident had had an effect on him, and maybe to some extent it always would. Natalie had told him that he'd closed himself off to relationships as a result of it. That he'd used his lifestyle as an excuse not to connect with anyone. That if he didn't take a risk, he might be alone for the rest of his life.

Bruce hadn't wanted to hear what she'd said. Instead he was angry with himself for allowing himself to trust her, even though he had every reason to trust her— she'd never done him any harm. Actually he was glad she'd been there that long-ago night; he couldn't imagine having been that vulnerable in front of anyone else. It hadn't been easy for Natalie to tell him how she felt and what she needed now. And she genuinely wanted him to be part of her life.

Maybe for a long time, Bruce thought, a part of him had been broken—the part that made him feel. But that wasn't true anymore. He *did* feel. And now that Natalie had gotten close to him, here he was, pulling away.

Yeah, maybe he was running again. He didn't deny that. He also knew there were IT consulting jobs he could take that were closer to Natalie—ones where he wouldn't have to fly nearly as often. Portsmouth Naval Shipyard was right up the coast, for one. He had connections there in a project right now.

But did he really want to risk staying in one place? Putting himself out there in a community again with the good, the bad and the ugly? Facing Bunny Faulkner?

*I love you.* He knew how much courage it had taken for Natalie to say that. She was Switzerland. It wasn't like her to commit herself like that and take the chance of being rejected by him.

The truth was…he didn't want to leave her. But, he didn't want to be in the community, either.

He couldn't stay here permanently. He couldn't give her what she'd asked for. And he never wanted to face Brian's mother.

Bruce shifted into Drive, and let that fast, sweet car carry him down Route 95. Less than an hour later, he followed the route for Logan airport in Boston, the signs clearly marked. He pulled off the exit ramp for the car rental return.

But it was strange. Instead of feeling as though he was home again, in the customary hub of travel where he had status and prestige, he really did feel as if…it was a very lonely place.

Lots of people around, yes, but to them, Bruce could be anybody. He was important and memorable only because of his frequent flyer card.

He pulled to the side of the road. Ahead of him were the spiked gates jutting over the pavement that led to the car return garage. Once the car rolled over those spikes, there was no backing up. No do-overs, or the tires would shred.

It was strange, but the sight of those sharp metal spikes made him pause.

He leaned his head on the steering wheel. All day he'd been going over and over the pros and cons of both choices: stay or leave. All day the final choice had always come down to *leave.*

But that was his mind talking. His gut wanted to go home to where people knew him. To *her.*

On a whim, he checked his phone. But no, Natalie hadn't called him. There were no missed calls at all.

Disappointment sank heavy in his gut. And that's when he knew. That's when he knew the right decision for him: he was turning around and heading home.

And just like that, the phone jumped in his hand. He jumped, too. He didn't even check the number—he *knew* it was her.

"Hello! Natalie?"

There was a pause. "Mr. Cole?"

His heart dropped. "Yes?"

"This is Ruth at the Beachwood Home. I'm very sorry

to tell you that William suffered a stroke and a fall this afternoon. He was taken by ambulance to Wallis Point Regional Hospital."

"What?" His fingers tightened on the phone. "Is he going to be okay?"

"Sir, I can give you the telephone number for the hospital if you'd like."

"I'll be there in an hour," Bruce said. "Less than an hour. I'm leaving right now."

## CHAPTER SIXTEEN

THIS WAS WHAT FAST CARS were made for. In the fading twilight, Bruce pushed the beautiful machine to its limit. The traffic was sluggish, but as Moon had said, he must have had somebody up there looking out for him. For once in his life, the left lane seemed to open up for him, and he passed no speed traps or state troopers sitting concealed with radar guns.

As Bruce sped north, he called the hospital twice. Bruce's name was on his grandfather's papers, so they spoke to him. A quiet, serious doctor gave his opinion. "We're checking him out, but at his age, falls are serious."

The road grew blurry again, but Bruce willed himself to see clearly, to stay in his lane. He had to get home. Whether Gramps recognized him or not, it didn't matter. He'd been wrong to leave without saying goodbye. He would never do that again.

For the first time in years, he began to pray.

NATALIE WAS SITTING with Otis in her lap when she got the phone call. She was still in a state of shock over Bruce leaving town. Every few minutes she had to grab for her box of tissues.

But the number on the phone wasn't familiar. She

almost didn't answer it, but she had to, in case it was a client calling. "Hello?"

"Natalie Kimball? This is Gail, from the Beachwood Home."

Natalie sat up. "Is William all right?"

"That's why I'm calling. He had a fall and has been taken to the hospital. I saw your flyer on the wall, and I remembered that you came with William's grandson to visit him a few times."

"Is Bruce with him?" she asked shrilly.

"Not yet, but my supervisor talked to him. He's about an hour away, and he said he was on his way back. I'm phoning you because, well…" She paused. "Technically, I'm not supposed to, but you are Bruce's lawyer. We all like William and we feel terrible. He was crying for his grandson after he left, and now he's very frightened. I knew you lived close by in town and—"

"Wait, William was asking for Bruce? By name?"

"Oh, yes. He talks about Bruce all the time. He loves that Bruce takes him out on visits to the community. Well, William isn't exactly a chatterbox, and he doesn't remember everything, but he has his lucid moments and he communicates in his way." She laughed. "He really is a rascal at heart. But you know that, I'm sure."

Natalie put her hand to her heart. *Oh, Bruce. William does remember you.*

"Where is William now?" Natalie asked.

"At the Wallis Point Hospital emergency room. One of our staff is with him, but he'd probably appreciate seeing a friend until his grandson can get there."

"I'm on my way. Thank you for calling," Natalie said.

WHEN NATALIE ARRIVED at the hospital, William was off in the radiology department, getting an X-ray. She strode to the administrator's desk, asking to see him when he returned.

But she didn't have long to wait, because within minutes, Bruce came running through the doors. Her heart soared to see him. "Natalie!" He caught her in an embrace. "How is he?"

"We'll find out together," she said. "He's in tests with the doctors."

Bruce pushed her hair behind her ears and gazed at her as if she'd been lost to him for years. How could she let him go again after they saw this through together?

Bruce took her by the hand and led her to a relatively private space, near the windows overlooking the setting dusk outside. They were out of earshot of the other people waiting.

Taking both her hands in his, Bruce gazed into her eyes. Everything seemed different about him.

"You can see William now," a nurse interrupted them.

They followed her. William was lying in a bed. He had tubes hooked up everywhere, and his face seemed as pale as the sheet. Bruce's expression grew anguished. He sat by his grandfather's side and leaned over him.

Natalie positioned herself to read his lips.

"I'm here with you," Bruce was saying to him. "I'm not going to leave. I'm right here with you."

Natalie's hand went to her mouth. He'd said these words to Brian, too. She was shot back in time, looking through a fifteen-year-old's eyes, as Bruce Cole leaned over his friend's body and spoke in that same tone, with that same anguished look.

She dropped into a chair.

Back then, she'd stood apart and had only watched. These were words he'd said, over and over. "I'm sorry I left you. I'm sorry I didn't listen. But I'm here now. I'm here, and I won't leave."

There was no feeling of belonging that matched what she felt when she was with Bruce. Nobody loved like him.

And she had let him just walk away? What a mistake. She wasn't making that one again without trying harder.

She walked over to Bruce and squeezed his shoulder. She wasn't fifteen anymore, and she wasn't holding back.

He turned and looked at her with love in his eyes. There were tears, too. He stood. "Natalia, sweetheart. I was on my way back to you when the home called me. Even before I knew William was sick, I couldn't leave."

Her heart hammered. But she smiled at him. "Thank you for telling me."

He gave her a bear hug. He put his mouth directly behind her ear and said, "I'm ready to try."

Nothing he'd ever said had made her so happy. She squeezed him tighter. Never, ever would she let him go. Never, ever would she take him for granted.

Hours later, after they left Gramps's bedside, Bruce laced his fingers into hers and led her from the hospital to the darkened parking lot.

William was going to be all right. Miraculously he hadn't broken his hip in the fall. His stroke was mild, and his doctors anticipated he would be returned to his rest home within a day or two.

Natalie assumed that Bruce was driving them back

to her cottage. But he swung the car into the parking lot of the twenty-four-hour store near the police station.

He kissed her before he got out. "I have one more errand before I take you home for good. Will you come with me to Bunny Faulkner's house?"

In the light from a streetlamp, she could see the seriousness in his face.

"I need your help, Natalia. I need you there with me while I do this."

She swallowed, the lump in her throat growing. "You have me," she whispered. "I'm here for you."

He nodded, and with a last squeeze to her hand, he went into the store alone. Ten minutes later, they pulled into Bunny Faulkner's driveway. She and Bruce stood on the stoop, ringing the doorbell, Bruce with a box of chocolates under his arm. He'd told her that when he and Brian were kids, whenever they'd gotten into scrapes—and there were many in those days—they had always begged Mrs. Faulkner's forgiveness with a gift of her favorite chocolates. Bruce said she had never stayed mad at them for long.

Natalie hoped it would be okay. She had no way of knowing. Bunny could easily throw them both out.

When Bunny answered the door, she was wearing a bathrobe, and a TV behind her was playing a rerun of a family sitcom.

Bruce held out the box of chocolates. "I'm long overdue," he said to Bunny. "I hope you can forgive me."

Natalie blinked, trying to hold back her tears. She smiled at Mrs. Faulkner as best she could through the stinging in her eyes. "Hello, Bunny. Can we please come in?"

Bunny opened her door. For the next hour Natalie

listened as Bunny showed Bruce the same photos she'd shown Natalie earlier in the day. She went to the kitchen and made Bruce some coffee and brought him a honey-dipped donut. Brian's favorite.

It was as if a dam had broken. There were no great revelations. No apologies, exactly. Just a visit to a lonely woman and an hour spent on her sofa, listening.

On the way out, Bruce stopped at the end of the walk-way. With the moonlight shining overhead and the june bugs pinging against the screens, he glanced back at Mrs. Faulkner's house.

"I'm gonna visit her again next week," he said to Natalie. "I think it does her good to be reminded of the old days."

"It does," Natalie agreed. "And how about you?"

He smiled at her, and it was his familiar, boyish smile. It struck her then that she was seeing the old Bruce, the true Bruce, the one she thought had been lost forever. He looked the same as he had back then, before the accident, but his eyes were older and wiser.

He leaned over and kissed her. "I took the long way home, sweetheart, but I'm here now, and somehow, I need to figure out a way to stay."

"I'll help you," she said.

# CHAPTER SEVENTEEN

Two weeks later Bruce looked out over a sea of young people in caps and gowns, seated on folding chairs on the football field where Brian Faulkner used to snap the ball to him on so many autumn Saturdays.

Bunny Faulkner had asked Bruce to present the scholarship in Brian's name this year. He'd spent more time with Bunny over these past two weeks. He felt a lot better than he had in years.

In his lap, he squeezed Natalie's hand. She smiled up at him, and in his heart he knew that everything would be okay.

"Bruce Cole," the high school principal announced, and Bruce rose from his seat on the sidelines and strode over the grass to the podium. He took the mic and gazed out at the people of Wallis Point.

Maureen sat watching in the bleachers, her hand in her new husband's, their kids in seats beside him. Even from here, he could tell she was beaming at him. Gramps was with his friends nearby, Bruce's ball cap on his head. Bunny had come, too, accompanying Natalie's parents, who were leaving tomorrow for their RV adventure, their financial future securely in Natalie's hands.

He lifted the mic. "The scholarship I'm presenting today was named for Brian Faulkner, my best friend and a good son to Bunny. Brian was a great student, one of our school's best athletes and friend to many people here today."

Bruce paused for a moment. "Those of us who knew him have never forgotten him." His voice caught, and he took a breath. From her seat, Natalie nodded encouragingly at him. He smiled slightly, thinking how lucky he was. Just before he continued, the sun came out from behind the clouds, and students in the audience blinked and shaded their eyes.

A glow seemed to fill him. He could almost imagine Brian standing beside him, laughing in his ear.

"The scholarship this year goes to Richard Hannaford."

The audience clapped and cheered for Jimmy's nephew, who hustled to the podium to receive the envelope Bruce passed him. Natalie, not Bunny, had chosen the recipient, though that was a secret Bruce was keeping—a good secret. He shook Jimmy's hand solemnly, and then returned to his place beside Natalie.

"I love you," he mouthed when he sat down.

She didn't say anything; she just gazed at him for a long time, her eyes teary.

She didn't know it yet, but he'd come up with a plan for staying. He would spring it on her tonight, on that dinner-date he'd planned weeks ago, but had been saving for just the right moment.

He didn't have everything worked out yet, but he was getting there. First was finding a place to live, then an assignment nearby. He was taking it day by day.

"Mr. Cole?" he heard behind him, after the ceremony was over.

He turned. Was someone looking for his father?

A short, skinny kid, about thirteen or fourteen years old, stuck out his hand. "It's my dream to go to the Naval Academy."

"Yeah?" He smiled at the kid as he shook his hand. "It's a great place. That's a good dream to have."

"C-can I talk to you about it sometime?" the kid stammered.

"Sure," Bruce said. "I'd be happy to. Anytime."

"Did I really just hear that?" Natalie murmured beside him after the kid left.

He folded her into his arms. Hard to believe he'd once thought he could never come home. "That depends. Do you think a road warrior can ever really settle down?"

"I don't know about the rest of them," Natalie said, putting her lips beside his ear. "But I know this one can."

\* \* \* \* \*

COMING NEXT MONTH FROM
# HARLEQUIN® SUPERROMANCE™

Available January 2, 2013

## #1824 THE OTHER SIDE OF US
### by Sarah Mayberry

After a few less-than-impressive meetings, Mackenzie Williams and Oliver Garrett have concluded that good fences make good neighbors. The less they see of each other, the better. Too bad their wayward dogs have other ideas, however, and won't stay apart. The canine antics bring Mackenzie and Oliver into contact so much that those poor first impressions turn into a spark of attraction...and that could lead to some *very* friendly relations!

## #1825 A HOMETOWN BOY
### by Janice Kay Johnson

Acadia Henderson once had a secret crush on David Owen. Then they went their separate ways. Now they're both back in their hometown trying to make sense of a tragic turn of events. Given what's happened, they shouldn't have anything to say to each other. Yet despite the odds, something powerful—something mutual—is pulling them together. Maybe it's the situation. Or maybe they're finally getting their chance at happiness.

## #1826 SOMETHING TO BELIEVE IN
*Family in Paradise* • by Kimberly Van Meter

Lilah has always been the quiet, meek Bell sister, the one to follow what everyone expects from her. Then she meets Justin Cales. The playboy turns her head and she allows herself to indulge in a very uncharacteristic and passionate affair. But when that leads to an unexpected pregnancy, Lilah discovers she has an inner strength she has never recognized

### #1827 THAT WEEKEND...
by Jennifer McKenzie

A weekend covering a film festival is what TV host Ava Christensen has been waiting for—her dream assignment. But not if it means being alone with her boss! Jake Durham recently denied her a big promotion, so Ava wants as little to do with him as possible. That's virtually impossible at the festival. Somehow, though, with all that time together, everything starts to look different. Must be the influence of the stars...

### #1828 BACK TO THE GOOD FORTUNE DINER
by Vicki Essex

Tiffany Cheung has tasted big-city success—and she's hungry for more. So when she ends up at home, working in her parents' restaurant, all she wants is to leave again. Nothing will change her mind. Not even the distraction of Chris Jamieson, her old crush. Yes, the adult version of him is even more tempting—especially because he seems equally attracted. But her dreams are taking her somewhere else, and Chris's life is deeply rooted here. There's no future...unless they can compromise.

### #1829 THE TRUTH ABOUT COMFORT COVE
*It Happened in Comfort Cove* • by Tara Taylor Quinn

The twenty-five-year-old abduction that cold-case detectives Lucy Hayes and Ramsey Miller are working together is taking its toll—especially with their attempt to ignore the intense attraction between them. The effort has been worth it, because they're close to solving this one. And once they do, then maybe they can explore their feelings. But as they get closer to the truth, they aren't prepared for what they discover!

---

*THE OTHER SIDE OF US*
A brand-new novel
from Harlequin® Superromance® author
Sarah Mayberry

*After a not-so-friendly introduction to Mackenzie Williams,
Oliver Garrett is looking to make a better second
impression…and he may have found it, thanks to
their dogs! Read on for an exciting excerpt
from THE OTHER SIDE OF US by Sarah Mayberry.*

OLIVER searched the yard for his dog, Greta. Finally he spotted her doing a very enthusiastic doggy meet and greet with Mackenzie's dachshund.

*How did he get over here?* Obviously there must be a hole in the fence between their properties.

Suddenly Oliver saw his best chance at a second meeting with his neighbor. Mackenzie would be grateful if he returned her wayward pet, wouldn't she?

He scooped up the dachshund, who wriggled desperately, but Oliver kept a tight grip the entire walk to Mackenzie's.

"Why do you have Mr. Smith?" she asked, frowning as she answered his knock.

"Your dog was in my yard. Seems our fence has a few holes."

"Thanks for bringing him back." Her tone was warm, even a little encouraging, he thought.

As he was about to respond, the phone rang inside her house.

"I need to get that." She was already closing the door.

"Fine. But we should talk about the fence or the dogs will keep visiting."

"I'm sorry, but I really need to take this call." There was a distracted urgency beneath her words.

He opened his mouth to respond, then stared in disbelief as the door swung shut in his face for the second time that day.

"You cannot be serious."

Okay, so he got the message. She was too busy for a friendship. Fine. He and Greta could live here happily *without* knowing their neighbors.

*Oliver may have given up on a relationship with Mackenzie, but it seems Greta and Mr. Smith may have other plans! Find out in THE OTHER SIDE OF US by Sarah Mayberry, available January 2013 from Harlequin® Superromance®.*